"Which wo[...] your choice, Els[...] you not consider I do not favor this union either?"

Confusion marred her features. She fisted her hands on her hips and glanced upward. "Did you argue against this marriage with King William?"

"Aye."

"Yet he convinced you?"

"*Aye*."

When she returned her gaze to him again, resolve and a bit of stubbornness filled them. "Why, Magnar?"

"The king will permit me to continue with my duties with the elite guard, including an important task which requires my attention after our marriage."

Chewing on her bottom lip, she nodded slowly. "Then you will be absent most months from Steinn?"

"Most assuredly, and when I am there, Erik will be my focus."

Her face softened as she moved slowly toward Magnar. "Therefore this marriage is in name only for Erik's protection, aye?"

Annoyed with the direction of his thoughts, he looked away. How Magnar longed to tell the lie on the tip of his tongue. The word ached to be released. He turned and stared into her jeweled eyes in an attempt to offer her any hope of what she wanted to hear.

When she placed a hand on his arm, she whispered, "Tell me honestly, Magnar."

He swallowed and removed her hand from his arm. Placing it securely over his heart, he stated, "Our marriage will be binding in all ways, Elspeth—in name *and* body. You may worship your God and I shall do so with mine, but ken this, you will be *mine* completely."

Praise for Mary Morgan

"If you love time-travel romance with independent heroines and virile heroes, you'll love this book. Fans of *Outlander* will love this one."

~N.N. Light Book Heaven

~*~

"Readers who enjoy romance blended with a combination of history and the mystical will be utterly enchanted by this clever 'weaving' of a tale."

~Long and Short Reviews

~*~

"Morgan's stories are as unique as they are brilliant. They are compelling, bold, and so very successful. To Weave A Highland Tapestry (A Tale from the Order of the Dragon Knights) was everything I had hoped it would be and then some."

~Coffee Pot Book Club

~*~

"A fascinating timeslip romance that takes us back to visit the "Dragon Knights" we have met in previous books in the series."

~Warrior Woman Winmill Reviews

~*~

"Mary Morgan weaves a delightful and enchanting tale around the reader's heart with this spellbinding magical romance!"

~InD'tale Magazine, February 2020 Issue

Magnar

by

Mary Morgan

The Wolves of Clan Sutherland

Magnar

Cover Art by *Abigail Owen*
Editor *Amanda Barnett*

The Wild Rose Press, Inc.
PO Box 708
Adams Basin, NY 14410-0708
Visit us at www.thewildrosepress.com

Publishing History
First Fantasy Rose Edition, 2020
Trade Paperback ISBN 978-1-5092-3289-5
Digital ISBN 978-1-5092-3290-1

The Wolves of Clan Sutherland
Published in the United States of America

Dedication

During our trip several years ago to Northern Scotland and the Orkney Islands, my husband and I were fortunate to have a personal guide escort us. David Ladd was exceptional in his knowledge—from referencing the names of flowers in the most obscure places to the wildlife and history, especially during our travels on Orkney. He took us on an amazing adventure, oftentimes off the well-worn path, revealing spectacular vistas. I shall always treasure our time with him and for allowing me to crawl into the Tomb of the Eagles in South Ronaldsay, Orkney. For a few hazarding moments, I worried David and my husband when I had trouble getting out of the small tomb.

~

I dedicate this story to David.
Thank you for providing me
with a vast wealth of inspiration for Magnar!

Glossary of Old Norse Terms

Hamnavoe - Current day town of Stromness, Orkney
Hnefatafl - Viking chess
Kærr - Dear, close, beloved
Kirkjuvágr - Kirkwall
Njörd - God of the Sea and Winds
Orkneyjar - Orkney
Skald - Norse bard/poet
Skinnleikr - Viking skin throwing game

The Nine Noble Virtues of Wolf Lore

* Learn to control the beast within. If not, the man will cease to exist.

* First lesson for the wolf—the man is always Alpha.

* Scotland is our home. *Orkneyjar* calls to our soul.

* When conflicted, follow the path of the stars. Odin will shine his light upon you.

* Keep your weapon as strong as Thor's hammer.

* Discipline your beast to honor the code of the Brotherhood.

* Honor the Gods. Do not beg at their feet for mercy.

* When All Father calls you to His table, storm proudly across the void.

* Remember your ancestors and honor their wisdom.

Prologue

What began as a magical, whispered thought deep within a dark forest between a druid, raven, and Norse Seer, eventually took shape within the minds of seers and druids who belonged to five ancient clans that carried blood from both the Norse people and the Picts.

While feuding clans and marauders continued to ravage the Scottish realm, the blood of their victims seeped into the land, and the people wept as they cried out for vengeance. Despite the pleas for war from their people, the chieftains, after seeking counsel from their druids and seers, sought another plan to ease the conflict tormenting the clans.

These chieftains called for an order of guards to protect their current king and those who would follow to reign over Scotland. Though these ancient clans had ties to two different countries—Norway *and* Scotland, they deemed the strongest king should rule over both.

After much debate, they came to a settlement. If the King of Scotland was to govern over both countries, he would require strong men to protect, serve, and even spy on his behalf. Men whose bloodline would be filled with the magic of the Norse God Odin and the Pict God Dagda—a bridge linking all of the people's beliefs.

The runes were cast on a stormy night, and the men were chosen. 'Twas on a Moon Day within the Black Frost month on *Orkneyjar*, that the blood of a wolf and an eagle were mixed with a powerful magic.

Each man selected from these ancient tribes entered the stone chamber—to be one with the bones of the wolves. What emerged was dominant and commanding—feared by those who witnessed the pairing of each man with his wolf.

And as the centuries bled into the next within the boundaries of Scotland, the wolves became more of a myth—one told by bards on a cold winter's night. Especially the tales of the leader of these mighty wolves. Known as the barbarian, Magnar MacAlpin is honor-bound to one clan. Loyal to one man—King William *The Lion* of Scotland.

Without his knowledge, evil stalks this warrior. Eventually, the lines between predator and prey will blur, leaving behind a deadly carnage in its path.

Though this warrior moves with stealth-like mastery, he is cloaked by the veil of darkness. The light of the full moon shimmers not from the steel of his weapon, but the silver within his eyes. He walks between the shadows of man and wolf—descended from the first and tied to the second.

Magnar from the house of Alpin, King Kenneth MacAlpin.

This is his tale.

The MacAlpin Wolf Saga.

Chapter One

Orkneyjar Isles ~ Early June 1206

Bracing his forearms on the bow of the longship, Magnar ignored the rough edges biting into his skin. He kept his focus fixed on the shore near the town of *Kirkjuvágr* on the *Orkneyjar Isles*. The land beckoned him toward her alluring bosom, tempting him with a song of welcoming. Stirring the blood flowing through his veins and calling forth the beast within his body.

Magnar clenched his jaw at the invasion. *We shall not linger long on this isle.*

How long had he been gone this time? Twelve moons? Or was it thirteen? Time merely concerned him when there were tasks to complete for his king. Furthermore, there was no need to seek the solace of the land here. The last time he walked on these shores, it was to his ship after harsh words were spoken in a conversation with his mother.

And on that day, he vowed not to return until man and beast had tempered their anger.

His beast rejoiced at the summons from the Seer, but Magnar still fumed at the order. No doubt she would demand that he meet with his mother and mend the rift. He'd considered refusing. Even crushing the missive within his fist that spring day when the messenger placed it in his hand.

The Seer refused to state clearly her reasons for the visit, and this inflamed his anger. Regardless, he could not disobey her request. A vow he made when he took an oath to protect both countries upon his initiation into the elite guard.

As he stared out into the depths of the sea, images from another time sifted through his memories.

"What are you?" she demanded in a raspy voice, heavy from the smoke within their small enclosure.

"A man," he affirmed with steely calm.

"Nae." She shook her head. "What are you?"

He placed his palms upon the coarse wood of the table. "A man."

She smacked the table with her gnarled fingers. "What are you?"

Magnar fought the surging power within his body. His fingers dug into the wood, leaving ugly scars within the grain. The wolf gnashed his teeth within him—more at the fury of Magnar's denial of what he truly was.

Controlling his beast was easy. Yet resisting the Seer would only increase her wrath. "A man."

Fury blazed in the depths of her eyes.

"And a…wolf," he affirmed with contempt for uttering the words out loud.

A blast of sea spray snapped Magnar out of his thoughts from a bitter reminder of the lesson he had learned in his youth. After his terse words with the Seer that day, she'd ordered him to remain in his wolf form for one full month. He'd nearly gone mad.

Not since that time had Magnar challenged the Seer again. Nor the woman who replaced her after her death.

And never *had he* allowed the wolf to roam free for

more than one day. A vow he made to both—man and beast. An oath that had kept them alive.

The longship rose high and slammed back down with a violent force, knocking one of his hardened warriors from his stance by Magnar's side.

Wiping the water from his eyes, he rose to his full height.

"The air is warm," remarked Rorik, resuming his position.

He rubbed a hand over his jaw. "Then Odin favors our return. If not, storms would hinder us from landing."

"I feared the tempest we left behind in Scotland might follow us on our journey."

Magnar glanced at his friend. "You sense the unrest, too?"

Shrugging, Rorik leaned against the bow. "A whisper on the breeze. Not a prophecy."

"Are you now a soothsayer?"

"Nae, *nae.*" Rorik turned away from the approaching shoreline. "Be careful the words you speak, or Ragna will hear you and cast out my tongue and eyes."

Magnar snorted in disgust. "The Seer poses nae threat to you or the men on this ship."

"Do you not fear her? Even when she called you home—"

"This is *not* my home," interjected Magnar tersely. "Furthermore, when did you ever fear a woman?"

Rorik shook his head solemnly. "Ragna might be young and a beauty, but she is the Seer and mighty powerful. And when will you make your peace with both countries?"

He regarded his friend for a few moments and then cast his sight outward. "When they stop calling me the *Barbarian of Orkneyjar.*"

His friend arched a brow but remained silent.

Magnar blew out a frustrated sigh. "Since I chose to further my training in Scotland—" He waved a hand dismissively. "—the people here regard me as a savage. As if they are any better, aye?"

Rorik shifted his stance. "Have not the Northmen judged themselves above all others?"

Chuckling softly, Magnar nodded. "We are a mixture of both—Scottish and Northmen blood. An advantage for us. Nevertheless, we must endure this hostile greeting each time we set foot upon this land."

"You are incorrect. It is merely fear that makes them lash out. There are a few who might envy what we are but many honor us. I ken they fear you more than any other wolves."

"Nae matter. We shall remain nae more than one night."

"Are you not curious as to why the Seer has called you home?" asked Rorik, running a hand through his beard.

Magnar bit back the words to remind his friend again that this was not his home. "Her summons was not detailed."

"Are you worried?"

"Not the word I would have chosen," stated Magnar, bracing his hands on the bow. "Annoyed. She removed me from an important assignment tasked by King William."

"I heard it was given to Ivar."

"Without my blessing," added Magnar.

Rorik smacked him on the back. "Aye, you are our leader, but even you cannot ignore an order given by King William."

Magnar fought the smile forming on his mouth. "True."

He inhaled deeply as they drew near their destination. The bloody scent of his previous training haunted him here on the *Orkneyjar Isles*. This land was unlike his wild and rugged Scotland. Too ancient. Too barren. Too much magic.

Though he was born on *Kirkjuvágr*, his heart belonged to another country.

Magnar raised his fist, a sign for the oarsmen to slow their speed. He noted, as they drew even closer, the arrival of several men on horseback. The stiffness in his shoulders disappeared when Berulf, his old friend, waved to him. After returning the gesture, Magnar waited until the longship came closer to the beach, and in one swift move, he jumped over the side.

The seawater came up to his waist—a frigid welcome back, and he embraced the cold. He gave no care to the shouts from the men on the ship. Or the bark of laughter from Rorik, who followed his lead and jumped overboard. Making long, steady strides, he greeted his friend on the sandy shore.

"Hail, Magnar!" exclaimed Berulf, embracing him in a strong hug.

Magnar smiled. "Greetings, *old* friend. The Seer foresaw our approach?"

Berulf laughed. "She did, and I am not too *old* to spar with you."

"Do I detect a challenge in your tone?" Releasing his hold, Magnar stepped aside and approached one of the horses.

"Always."

"When you have bested this man, you can fight with me," teased Rorik, smacking Berulf on the back in greeting and handing Magnar his axe. "A fine welcome to see you here."

"If I recall, you owe me a barrel of *uisge beathe*," remarked the man.

Rorik pointed over his shoulder at the men offloading supplies. "Done."

Magnar placed a gentle hand on the animal. "You have brought my father's horse, Alf." Different emotions engulfed Magnar as he stroked the horse's rich chestnut mane. When his father had died years ago in Scotland, Magnar's mother had taken the horse with her to *Kirkjuvágr*. She vowed to never return to a land that stole the man of her heart.

Berulf approached on the other side. "I knew you would want to ride him on your journey to Ragna."

The horse snorted softly.

"Aye, my friend. I have been away far too long."

"After you have visited Ragna, come seek me," said Berulf.

Magnar secured his axe to the side of the animal and then mounted his horse. "I look forward to sharing a cup of ale with you."

"And a game of *hnefatafl*," suggested the man as he walked toward his horse. "Come, Rorik. You can tell me about your adventures."

Rorik quickly swung a leg over his horse and asked, "Do you not mean the women I have met?"

The roar of Berulf's laughter followed Magnar as he rode off toward the hills. Giving his horse free rein, he allowed the animal to gallop over the lush grassy landscape. The wind slapped at his face, and he inhaled the salty tang of the sea mixed with the land. Embracing the elements, Magnar relaxed and allowed the tension to ease from his body.

Onward they traveled through rolling hills until they reached a dense forest of ash and yew trees. When they entered, a silence, devoid of birdsong and animals, descended around them. Magnar slowed his horse. Sunlight glimmered through the canopy of branches as he followed the narrow path. Rune markings dotted several trees, guiding him farther into the sacred forest.

Approaching two giant yew trees, Magnar dismounted from his horse. "Stay steady, Alf." After giving the animal a gentle pat, he moved gradually forward. Ducking under heavy limbs, he followed the stream flowing between more yew trees. Ragna's cottage appeared in a small clearing. Wood smoke curled in a lazy circle upward.

Magnar approached the entrance, and then waited. The Seer knew all who drew nigh—be it man or animal. Moments ticked by in frustrating silence. He fought the urge to shout his arrival, but it would do no good. Ragna demanded patience and respect. And he was honor-bound to give her both.

"You are early, Magnar, from the house of Alpin," responded a familiar voice coming from around the back of the cottage. "I thought you would bide your time and rest your bones at the house of Berulf." As the Seer came into sight, she shifted the bundle of herbs in her basket to her other arm.

He clasped his hands behind his back. "Your request was marked urgent."

"And yet, you took your time crossing the sea." Brushing past him, Ragna dropped the basket by the entrance of her cottage.

"I had matters to attend to for King William."

She eyed him skeptically. "The Lion can survive without one of his guards, even if you are the leader of the King's guardians."

His gaze never wavered from hers. "Forsooth he parted with *two*. Rorik travels with me."

She shook her head. "This does not concern him."

Deciding it best to end this topic of conversation, he asked, "Why did you send for me, Ragna?"

After sweeping her braids over her shoulder, her brow furrowed. "You are as impatient as my goat."

Magnar let out a growl.

"Temper your beast," she demanded, wandering into her cottage.

Unclenching his hands, Magnar exhaled slowly and followed her inside.

As his eyes adjusted to the dark interior, he waited.

She gestured to a bench by the hearth. "Please sit. You are blocking the sunlight."

Biting back the curse he wanted to fling outward, he did as she ordered.

Ragna approached, holding a sealed parchment in her hands, and sat on the opposite bench. The firelight danced off her dark locks. "Since you still lack patience, I will be direct with my words. Your mother, Olga, has passed from the realm of the living. She is dead."

Her words slashed like a blade through his heart. Immense pain blinded him, and Magnar stood abruptly. Dizziness swamped his senses as he fought for control.

Tongues of flames from the fire snapped and hissed at him.

The enclosure was too confining.

His inner wolf howled, and he longed to rage with him. Suppressing the urge to shift, he clenched his hands at his sides. "How?" His question barely a whisper.

The Seer's features softened. "Her heart."

Instinctively, Magnar rubbed his fist over his chest. Guilt haunted him. Quickly slamming the door on his last discussion with his mother, he asked, "When?"

"Three months past."

Closing his eyes, he lowered his head. Pride had kept him away. Kept him at a distance from seeking forgiveness. Or offering an apology. First, his father. Now, his mother. Gone. Forever.

"She had penned three letters."

He snapped open his eyes, confused. "Three?"

The Seer tapped the parchment against her knee. "One was for me. One for you, and I am not permitted to disclose the last name until you have read yours first." She stood slowly. "If I may ask, why did you not mend the rift with her? Often times, your mother sought solace in the runes with me, but would not speak of the conversation she had with you before you left. Can you share anything?"

"Besides her constant talk of me taking a wife? Are you certain you don't know?" He laughed bitterly. Raking a hand through his hair, Magnar stormed out of the cottage. Where did he begin to tell the dreadful tale of what he found out over a year ago? One so epic, he silenced his mother with his burning words as he stormed away in disgust.

He lifted his head skyward, allowing the sun to warm his chilled bones. He heard the Seer's gentle footsteps behind him.

"If you have nae wish to discuss the conversation, I will understand. She kept the words tucked inside her heart and soul, refusing to share anything with me."

Blowing out a frustrated sigh, he glanced over his shoulder at her. "My mother confessed to having another son. My twin."

Clutching the parchment to her breasts, Ragna's eyes widened in shock, and she took a step back. "*Nae.*"

"Even her secret remained hidden from you," stated Magnar in a soft voice. Weary from the news, he brushed a hand down the back of his neck.

"Twins cannot be firstborn," she declared, moving to his side. "The magic was woven firmly, so there would be nae risk of harm. *Or* challenge."

"Apparently, something went wrong with the *magic*," he replied dryly.

Ragna touched his arm. "What happened to the other babe?"

"My father took him far north. Away from the isles."

"Norway?"

He shrugged. "I did not ask." Glancing sharply away, he confessed, "I spouted harsh words, damning both my parents when she told me last spring. I then left for Scotland."

Ragna moved away from him. Bending down on one knee, she placed her palm upon the ground. Slowly, she began to draw spirals in the dirt with two fingers. Dry leaves whirled around her as the wind lifted the strands of hair around her face. "Your *new* journey begins now, Magnar."

She stood and turned toward him. Holding out the parchment, she added, "You must mend this rift that has split the fabric of your family. I shall consult the runes and tides. There is a reason two were born first in the house of Alpin. Go home, Magnar. See what you can learn from there. Watch the signs. Listen to the whispers in the breeze. Seek out the eagle near the tomb of bones. If there are two, there is a purpose—one your parents refused to consider. A lone wolf can do as much harm as an entire pack."

His hand shook as he removed the parchment from her fingers. When he rubbed his thumb over his mother's script, his grief returned in force. He swiftly banished the emotions. After carefully tucking the missive into his belt at his side, he gave a slight bow to the Seer. "My plans were to stay for one night."

She closed her eyes as if pondering some message from the Gods or Goddesses. The air stilled and warmed around them. A prickling of awareness skimmed across his skin. His inner beast lifted his head, and Magnar waited.

Exhaling slowly, Ragna opened her eyes and smiled. "Wait *two* nights and then journey back to Scotland."

Without giving him time to counter her reasoning, she retreated back into her cottage.

He curled his lip in disgust and started walking in the direction of his horse. "I pray it was the Gods who spoke to you, Ragna. For I shall stay nae longer than I deem necessary."

As his steps led him through the darkness of the

forest, Magnar sought to soothe the ache he would no doubt encounter when he reached his parents' home.

Chapter Two

Shielding his eyes from the intense sunlight, Magnar shifted uneasily on his horse. Try as he might, the onslaught of his mother's loss overtook him. The massive dwelling where he had been born now stood vacant, high on the hill overlooking the sea. Ghosts of the past lingered, particularly by the entrance where his mother often greeted him. Her keen insight on his arrivals was one she never shared with him. He and his father believed the woman was part seer, and she often imparted wisdom from the animal world as well.

He dismounted slowly. Honor bid him to walk the last few steps to the home. She waited in the whisper of the winds, gently blowing the wildflowers gracing the land. As Magnar's steps led him closer, his vision blurred, and he wiped a hand over his forehead.

His gaze traveled to one of the shuttered windows on the upper floor where they held their last conversation. He fisted one hand and then unclenched it slowly.

"Will you not listen to me? Can you not try and understand what we had to do to protect you both?" pleaded his mother.

"Nae!" Magnar pounded the wall with his fist. "You gave nae regard to my brother. You did not give us a chance. Did you worry for our safety, or was it too much to raise two as part man and wolf?"

"*Listen to my account before you pass your judgment.*"

"*Like the ruling you gave my twin?*" He looked down on her in disdain. "*Do you ken where he is now? Perchance death has claimed him already?*"

Her gasp echoed around them. "*Do not speak such words! I ken you are angry—*"

"*Aye!*" He dismissed her with a slash of his hand through the chilled air. "*From the moment we were born, the lie was woven and spewed forth these five and twenty years.*"

She brushed a hand over her gown and stood. "*As always, Magnar, you are quick to anger without hearing the full account. I cannot fathom why King William chose you as the leader of the Wolves of Clan Sutherland. How can you lead when you have gained nae wisdom?*"

"*You ken nothing!*"

Shaking her head, she countered, "*Wrong. I am older, wiser, and was the wife of one of the finest elite guards who roamed Scotland.*"

"*Apparently, you both lacked wisdom when it came to parting with your blood kin.*"

Her mouth thinned in disapproval of his words. "*Again, I ask, will you not hear my account?*"

Without uttering a reply, Magnar stormed out of the house.

"I should have listened more to your wisdom, Mother." Pushing the door to his home open, Magnar stood still at the entrance. Scents of drying herbs assaulted him, and he took in deep calming breaths. His mother's presence lingered everywhere—from the neatly stacked bowls on the shelf, to her wrap draped over the chair by the hearth.

Taking slow steps inside, he wandered with no purpose throughout the home and opened all the shutters. Though the day was warm, the sunlight did little to heat the place or his bones. Noting the lack of dust, he pondered who had kept the place tidy. His mother would have been honored.

He touched the missive at his belt and prayed the answers he sought would be revealed in the parchment.

Before he attempted any reading, Magnar required something to parch his thirst. Searching the shelves lining the back of the house, he came upon a jug. Lifting the covering, he sniffed the contents.

"Mead will have to do, though I long for something stronger to drink." Pulling down a cup from the top shelf, he went to the large table in the center of the room.

Weary from his grief, Magnar slumped down on the bench. He poured a hefty amount, and then drank fully. After wiping his mouth with the back of his hand, he refilled the cup. Removing the parchment from his belt, he broke the seal. He drew in a long breath and released it slowly as his fingers unfurled the document.

My dearest son...

Since the day you left in anger, I have waited patiently for your return. As spring turned into summer, and autumn soon became cloaked with winter, I know it to be important to pen this missive. Call it insight, but my days are lessening here in this world.

On the day my sons—both part wolf—entered into the world, your father and I made a vow that only one shall rule. Even after consulting the Seer, we deemed it wise that one twin stay with us and our other son to be raised in the far north. The future was murky, and darkness surrounded the Seer's visions. We made her say a vow to keep the secret locked within her heart.

Determined to keep you both safe, we made the only decision we were able to at the time. Your brother was entrusted into the care of a good family on my father's side. They helped him go through his own training and kept his secret about his lineage and what he is from their people.

As you are part of an ancient order, you have heard the tales spoken around the fire. You ken the mantle you assume as an elite guard. There can never be more than one born within a family. You both would fight for control. For power. For the right to be first-born and a leader.

I beg you not to find fault with us, Magnar. Seek out your own wisdom. Seek out your brother. Aye, he lives. I have received correspondences each year from the family we gave him to, except for the last two.

He left the family to go with a group of Northmen traders who were not honorable.

I pray one day you shall forgive us. May Odin grace you with long life, and Thor the strength to battle your enemies. Let not your brother become your foe.

His name is Thorfinn. Find him and make peace, Magnar. I have seen the vision.

Remember my love always.

Magnar released the parchment and stared at the curling edges. "What vision have you seen, Mother? A harbinger for good or bad?"

The walls of the house appeared to be closing in around him. After draining his cup, he stood abruptly. Grabbing the jug of mead, he fled to the comfort of sunlight and fresh air.

A great shudder wracked through his body. "By the Gods what am I to do?" He glanced in all directions to discern any message. "Give me *something*, All Father! Speak to me!"

The wind slapped at his face, mocking him. He clenched his jaw. "Must my plea be heard by the God of Justice, Forsetti?"

Waiting for several heartbeats, he shook his head.

Walking the land, he traveled far until he came upon a favorite spot of his father's. There he slumped against an ash tree. He tilted the jug to his lips and guzzled deeply. The view of the sea commanded he return home to Scotland, but Magnar was not ready.

Nor did he believe the next day would call him back either.

****

The scent of another reached him before he heard the footsteps. Keeping his eyes closed, Magnar waited for the intruder to approach. His mood was foul, and he welcomed no one.

"Leave, Rorik," he uttered tersely.

The man ignored his order and sat beside him. "I have brought food—"

"Unless you have something stronger than mead, you can depart."

"As I was saying, I brought food in the form of smoked cod, goat cheese, dried hazelnuts, blueberries, and fresh bread. And you should see the beauty that provided this good fare. She has a comely shape, full breasts, and a face that would tempt Odin himself."

Magnar cracked opened one eye. A dull ache throbbed behind his temples. "Did said lass have a name?"

A mischievous smiled tipped the corners of the man's mouth. "She will profess her name when the crescent moon rises high in the sky. We are meeting later. She was not allowed to speak much, as I traveled with Berulf to his house. The lass met us halfway in the company of an older woman."

Letting out a snort, Magnar closed his eye. "Be warned. Sounds like the lass has a watchful father, or worse, many brothers. I am positive they have heard that *Rorik the Charmer* has returned to *Orkneyjar* and is roaming the hills in search of his next prey."

"I am offended. You make it sound like I am stalking the lass for my next meal."

Magnar roared with laughter—the effort costing him, and he winced from the pain. Opening his eyes, he rubbed his temples. "Albeit a pleasurable meal, aye?"

Rorik winked and braced his arms over his bent knees. "Might I remind you that all my *pleasing* conquests give of themselves freely?" He glanced sideways at Magnar. "One look at this handsome face and they are smitten."

Reaching for a portion of food, Magnar responded, "One of these days, some father or husband will take a blade to your *handsome* face, Rorik."

The man chuckled softly and withdrew a skin from the satchel of food. "Never."

"Please tell me that is not mead?"

Rorik removed the cork and took a swig. "Ale. Eat first. Then you can share what troubles you."

The wolf growled within Magnar. Ignoring his beast, he proceeded to eat some smoked cod. Afterward, he removed the cloth covering from the bread and ripped off a huge piece. Searching for a small jar in the satchel, he smiled as he removed the lid. After dipping the bread into the creamy goat cheese, he savored the first bite. While continuing to eat his meal in silence, he watched the last rays of sunlight slip over the edge of the sea.

When the first star graced the evening sky, Rorik handed him the ale skin. "The gloaming is always a favorite of mine," he confessed.

Magnar took a sip of the ale. "It marks a shift from day to night."

"And man to wolf."

"Aye," acknowledged Magnar, handing the ale skin back to Rorik. "In a blink of an eye, one blends into the next." He stood and placed his hands on his hips. "We are staying longer than I intended."

"What about the king?"

Scanning the vast ocean, he replied, "For once, our king must wait. The news I shall bring him will alter much within the brotherhood."

Rorik stood and approached by his side. "Can you share this news? Or must I rely on your trust?"

Narrowing his eyes in thought, Magnar turned toward his friend. He realized this news should be shared first with their king, but Magnar's loyalty remained true to his brothers within the elite guard, especially Rorik. Most of their early commissions were fought together, and a bond formed between the two men. Though Magnar was the leader, he allowed Rorik more freedom than the other men. "The rift that tore through my family was from knowledge I have a brother—a twin. This is why I stayed away for too long."

"Loki's balls, nae! 'Tis not possible!"

Remorse filled Magnar once again, and he turned away from the man. "In truth, bitter words were spoken between my mother and me—ones that will haunt me for the rest of my days. I never made peace with her. Upon my return, the Seer presented me with a letter from my mother."

"What are you planning?" Rorik's question was laced with concern and fear. The emotions rolled off him in waves—slamming into Magnar. His inner wolf gave a low growl.

"With consent from our king, I will search for my brother. I must make amends to our family. He is my kin."

Rorik paced in front of him. "'Tis dangerous to seek out the man. Two cannot be in the same house."

Slamming his fist into his palm, Magnar argued, "Then let us begin a new law within the guards. He was forsaken by an ancient creed. Even the Seer did not predict this birth. I ken it was destined by the Gods as a new beginning."

"'Tis a curse," spouted Rorik. "Between good and evil. You cannot be certain your brother does not wield the dark magic. To pursue this path and find him might result in death for all of us."

"Nae!" shouted Magnar, his words echoing along with the roar of the ocean. "Hear my words, Rorik, from the house of MacNeil, you will not interfere with my decision to bring my brother home. He belongs with the brotherhood. In the letter from my mother, he abandoned the family that raised him and fled with Northmen traders."

Rorik's face was tight with strain when he spoke.

"Have you not considered what the man wants? Will you drag him into the brotherhood, snarling and snapping at your heels? Order him to become the lesser? Bind him with our laws and force him to obey a king he may not be loyal to?"

Magnar shrugged. There was a truth to his friend's words, but he remained steadfast in his belief to unite his brother with the other wolves. "Nevertheless, he is a wolf. I have to take into account his training and what his foster family has shared with him. We do not survive alone, Rorik. You ken this well. This is why I must search for him. Besides, King William will welcome another guard. Is he not spouting that there are not enough of the elite guards to do his bidding?"

Rorik scratched the back of his neck. Bending, he retrieved the ale skin. After guzzling deeply, he handed it to Magnar. "What does the Seer advise?"

Refusing the drink, Magnar moved away from the tree. "What the Seer does best. Give you puzzle pieces to sort out. I can share she was shocked to learn the knowledge there was another wolf born into the House of Alpin. In truth, the previous Seer chose not to share this knowledge with Ragna before she died."

Rorik stepped near him. "How many days are you planning on staying here?"

"Nae more than two." Magnar inhaled sharply.

His friend gave a weak smile. "Come back into the village. Perchance there is a comely lass to entice you and warm your bed on this night."

"*Tempting* as that may sound, the land beckons me."

Rorik shook his head slowly and walked away. "You mean the *wolf* calls to you. Forgive me for saying this, but you are becoming a monk, my friend."

He snarled. "I do not follow the *monks*' beliefs. And I did not ken you were watching my carnal pleasures with such a keen eye."

Rorik glanced sharply at him. "You ken well my meaning. I will say nae more."

Magnar watched as the man gathered the remainder of the food items and shoved them into the pouch. "I shall meet you at the shore in two days. If my plans change, I will send a message."

Rorik waved at him over his shoulder and disappeared into the darkness.

Returning his attention to the sea, Magnar scratched at two days' growth of beard. Though the temptation to sink his cock between the soft folds of a woman was a heady desire, he could ill afford to spend time slaking his pleasures. Other pressing matters required his attention.

After stripping free of all his clothing, he inhaled slowly, allowing the magic to build within his body. The waves of the ocean echoed all around him as power flooded his veins. On the exhale, he shifted in a shimmer of gray lights and transformed into the wolf.

Shaking off the lingering energy, he swiftly glanced in all directions.

Gifted with agile speed since birth, Magnar took off running over the hills. The moist, musty scent of the earth filled his nostrils, urging him onward. Past his home, past the village, and upward toward the crest of the large hill by the ocean. Time no longer existed. Only the elements surrounding him.

The man became the wolf—a freedom both relished.

Small animals quickly dodged out of his path, most likely in fear of becoming his next meal. But the wolf cared nothing about them. Traversing over the rocky incline, he steadily moved quietly toward his destination.

The moss-covered stone structure loomed in the moonlight. The wolf padded toward the entrance. Sniffing cautiously, he hesitated before ducking low and entering the enclosure. Once inside, the wolf went to the back where the bones of many eagles lay scattered in a crescent form.

Stretching out his front paws, the wolf became the man.

With a shudder, Magnar scooted against the cold stone wall and brought his knees to his chest. Closing his eyes, he whispered the words of magic to the Gods of Norse and Pict to show him the path to where his brother now resided.

Chapter Three

Thurso, Scotland ~ Castle Steinn

Smoke filled Elspeth's vision as she tried to ease into a better position within the stables. The fires continued to ravage the outer bailey, leaving her with no clear path to flee. The stench of dead bodies coated the back of her throat, and she cupped a hand over her mouth to keep from heaving what little she had in her stomach onto the ground. Fear cloaked her as surely as the haze surrounding her.

A tiny hand tugged on her cloak, reminding Elspeth to temper her emotions. She bent down and placed a finger over her nephew's lips. "You must be silent, Erik," she whispered.

The lad frowned. "Like my friend?" He patted the pouch secured on a belt at his waist.

Giving him a weak smile, she nodded. "Aye, like Sir Mouse."

He lifted his chin and returned a smile of his own.

Standing, Elspeth quickly scanned the entrance again and deemed their only hope of staying alive meant they had to flee on foot. None of their horses were inside, and she had nae time to dwell on what happened to them. To remain within the castle walls with the enemy would bring death to her nephew—the new chieftain of Steinn Castle.

Wrapping an arm around Erik, she fought the wave of pain burrowing into her chest from witnessing her brother, Thomas' death at the hands of one of the Northmen invaders. Only two days prior, he'd opened the gates, giving them a warm welcome. They came to discuss plans of trading. However, war against the King of Scotland was their true strategy, and they wanted Thomas to ride with them. When he argued against this traitorous idea, his life became forfeit.

A scream ripped through the air, snapping Elspeth out of her thoughts. They could not stay hidden forever. Their home was under attack and being pillaged. She needed to get Erik to safety.

Crouching down beside the lad, she whispered, "We need to leave now. There are nae horses. Not one word shall pass from your lips until I give the order. Do you ken my meaning?"

"Did I not keep my tongue silent when we passed Robbie's dead body?"

She sighed. "Aye. But we may encounter more of the dead, and we have lost our guard."

"I am not a baby," he protested, stomping his foot.

Elspeth stood slowly. "I will hold you to your word." She held her hand outward.

When he grasped it firmly, he responded, "As the future chieftain, 'tis important."

You are now my chieftain, Erik Gunn.

Quickly settling her jumbled nerves, Elspeth moved them along to the entrance. Unable to see anything or anyone clearly, she feared she was leading them into danger.

Erik tugged on her hand.

"For the love of Mother Mary," she bit out under

27

her breath.

Her nephew pointed to the back of the stables. "I ken another way out."

Hope flared like the dawn of a new day. She nodded and gestured him back inside, allowing him to take the lead. When he entered one of the stalls, Elspeth wanted to protest. She watched in stunned silence as Erik removed one of the boards at the back of the stall. His small fingers deftly slid another board to the side. Though the opening was small, she judged they both could fit.

Elspeth went to her nephew's side. "Where does this lead, Erik?"

"Away from the bailey and to the kitchen gardens."

She narrowed her eyes in thought. "But we shall be trapped behind the wall."

Erik snorted. "Nae."

Before she could counter his response, shouting and curses flew near the entrance to the stables. Time was now their enemy.

Elspeth tugged on her nephew's arm and gestured him through the narrow space. The steps of an approaching man spurred her into action, and she followed Erik. Her leg scraped on the rough wood, and she bit her tongue to hold back the curse. There was no time to cover their escape, and Elspeth said a silent plea that God would see them safely away.

Quickly standing, she withdrew her dirk and took off down the small path. Fear kept her focused on following her nephew. If the enemy came upon them fleeing, Elspeth would do all in her power to fend them off until Erik managed to get away.

A bird flew out from a nearby bush, and she almost

let out a scream. Wisps of smoke curled around them reminding her of eagle's talons, and she fought the growing fear of being captured. Her steps slowed as they approached the kitchen gardens. Erik darted past the main entrance. Concern filled her as she moved past the apple trees. "You must be daft, Erik. You are leading us into a corner," she muttered with impatience.

When she came upon him, the lad was pointing upward.

"Sadly, we cannot climb over the wall." Her tone was resigned, and her shoulders slumped.

He gave her a look of disgust and ducked around the corner of the trees. Swiftly returning, he dragged forth a ladder.

Her eyes grew wide. "Sweet Mother Mary and all the saints," she whispered. "Now I ken where you go to in the early morn. You have been warned before for leaving the outer walls." She clicked her tongue softly, but a smile tugged on the corners of her mouth. "But how can we get down?"

Erik pointed to the tree. "This way," he uttered softly.

After casting a glance over her shoulder, Elspeth secured her dirk within the belt at her waist and helped Erik position the ladder against the stone wall. "Check in all directions before you go over the wall, aye?"

He nodded, his eyes gleaming brightly.

Squeezing his shoulder, Elspeth gently prodded him to proceed up the ladder. As she held her breath, she waited for him to cast his sight in all directions. And in a blink of an eye, her nephew slipped over the wall.

Exhaling slowly, she brushed a hand over her brow

and swiftly ascended the ladder. When she reached the top, Elspeth spotted the lad already standing by the base of the pine tree. As she straddled the wall, she did her best to shove the ladder away from view and onto the garden floor behind the trees.

Her heart beat rapidly with the hope of freedom as she grasped the tree branch and started her descent. Her gown snagged on one of the branches and she uttered a soft curse. Cautiously, she continued to make her way down.

With the ground firmly under her feet, she reached for Erik and embraced the lad in a hug. "Thank you."

He squirmed in her arms. "You are pleased?"

Releasing him, she smiled. "Aye. But we are not out of danger yet."

"Where are we going?" he asked quietly.

Unsure, Elspeth responded, "South."

The lad frowned. "If we go north, we can find friends to aid us. Father will need more men."

Sorrow filled Elspeth. Now was not the time to disclose to her nephew that the enemy traveled with two of their allies from the north and that his father was dead. South was their only recourse.

Turning back toward the wall, Elspeth bent and brushed away the moss and dirt from near the bottom. Swiftly removing a *sgian dubh* from her boot, she prodded a section of the wall free. She retrieved a small stone and stood. After securing her small blade, she sighed heavily.

Elspeth took hold of her nephew's hand. As she placed the stone in his palm, she said, "Wherever you go, Erik, you take a part of your home with you. Never forget what happened here today. 'Tis important."

He frowned, tilting his head to the side. "But—"

She closed his fingers over the precious piece of their land. "Nae more questions until we are far away from here. You must put your trust in me, Erik."

He nodded and placed the stone in the pouch secured at his side.

Elspeth cast her sight one more time at their home. She prayed the others within the castle had fled from the destruction imposed by the enemy. *Aye, King William will hear of this injustice, and we shall return to claim what is ours—yours, Erik.*

Returning her gaze to her nephew, she reached for his hand and started forward.

****

"Are you sure we are heading south, Aunt Elspeth?" inquired the lad for the fifth time in the last several hours.

Trying to maintain her patience, she replied, "Aye." She pointed upward where the sun shone brightly. "Did you not learn how to follow the movement of the sun's progress across the sky?"

"Aye, *aye*. I still do not ken why we have to travel so far," he protested, rubbing a hand over his stomach.

Elspeth realized they had not eaten since the morning meal yesterday. The madness began before the evening meal. When her brother had pulled her aside at the entrance to the great hall, his features were strained. Thomas instructed her to fetch Erik and leave with one of his guards. He feared his guests were not who they portrayed themselves to be and considered them to be dishonorable thieves.

She shoved what happened next out of her thoughts.

Scanning their surroundings, she heard the soft bubbling of water. If anything, they could refill their water skins. She pushed aside heavy tree limbs, hoping to get a better view. The sound appeared to be on their right. She judged the path to slope downward, and turned toward Erik. "Are you thirsty?"

"Nae." He wiped a hand over his nose and bent his head.

"We need to take advantage of refilling our water skins, aye?"

When he kept silent, Elspeth tugged on his arm. "Where is my brave warrior?"

His head snapped up. "You meant me?"

She waved her hand about. "Do you see another warrior standing with us?"

He visibly swallowed. "Nae. Only me."

Smiling, she nodded. "Correct. Warriors on a quest do not behave in a sullen matter, especially when they are hungry—"

The lad placed his hands on his hips. "Did I say anything about food?"

Elspeth fought to keep her mirth hidden. "In truth, you did not. Your countenance speaks another message, though."

Glancing around, he asked, "Where is this water?"

She tapped a finger to her mouth. "Why don't you show me? Your first quest, Warrior Erik."

Her nephew puffed out his chest and scampered away.

Following after him, she spied a thick blackberry bush, ripe with berries. "Thank you, God," she murmured.

She pondered if she should shout her glee at

finding some food or let her nephew search for the bounty. Shielding her eyes from the afternoon sun, she observed his small body already refilling his water skin.

Waiting patiently against an aging oak tree, she tried to ease the tension in her back. Upon his return, Elspeth handed him her water skin.

"The Gods have provided food for us, too," he announced in a cheerful tone.

"Gods?"

"Aye. Odin and Dagda." He pointed behind her. "Blackberries."

Elspeth did her best to temper her anger over his choice of words. It had been a constant battle between herself and her brother. This clash over beliefs and the new religion often left them spewing harsh words at each other. Indeed, her nephew continued to defy her request not to mention the old Gods. In truth, now was not the time to debate his choice of religion.

She dipped her head at him. "Your eyesight is keen, my warrior."

Smiling broadly, he dashed back to the stream. After refilling her water skin, he returned to her side.

"Let us consume the food *God* has graciously provided," suggested Elspeth.

Coming upon the bush laden with fruit, Elspeth went and sat on a fallen log. She motioned for Erik to pluck some of the berries. Unfastening her cloak, she removed the garment. The day was warm, and she offered another silent prayer that their journey would not be fraught with any foul weather.

Erik returned and dropped a portion of the ripe fruit into her lap and joined her on the log. Each enjoyed a respite while they ate their small meal. A rabbit skittered about in the dry leaves seemingly unfazed by their presence, and they both watched its progress through the forest floor.

"I miss Hilda's stew," uttered the lad quietly.

She popped the last blackberry into her mouth. "Aye. The cook did have a way of preparing a fine rabbit stew with cabbage."

He glanced at her sideways. "But I am not hungry enough to take my blade to our friend, the rabbit."

Elspeth chuckled softly. "You are a compassionate warrior, Erik."

Snorting, he finished the rest of his blackberries. "I might not be tomorrow."

As the tension eased somewhat from Elspeth's shoulders, she realized the time had come to speak with Erik about his father. After taking a sip of water, she placed the water skin on the ground. Brushing her hands over the folds in her gown, she turned toward him.

"I need to share some knowledge with you, Erik. It will not be pleasant to hear, but I ken you are a strong lad—"

"*Warrior*," he interrupted.

Nodding, she clasped her hands in her lap. "In truth you are more. You are now *my* chieftain."

His brow furrowed, and he shook his head. "Father is your chieftain, not I."

Elspeth swallowed. The lump of pain grew within her chest, pressing against her body. "*Sadly*, our chieftain was slain by the enemy. Your father is dead, Erik."

The lad's face paled, and he stood abruptly. "You lie!"

"Nae." She shook her head solemnly. "I speak the truth." Elspeth reached for his hand, but he scooted away from her.

"We have to go back. He needs our help," he protested.

Standing, she continued to speak in a calm voice. "I watched him die. He is gone from this world."

The terror that lit within her nephew's eyes scared Elspeth. She feared he'd take off running through the trees, so she went to his side and wrapped a firm arm around his shoulder. "You must trust me."

He struggled to get free. "Nae, *nae!*"

Tears smarted her eyes, and she blinked in an effort to keep them from spilling. "Are you not a brave warrior, Erik, from the house of Gunn?"

Burying his head against her waist, he poured out his grief.

Elspeth held on to his quaking body, allowing this time for him to shed his sorrow. Finally, she allowed her own tears to trickle down her cheeks as she wept with him. Sorrow engulfed them both.

The shrill cry of an eagle snapped Elspeth out of her misery. Darting her gaze in all directions, she half-expected the Northmen to come charging through the trees.

She brushed a hand over the top of Erik's head. "We need to keep moving and put some more distance between us and the enemy. We can follow the path of the stream."

Her nephew lifted his head. He wiped his nose with the back of his hand. Raw determination glittered back at her within the depths of his eyes. "One day, vengeance will be mine."

In that quiet moment, Elspeth witnessed the birth of a chieftain.

Chapter Four

"You are unwise in your move, old friend," remarked Magnar, studying the board with intent.

Berulf refilled his cup with more ale. "And as always, you insult me with your words. Might I remind you that it was I who taught you the game of *hnefatafl*?"

"Did I not win our last battle?" inquired Magnar as he moved his defender forward.

"It was a *first* in many moons," countered Berulf, glaring at him over the rim of his cup.

"Yet a win."

His friend narrowed his eyes and returned his attention to the game. "Are you boasting?"

Magnar watched him in silent study. Stirring the ire of Berulf was one that led to him winning. Would the elder fall prey to the trap again?

"Presenting the facts," replied Magnar.

The man grumbled a curse and moved one of his attackers.

Magnar smiled inwardly.

"Your meeting with Ragna must have gone well. You are still here."

Magnar's smiled faded, and he swiftly moved his king out of harm's way. Until he spoke with King William, he could not confess about his quest to seek out his brother. Another thought occurred to him. "She held news about my mother's passing," he offered, and then quickly added, "Have you heard of any thieving by traders without honor?"

Berulf's hand hovered over one of his war pieces. "Are you gaining knowledge for King William?" His question held a note of warning.

Magnar arched a brow. "My loyalty is to my king...*always*. But this is not for him."

After moving another piece across the board, his friend leaned back in his chair. "I was sorry to hear about Olga's passing. Many mourned her loss."

Keeping his focus on the game, Magnar nodded slowly. He had nae desire to speak further about his mother.

Silence hovered like an unwelcome companion. Flames snapped in the hearth behind them, and Magnar moved another piece on the board.

Berulf let out a soft belch. "There have been rumors of certain Northmen who are intent in regaining a stronghold in Scotland."

Returning his gaze to the man, Magnar frowned. "Continue."

He waved a hand dismissively. "As I've stated. Merely rumors. Their actions and deeds are not what you would call honorable. They make claims as traders, but in truth, they are seeking to stir the wrath within the country."

Magnar folded his arms over his chest. "Rumors?"

His friend shrugged. "Scotland's troubles are not my affair. These skirmishes come to us as messages on the sea breezes—from one man to the next. How am I to discern truth from a tale woven by another after a few cups of ale?"

"Nevertheless, you chose to tell me."

Berulf tapped a finger to his chin, surveying the board. "Did you not admit this knowledge was for you and not your *king*? Nae doubt you shall take this information to him." Shifting another piece, he announced, "I have you."

Magnar leaned forward and swiftly moved his king from being captured. "You are wrong, old friend. A few men intent on stirring the wrath within Scotland can be easily handled. I am certain your king did not approve this kind of plan, aye?"

"Is not King Inge *your* king, too?"

Magnar leveled a hard glare at the man. "You ken my loyalties are to both, but I serve only one—the Lion of Scotland."

Snorting in disgust Berulf shoved away from the table and stood. "Kings, men, wolves—you're all beasts, each trying to defeat the other." He went to the hearth and tossed more wood into the flames. The fire snapped and hissed.

Taken aback by his friend's words, Magnar shifted in his chair. "What ails you?"

The man glanced over his shoulder. "Will there ever be peace?"

Stunned, Magnar burst out in laughter.

"You find humor in my words?" snapped his friend.

Magnar held up his hands in surrender. "Forgive my laughter. 'Tis only shocking you would speak of peace when our people have been plundering for hundreds of years. There will always be differences, war, and men seeking to cause unrest. All for the love of *power*. You ken this, old friend."

Berulf blew out a sigh and went back to his chair. "I grow weary of the battle."

All humor vanished from Magnar. "Do your bones speak for you, Berulf the Axe? Or is your mind addled from too much drink?"

The man fingered with one of the war pieces. "Perchance both."

"The table at Valhalla is not ready to greet one of its finest warriors," remarked Magnar.

His friend chuckled softly. Slipping another piece across the board, he said, "Do not attempt to thwart the plan of All Father."

"I can always bargain with Odin."

"You tempt fate, MacAlpin."

"I deem I have my entire life," admitted Magnar, moving a defender in front of his king.

Berulf leaned back and stroked his beard. "Next time we meet, we shall talk of crops and the weather. I see this discussion has not kept my mind focused on our game." He tapped a finger to his head.

Magnar roared and smacked his hand on the table. The game pieces toppled everywhere. "Or leave the drinking to me and you can have water."

Reaching for his cup, Berulf grunted a curse and drained the remainder of his ale.

****

Narrowing his eyes at the glaring sunlight, Magnar waited for the small boat to approach the shore. Earlier, he had gathered some of his belongings from his former home and had them placed on board his ship. Instead of two days, his visit on *Kirkjuvágr* had grown to a sennight, and that had been more than enough. Strangely, though, he felt a small ache at leaving the

40

isle. He glanced over his shoulder in the direction of his parents' home. Others in the village would watch over and tend to the dwelling. Perchance he would return in six moons.

He watched Rorik dismount from his horse. The man staggered, and Magnar pondered if his friend got any rest in the past week. *You have had far too much drink and women. The sea journey back home will not be pleasant.*

Berulf approached Magnar's side. "I shall take care of the horses."

Magnar gave him a curt nod. "Thank you."

"Before you take your leave, the group of men plundering, instead of *trading* are known by a certain name. They barter for goods with precious amber stones, furs, and narwhal tusks."

The boat landed on the sandy shore. Magnar gestured to Rorik to proceed ahead of him. He turned toward Berulf. "Aye? And their name?"

"*Loki's Vengeance.* They seek to bring back the ways of the old Gods before Odin ruled."

The wolf within Magnar growled. "There is nae purpose or justice in vengeance in *this* world. 'Tis between the Gods, not us. They'd best serve Odin than stir his wrath."

"Have you forgotten the *edda*—the tales spoken by the fire? Loki will use any to gain power in all realms."

Magnar shook his head. "Surely the Seer would advise us of any threat of a battle, aye? Her magic would see beyond to the other side."

Berulf shifted his stance and scratched the side of his face. "Depends on whose side she seeks her power."

Leaning near the man, Magnar uttered softly, "Be

warned—Ragna would never betray her people for power. I am not overly fond of the woman, but I ken unfailing loyalty from her." Straightening, he added, "And I might remind you she has ears everywhere."

The man looked affronted. "Did I mention her name?"

"And yet she approaches."

Berulf let out a sigh and turned around. "Good morn, Ragna."

Ignoring his greeting, she continued past him. "Walk with me, Magnar."

He winked at his old friend. Magnar kept his steps slow as he kept pace with the Seer. "Have you come to give your regards at my passing from *Kirkjuvágr*?"

"Do not flatter yourself, *wolf*," she replied dryly.

The beast within Magnar gnashed his teeth. But the man remained composed.

When she came to the bend along the shore, Ragna paused. Shielding her eyes with her hand, she kept her sight fixed on a flight of sea birds gliding over the waves of the ocean. "Have you gleaned anything from the bones?"

"South appears to be the message," he replied, clasping his hands behind his back.

Chuckling softly, Ragna lowered her hand. "The Gods and Goddesses must favor you, Magnar. They refuse to answer me."

Her admission startled him. "I am unsure how to respond."

This time her laughter surrounded him. She tilted her head to one side, studying him. "Contrary to my certain gifts, there are times when the Gods and Goddesses choose *not* to deliver their messages through me. Often times, they judge it wiser to deal directly with another." Ragna turned fully toward him. "You have been chosen, Magnar. Tread carefully on this journey you have been given. There is a division in your lineage. The path is unclear."

"Before I undertake any quest, I must report to King William."

"Aye. Your king must be informed," she replied dryly. "You never did state the name of your brother."

Magnar turned away from her questioning gaze. "I did not ken his name until I read the letter from my mother. He is called Thorfinn."

"The Fates are definitely guiding you." The woman removed a sealed parchment from the belt at her side. Handing the document to Magnar, she added, "This is the third letter your mother wrote. You must see it safely to your brother."

As Magnar took the document from her hand, his anger surfaced once again at being denied a chance to know his twin. Yet he quickly suppressed the emotion. His parents were dead.

I shall right this injustice. My oath to you, Thorfinn.

After tucking the parchment securely inside his pouch, Magnar exhaled softly.

Ragna bent and picked up a shell along the water's edge. "If I may ask, are you considering bringing your brother into the brotherhood?"

He cast her a sideways glance. "You ken the rules. Only one from each clan."

A muscle twitched in her jaw. "I am familiar with the edicts proclaimed when the ancient order was birthed. You have not answered my question, which leads me to reason you're unsure of what you will offer him."

"Nae. But would you be comfortable with the knowledge, if I decide to *bend* the laws?"

She rubbed her thumb over the smooth surface of the shell. "Out of all the wolves, you are the most stubborn."

Magnar roared with laughter. Recovering quickly, he replied, "And here I thought you believed Rorik was the most stubborn."

Her mouth twitched with obvious mirth. "There is another word for that wolf."

Magnar's good humor vanished. "He is a man first, Ragna."

She tossed the shell out into the water. "Simply a wolf that prefers to sniff under the gown of any woman whom he desires."

Curious, he asked, "Why do you despise him thus?"

"Because he unleashes the beast within the man," she snapped.

Magnar arched a brow. "I suppose there is more to your account. The man has honor, as do all within the brotherhood."

She snorted and folded her arms over her chest. "You all have your own rules." Pointing a finger at the small boat, she continued, "Ask how many he bedded this week. Shameful."

Curious at her venom toward his friend, he asked, "Since when did Rorik's carnal appetites concern the Seer?"

She gave him a horrified expression and took a step back. "You...you misunderstood my meaning."

"I think not." He dipped a slight bow. "Until we meet again."

Without giving her time to respond, Magnar strode quickly across the shore. Tension between his friend and the Seer had always been a thorn in his side. He should have brought another on the voyage. Out of all within the brotherhood, Ragna despised his loyal friend the most. With each visit to the isles, the tension between them became more terse—each spouting harsh words at the other.

Upon reaching the boat, Magnar climbed inside and signaled for the man to proceed with rowing them back to the ship.

Rorik leaned his head against the edge of the boat, keeping his eyes closed. "What words of wisdom did the witch spout to you?"

"Your *shameful* appetites," confessed Magnar, watching for his friend's reaction.

Rorik cracked open one eye. "I do not recall seeing her at any of my meals."

He snickered softly. "*Carnal* appetites."

"Bloody interfering woman. Her words and tongue are as sharp as the sting of nettles. She should keep to her runes and bones. 'Tis not her concern."

Leaning forward, Magnar braced his forearms on his thighs. "I agree with you. Can you share why she loathes you?"

The boat rose and fell over a large wave, and his friend let out a groan. He rolled over and heaved the contents of his stomach into the sea. After wiping his mouth with the back of his hand, Rorik resumed his position in the boat. "You might as well confer with Odin, since I cannot give you an answer. The woman is foul-tempered and ugly as the Black Hills of Gorlean."

Magnar shoved the man's leg aside with his boot. "Might I remind you that those hills you speak of are stunning in summer months—filled with flowers."

Rorik placed a fist over his stomach. "All this talk of the woman has soured my gut. I have nae wish to speak of the vile witch any further."

Sea spray washed over them, and Rorik uttered a curse. "By the hounds, are we heading into a storm?"

Magnar threw back his head and roared with laughter. "'Tis a long journey, my friend. And you best pray to all the Gods and Goddesses we do not encounter any tempests, or your body will suffer greatly. I deem a prayer to the God of the Sea and Winds, Njörd, to keep back any threat of storms might aid you."

Rorik rolled to the side again and held his head over the boat. "If Njörd forsakes me, I give you permission to take your blade to my heart."

Chapter Five

Clamping a hand over her nephew's mouth, Elspeth stilled. She studied the area ahead. Several horses were tethered to low-hanging tree limbs. Her ears strained to pick up any sound of their owners. Birds chirped and darted within the thick forest, only adding to her frustration.

Time moved slowly, and Erik squirmed at being confined.

She brought them both to a crouching position behind a large gorse bush and released her hold on him. "I do not ken who is out there," she whispered.

Erik rubbed his eyes. "I say we take their horses."

Narrowing her eyes in thought, she pondered her nephew's plan. "What if there are others on horseback?"

"Then we ride hard and fast," he responded. He pointed to the small blade tucked in his boot. "I can always toss my weapon at any who may come for us."

You have learned to master the small blade, but you are not that good, nephew.

She tapped a finger to her chin with a better idea and smiled. "What if we take their satchels?"

His eyes grew wide. "Food?"

Elspeth nodded in agreement. "Can I trust you to stay hidden while I fetch the satchels?"

"I can help you," he offered, a grin creasing the

corners of his mouth and his eyes bright with the new challenge.

Her chieftain was growing in confidence. Since their conversation two days ago, he had tried to defend his right in doing things his way. Elspeth could not find fault with the lad. She required strength and courage during this hardship while they traveled the land, not a fearful lad. With no food, she tried her best to forage the forest for any signs of fruit or nuts. Though her nephew kept silent about his gnawing hunger, his strength was declining.

Placing a firm hand on his shoulder, she uttered softly, "Wait until I raise two fingers. When you see the signal, come forth with quiet steps."

He gave her a curt nod.

Elspeth rose from her position and studied the landscape once again. Swallowing the fear lodged in her throat, she darted out from the gorse bush. Making slow steps toward the horses, she tried to squash her uneasiness so as not to frighten the animals. Dry leaves rustled under her feet with each step she took.

Finally drawing near the first horse, Elspeth drew in a deep breath and released it slowly. Brushing her hand over the thick mane of the horse, she was rewarded with a soft snicker. Her fingers deftly removed the leather satchel before she crept along to the other horse. After safely procuring the second satchel, Elspeth glanced in all directions. Deeming it safe, she held up two fingers.

Erik swiftly approached by her side. She could ill afford to find out what the large pouches contained and motioned the lad to proceed through the thick pines ahead of her.

Onward they traveled along the edge of the stream until it narrowed through a thick part of the forest. When she noticed a stone pathway to the other side, she wanted to shout for joy. Though the water splashed over part of the stones, she judged they could cross safely.

Shifting the load on her shoulders, she moved ahead of Erik and halted at the edge of the water. After dropping their precious goods, she bent near the lad's head. "I will lead you across the stream, and then return for the satchels."

"I do not need help. I am not a baby," he protested.

"And if you slip and fall into the water?" she asked, her tone harsher than she intended.

He lowered his head and clenched his hands at his side.

"Aye. You would surely drown." Elspeth drew near his side. "A warrior—"

"Chieftain," he corrected.

She cast her gaze upward in an attempt to calm her nerves. "As I was about to say, a *chieftain* does not take risks unless he is prepared for the outcome. Can you swim, Erik?" She stole a glance at his features.

He sneered at her but held out his hand in surrender.

By all the saints, you remind me of my brother. So stubborn. Elspeth took his hand and led him carefully across the width of the stream. After safely seeing him behind a thick pine tree, she swiftly returned and retrieved the satchels. With careful steps, she made it across the stones and to Erik. Before disappearing through the forest, Elspeth gave one final glance over her shoulder to make sure no one was following.

Uttering another silent prayer, she slipped into the darkness.

****

"I reckon 'tis time to see what is in these heavy satchels," announced Elspeth.

Erik collapsed onto the forest floor. "About bloody time. I thought you were not going to stop until the sun went away."

She chuckled softly. "Nae. I only wanted to give us more time to slip away from the owners of these."

Scanning the area, she found a dry patch of leaves by the base of an oak tree. "I believe I have found a perfect spot for us to eat."

Though the air was brisk, her skin was damp from the effort of lugging the items, and she removed her cloak. Dumping the satchels on the ground, Elspeth stretched her arms over-head to ease the knots and tension from her shoulders.

Her nephew dashed over to the ancient oak and sat. She joined him and shoved one of the satchels toward him. "As my chieftain, I bid you to be the first to bring forth our bounty."

With eager hands, he lifted the flap and peered inside. Instantly, a frown marred his features and his shoulders sagged. "Nae food."

Her heart constricted, and Elspeth reached for the leather satchel. Carefully, she removed several rolled, sealed parchments. Tracing a finger over the red wax seal of a lion and along the graceful script, a tremor of dread washed over her. "What have we done?" she muttered.

"Perchance there is food in the second one," uttered her nephew quietly.

Ignoring him, Elspeth pulled out more documents. Icy wisps of fear traveled across her skin. *We have stolen documents meant for King William.* When she spotted the apples at the bottom, she blew out a sigh. At least her nephew could eat.

Drawing forth the fruit, she handed it to Erik. "Eat this slowly."

Elspeth expected him to utter a protest, but he took the offering and ate in silence. After removing several more apples, she returned the precious documents back inside the satchel. Her hands shook as she reached for the other one.

Upon opening the second satchel, she let out a choked sob. The smell of smoked dried fish assaulted her senses. "Thank you, Lord, for providing us this feast to nourish our bodies." She withdrew the parcels, one by one. After spreading them out in an orderly fashion, Elspeth unwrapped their fare. Not only was there fish, but small pies, bannocks, a wedge of cheese, and strawberries.

Erik dropped his partially eaten apple into his lap. He visibly swallowed as his gaze roamed their huge feast. "You…you first."

Smiling fully, she held out what she knew was Erik's favorite food.

"Smoked fish," he announced with glee, removing the parcel from her hand. When he took the first bite, he smiled and closed his eyes.

Elspeth retrieved the *sgian dubh* from her boot and sliced into the wedge of cheese. After taking several bites, she cut one of the pies in half and sniffed at the contents. "'Tis only onions, wild garlic, and mushrooms. Nae meat."

"I will eat that next."

Her eyes widened. "But you do not care for onions."

Her nephew pointed to their feast spread out before them. "'Tis food, Aunt Elspeth."

Nodding slowly, she handed him half of the vegetable pie.

As they ate their meal in contented silence, birds flitted down around them in hopes of catching a stray crumb or two. Elspeth crumbled a small portion of a bannock and tossed the bits outward.

Erik laughed as he watched their attempts to snatch all the crumbs from the forest floor. Joy infused Elspeth, and she settled back against the rough bark of the oak tree.

"Are you finished?" inquired her nephew, wiping his mouth with the back of his hand.

"For now. We must treasure this bounty of food. I cannot say when we will encounter another fare this precious."

"Aye. You are correct. We must not eat everything." With care, the lad wrapped the remainder of the food and placed the parcels back in the satchel. He reached for an apple and stood.

Elspeth watched as her nephew tossed the fruit playfully into the air. It was the first time since their escape from Steinn Castle that she'd witnessed a relaxed child at play. *Will I ever see this side of you again, sweet nephew? Or will the hardships of our journey harden you?*

On a sigh, she closed her eyes and let the cool breezes relax her limbs.

Blood spewed forth from his lips—his eyes wide

with horror.

Elspeth clamped a hand over her mouth to squelch the scream, yet it was lodged in her throat. There was nothing she could do for him. The blade had struck a deadly blow, ending his life in seconds.

He sputtered out one final word. One final request he required of his sister. Whatever the risks, Elspeth knew what to do.

Find Erik.

Elspeth woke on a choked sob, tears streaming down her face. Bringing her knees to her chest, she tried to control her racing heart. The images of that horrific night struck with a vengeance. "You should not have died, Brother. I promise to avenge the injustice and take back what is ours—what belongs to Erik."

"An enemy of the king is an enemy of ours," announced the low male voice.

Startled by the appearance of two men emerging from the trees, Elspeth stood abruptly. They reminded her of the Northmen who had descended on their home. Had she and Erik been found so easily?

One of the men bore a jagged scar across his chin. His dark, menacing eyes pierced into hers, and she trembled. Fear rooted in her spine as she swept her gaze in all directions for her nephew. Were there others? Did they have Erik tied up somewhere? She cursed herself for falling asleep and allowing harm to come to the lad. She was his last protector, and she had failed.

"Who is this Erik you speak of?" asked the other man, steadily approaching her. His lip curled in disgust as he slowly unsheathed his sword.

Hope flared within her. *Thank you, God! The lad must have fled.*

She swallowed in an attempt to calm her voice. "It was only a dream."

Her breathing hitched as she watched the pair advance toward her. The tree held her trapped without a means of escaping. All hope of seeing her nephew to safety had been for nothing. She blinked back the tears smarting her eyes. *Seek me out at Heaven's gate, Thomas. I pray I find you there.*

Somewhere a spark of courage wove its way into Elspeth's quaking body, and she lifted her chin. She clamped a hand over the dirk at her belt.

Both men halted.

"I will not go willingly," she stated with determination, withdrawing her dirk.

The man with the scar smiled slowly. "Care to make a wager, Ivar?"

"Aye. I say you can disarm her in two seconds, Bjorn."

"Nae, Ivar. She will drop the blade on the ground *willingly.*"

"You tempt fate, my friend."

The man called Bjorn sheathed his sword.

Cold sweat broke out along Elspeth's body. The eyes of the monster turned from pale blue to black in a second, followed by a blood chilling growl. Her grip tightened as she stepped away from the oak.

"Then let death take me, but you *devil* shall not," she whispered.

"Nae! Leave her alone!" shouted Erik, as he came charging to her side with his small blade held outward at the monsters.

Everything tumbled in a flash of colors and movement. Where only moments before Erik had been standing in front of her, he was now bound in the arms of the monster called Bjorn. Her blade had been wrenched free from her hand and now secured in the hands of the other monster.

Erik continued to squirm and thrash in an attempt to free himself.

"Stop!" snarled Bjorn.

"I beg you, please release my nephew," pleaded Elspeth. "He means you nae harm. Erik—"

"Erik?" The man glanced swiftly at the lad struggling to free himself.

"Aye. 'Tis my name, you savage. I am the chieftain of Castle Steinn." Her nephew met the stony glare of the monster.

The blood drained from Elspeth's face. Dread invaded every pore within her body. The lad had revealed too much. She clutched a fist to her chest. "Nae," she mumbled.

Shock registered across her nephew's captor, and he instantly released his hold. Placing Erik on the ground, the man was rewarded with a kick to his shin, but Elspeth doubted he even felt the attack.

Erik promptly returned to her side. Though she saw the fear reflected within his eyes as he took a hold of her hand.

"For the love of Odin, how can this be?" asked Ivar. "Why are they here? And why did they steal our provisions?"

Confusion marred the features of the one called Bjorn. He stepped away and went toward the satchels.

"We were hungry," blurted out Elspeth. "I...I did not ken about the important missives for the king." She grew weary of the battle with these men and prayed they would spare their lives.

Bjorn handed the satchels to Ivar and then regarded Elspeth. "I ken the chieftain of Castle Steinn. He goes by the name of Thomas."

Elspeth drew her nephew closer to her side. "My brother was slain days ago. This is his son, Erik."

The man blew out a curse. Raking a hand through his hair, he withdrew his sword. The light danced off the blade.

Unable to move, Elspeth held her breath for the fatal blow to slash across her body. Yet it never came.

Bjorn knelt on one knee and placed his blade on the ground in front of Erik. "As I made an oath to your father on the day he became chieftain, I do so again in front of you. My blade and sword arm are yours. Though my allegiance is to King William as part of the elite guard, I pledge to protect you and those under your protection. We shall see you and your aunt safely to the king."

Erik moved away from the safety of Elspeth and placed his tiny hand on the man's shoulder. "Thank you, Bjorn."

The other man came forward and did the same in front of her nephew. Elspeth watched in stunned silence at the change that had come over these men. From enemy to angels sent from God. Once, she had heard her brother speak of the special guards that worked for the king. He regarded them with the utmost respect, but feared them as well. Elspeth tried to recall something else her brother had mentioned about these men.

Bjorn dipped his head toward her. "Forgive us for the harm that has befallen you. These lands have seen many come under attack. We cannot be led astray even by a lone woman and lad traveling these parts. Had we known who you were, I can assure you a much kinder approach. How did you come to be so far away from the castle?"

Elspeth laughed bitterly and moved away from her nephew, who was now speaking softly to Ivar. The air had chilled considerably, and she went to retrieve her cloak. She glanced sharply at Bjorn. "During the battle after the death of my brother, I managed to find Erik and flee the castle."

"Then how fortunate we were in the area."

"And that you had food," added Elspeth, giving the man a tight smile.

He scratched the side of his face. "Aye. In truth, we were on our way to your brother. We had a writ from the king for him." Bjorn cast his sight to her nephew. "Which now must be read to the new chieftain."

Brushing out the leaves and dirt on her cloak, Elspeth wrapped the garment around her shoulders. "Nae need. My new chieftain might be a lad of seven winters, but I can assure you, he is capable of reading the script of King William."

Chapter Six

Castle Vargr, Scotland ~ Clan Sutherland

With steely calm, Magnar waited for his king to respond. King William stared aimlessly out the arched window. The man had neither moved nor uttered a word since Magnar had shared the news about his twin brother.

The air within the small chamber felt chilled even with the heat of the fire in the hearth.

Upon his return to the Earl of Sutherland's stronghold, Magnar had immediately requested a meeting in private with the king. Aye, he realized his grave error in not reporting the information his mother shared with him earlier last year. But now was not the time to ask the king for his absolution.

By outward appearance, the king was not pleased. And Magnar offered no apology either.

"Do you believe in the one God?" inquired the king softly.

Magnar gritted his teeth. *You ken who we are and what you call our heathen ways.* "I follow the old beliefs."

William glanced sharply over his shoulder at him. "That is not what I asked."

"I do not ken your God. So, nae."

The king resumed his focus on the landscape

below. "'Tis a pity."

Unsure how to reply, Magnar remained silent. He could not fathom this direction of conversation.

"I do not ken why God has deemed men to be part man and wolf." He gestured outward. "To me, magic is evil."

Magnar shifted his stance. His respect for his king was absolute, but the man's words unsettled him. His blood flowed with the magic of the old beliefs. Ancient, commanding, and a verra part of his soul. Had the time come for the king to disband the ancient order?

"Yet those within the brotherhood are honorable, loyal, *and* good men," uttered the king softly. "Perchance one day you will seek out my Lord." He turned from the window. Crossing the room, he came and stood before Magnar. "The news you have brought me disturbs the balance within the brotherhood. Is this a new evil that will threaten us?"

Magnar blew out a frustrated breath. "There shall always be battles between good and evil. Do not your own holy stories speak of two brothers—"

"Aye, the Scriptures," interjected William, rubbing a hand through his beard. He narrowed his eyes. "You have heard the tales?"

Giving the man a tight smile, Magnar nodded. "Call me a well-read heathen."

William chuckled and wagged a finger in front of him. "Be warned. Brother Calum does not favor those who read his scrolls. He considers the holy words sacred and not to be viewed by any except members within the order of monks and bishops. I find nae objection to others reading what has been written down. I believe these teachings should be read by any who wish to learn about our Lord. Yet I am not ready to battle the bishops over the teachings of theology."

Shrugging, Magnar replied, "Then tell Brother Calum not to leave his parchments lying around for others to read."

The king arched a brow. "I have only witnessed him doing so in his chambers here and at the abbey."

"I studied with Brother Stephen many moons ago in an attempt to gain insight into the thievery of certain relics. I grew curious during my time there and came upon the scrolls lying on a table. I did not ken they belonged to Brother Calum."

"Interesting," mused the king. "Brother Stephen never mentioned your visit. Currently, the holy scrolls are under the care and protection of Brother Calum."

Curious, Magnar asked, "Would you have forbidden me from entering the grounds of the abbey?"

William shook his head and started for the table. Reaching for a jug of ale, he poured some into two cups. He handed one to Magnar. "All are welcome at God's table. Especially those who wish to learn about our Lord. If I had known, I would have greatly approved of the monks sharing the knowledge with you. As you ken, there is only one amongst you who follows our belief."

"Aye. Gunnar," admitted Magnar. It proved to be an endless topic of conversation within the brotherhood. The lone man who refused to join in their feast days.

William laughed. "You should name him Gunnar the Peacemaker.

"And all are welcome in the house of Odin," offered Magnar.

The king snorted and gestured for Magnar to take a

seat. "Nevertheless, we must decide on what to do about your brother."

After taking a sip of ale, he leaned back in his chair. "I must first find Thorfinn."

The king's lips thinned. "Where?"

"I reckon he is here in Scotland."

"Purpose?"

"Unsure."

William studied him. "Are you undecided on what to share with me?"

"To spout untruths without any facts is not wise," countered Magnar.

"What can you share, *MacAlpin*?" The king's words held a note of impatience.

"The only truth I ken. He travels with those not honorable. They plunder and destroy all in their path. I have gathered information from local villagers on my return from *Kirkjuvágr*."

The king stared into the flames. "I have sent missives with Bjorn and Ivar to all the chieftains in the north. They will be gone for several more weeks. News has reached me of the increasing skirmishes of several bands of Northmen. They steal, rape, and burn everything. Those who manage to flee speak of an evil monster who leads them. There is talk of fear amongst my people of King Inge invading our shores."

"I can assure you the King of Norway has nae desire to claim this part of Scotland," professed Magnar.

William returned his gaze to Magnar. "Have you spoken with him recently? Or do you give your account on those from *Orkneyjar Isles*?"

Frowning, Magnar responded, "Those who are

loyal to King Inge are *loyal* to me."

The king waved his hand dismissively. "We must end this conflict and find out who is at the heart of these mercenaries. A few men creating mayhem is easy to put down. But when a threat of this extent invades much of northern Scotland, I want it vanquished immediately."

Both men turned when Alexander Sutherland entered the chamber. The earl's features seemed strained as he approached. "We have a new threat," he announced.

King William stood abruptly. "Explain!"

"Ivar and Bjorn have returned. They bring with them Lady Elspeth Gunn and her nephew, Erik. They found them wandering the hills far away from Castle Steinn after a battle was fought."

Magnar placed his cup on the stone floor and stood slowly. A tremor of unease slid across his skin. "Where is their chieftain?"

Alexander rubbed a hand down the back of his neck. "Slain. The castle taken and parts burned. This is the only information disclosed to me from Bjorn. He requests to speak to you about the new chieftain."

"God's blood!" William tossed the remainder of his ale into the fire. "The nephew you speak of is in truth, the new chieftain of Castle Steinn."

"Nae," uttered Alexander in a shocked tone. "He is but a wee lad."

"Who will require guidance," interjected William. "Have proper chambers prepared for them. I shall meet with both of them now. Where are they?"

"I have cleared the great hall and placed them near the hearth."

"Good. For now, we must contain this news."

Dark fury burst within Magnar. He counted Thomas Gunn a loyal and good friend. He knew of his sister, but never had been introduced. Sadly, he had not visited with Thomas in many years, especially after the death of his wife in her childbed. The beast within him howled in protest and sorrow. He clenched and unclenched his fist, yearning to rip apart the person responsible for ending the life of a good man. "I shall speak with Ivar and Bjorn."

The king shook his head and made for the door. "Nae. Attend with me while I speak with them. You can glean any wisdom from their accounts. This threat across my lands will cease!"

After giving the king a curt nod, Magnar followed him out of the chamber.

****

Elspeth smoothed the folds of her gown, doing her best to brush the smudges of dirt staining the garment. Upon her arrival, she was told of King William being within the castle, and her nerves skittered. The food she had eaten earlier in the morn had quickly soured. However, Erik appeared eager to meet the king, despite his appearance. He continued to converse with Bjorn and Ivar as if they were kin. Even Lord Sutherland had taken an interest in what her nephew was saying before he departed the hall. Part of her realized this was Erik's way of dealing with the death of his father. Although she understood the young lad was merely waiting for the day to avenge his father's death.

You have found allies, Erik. Your father would be proud.

The flames from the hearth snapped, startling Elspeth. When the doors to the great hall opened, she pushed back her chair and stood. The man striding forward with Lord Sutherland following required no introduction. She had heard the tales of the tall, red-bearded king from her brother. Clasping her hands together to ward off the trembling within her body, she waited for him to acknowledge her.

Erik had left his companions and stood next to her. As the king approached, she dipped a low curtsey.

"I am saddened to hear of the loss of your chieftain—a loyal father *and* brother to you both," proclaimed the king in a low voice.

Words she wanted to offer in response lodged within her throat like a hard bannock as she rose upright.

"Thank you," whispered Erik, giving the king a bow.

"Aye. I can see courage in you as the new chieftain, Erik."

Erik beamed from the king's praise. He glanced up at Elspeth. "My aunt helped to get us free from the Northmen."

The king looked her way. "Indeed. A brave woman." Returning his attention to Erik, he motioned for him to take a seat. "You must share your account with us. You were fortunate to come upon my other guards, Bjorn and Ivar, but this is my most trusted guard, Magnar."

Slowly, Elspeth turned around at the mention of the other man. When had he entered the hall? She'd heard no other footsteps. Yet there he stood, looming over her as she lifted her head to meet his gaze. A giant with piercing blue eyes, long fair-colored hair, and a silver torc around his massive neck.

Another bloody heathen Northman!

Determined not to be swayed by his handsome features, she swallowed and took a step back.

The man approached. And Elspeth continued to back away.

He paused and tilted his head to the side. "You might want to halt your steps, Lady Elspeth."

His words skimmed across her skin and to the pit of her stomach. He was too near. His gaze made her dizzy, and her heart pounded against her chest. She would not be dismayed by his words. Elspeth shot him a haughty glare and lifted her chin. "Do not tell me what I shall do."

The man arched a brow and mirth danced within those eyes. "Unless you heed my words, you will fall back into the king."

Horrified, Elspeth glanced over her shoulder. King William was directly behind her. Beads of sweat broke out along the back of her neck. *You are a lady of the house of Gunn. What is wrong with you? He is only a guard for our king!*

Returning her attention to the man, she gave him a curt nod, unable to utter another word.

Elspeth scooted to the side and went around the table. Taking a seat across from her nephew, she watched in stunned silence as the giant approached and sat beside her.

"You were fortunate Bjorn and Ivar came upon you both. The forest is not a place for a young lad and woman to be traveling alone, especially without guards."

Elspeth held back the barb she wanted to toss out at the man. She decided on a more blunt approach. "The *young lad* is a strong warrior. And I am not some feeble maiden."

Reaching for a jug, Magnar poured the wine into two cups and handed her one. "Aye, I can see the fire in your eyes—strong *and* stubborn. Nevertheless, harm would have surely befallen you and your warrior, if you had continued on your journey."

Sweet Mother Mary! She fully understood the risk they took by fleeing. Certainly, she did not need to have this man rebuke her for taking action and seeking help. The man's presence surrounded her, and she longed to remove herself to another position at the table. Elspeth took a huge sip of the wine and then another. Glorious warmth invaded her body like a warm blanket, helping to ease the tension.

She swirled the wine within her cup. "I can assure you, *Magnar*, if Erik and I had remained at Castle Steinn death would have claimed us." She met his steely gaze. "It would have been *stubborn* and *foolhardy* to remain. Fleeing to protect my chieftain was my only choice."

He chuckled softly. "And I do not disagree with your decision."

"Then why mention anything?"

"Simply making a statement regarding my men and how their actions led them to you," he replied and then drained the wine in his cup.

"I thought they were the king's men?" disputed Elspeth.

A muscle twitched in his jaw, and he placed his cup on the table. "Aye, but I am their leader."

Confused, Elspeth started to object when boisterous laughter resounded from the king and other men. Erik was giving his account of how they stole the satchels of food. Except his interpretation was not entirely correct. Her nephew omitted the part where it was her skill and keen eyesight in retrieving the items.

Tapping her fingers on the table, she tried to draw her nephew's attention toward her. To rebuke him in front of the king would be beneath her. However, Erik would surely hear her displeasure at his fable when they were alone.

Magnar leaned near her. "Does the lad speak the truth? Or do I hear boasting?" he asked softly.

His warm breath caressed her cheek, and she dared to meet his heated gaze. "How do you ken?"

"The lad has captured the attention of the king. I have witnessed it among many men—young *and* old. 'Tis a custom to boast after a great victory. Besides, when someone is plied with wine, the truth is skewed to fit the bard. 'Tis a good story."

Elspeth blinked as if coming out of trance. "Wine? Erik has been drinking *wine*? Did someone not think to mix it with water?"

"Aye!" proclaimed Erik, lifting his cup high. "A chieftain always has drink with his meal."

Standing abruptly, she glanced around the table. She wanted to shout at them all. Did they not understand how exhausted they were? From the moment they arrived at Lord Sutherland's castle, they were ushered into the great hall to await the king. No food given. Only wine served. Bright red splotches covered her nephew's cheeks.

Moving away from the table, she went to her nephew and placed a firm hand on his shoulder. "My king. If you would be so kind, I shall see Erik to his chamber."

King William smiled. "Do not fret, Lady Elspeth. There was not much wine in his cup. I deemed it best to acknowledge his new position as chieftain with a small amount."

Relief coursed through her, and she gave him her best smile. "Then with your consent, may I fetch him some food from the kitchens?"

The king rose from his chair. "Lord Sutherland has prepared chambers for you both.

"I shall send a woman to attend to you. Another will bring food for you and Erik," announced Lord Sutherland.

"Chambers in the south tower?" asked Magnar, taking a hold of her elbow.

Lord Sutherland gave him a slight nod.

Startled once again by the man's silent movements, Elspeth remained mute, trying to control the warring emotions from the man's touch. The heat of his fingers seared into her gown and onto her skin.

Giving the king a small smile, she permitted Magnar to usher her out of the great hall. Erik kept a steady pace with their movements as he continued to entertain their overly bold guide with yet another tale of how they escaped their home.

Her steps slowed as the torchlight danced off the giant tapestry hanging on the wall near the stairs. The eyes of a white wolf bore into Elspeth as she drew near. Though only the head of the animal was represented within the woven threads, she half expected the wolf to jump out at her.

Elite Guards. Wolves. King William.

Elspeth returned her attention to the man holding

her in his grip. "I heard my brother *once* mention the elite guards for the king. He spoke with reverence *and* with fear. They are loyal to the king but had one leader—*one* who all of Scotland should fear because of his magic."

The man's eyes darkened, and a smile tipped the corners of his mouth. "Your brother was wise in his account."

Elspeth's heart pounded fiercely within her chest. "*You* are the leader of the Wolves of Clan Sutherland."

Chapter Seven

"You fight like a dog, Ivar!" Magnar spat on the ground in disgust. Even though the day was brisk, beads of sweat rolled off his body.

A low growl came forth from the man. "And you nae better than a woman."

"Harness both—man and beast," ordered Magnar, wiping the moisture from his eyes.

When Ivar lunged at him, Magnar attempted to block the blow. The result was a gash to his forehead from the man's blade.

"You might be my leader, but you cannot tell me how to fight in the lists."

Blowing out a curse, Magnar tossed his sword onto the ground. Out of all the warriors, Ivar continued to challenge him. Clenching and unclenching his right fist, he sneered at his foe in the lists. "Then let us see who can draw first blood without using a blade."

Ivar snarled. "Blood already seeps from a cut above your eye."

Pointing to his sword, Magnar argued, "From the blade—not a fist."

The man tossed his blade aside and charged forward. The battle between the two began in earnest, each determined to injure the other. Magnar leveled a mighty blow to Ivar's chin, but the man righted himself quickly and returned to the fighting. Each continued to struggle for balance and victory between grunts, curses, and blows. Yet not one drop of blood was drawn forth.

When the man dropped to the ground, Magnar held up his hand in warning. "Do not resort to the animal."

"Is it not what we are?" taunted Ivar, pounding the ground with his fist. "Man *and* wolf? To fight as both is folly. The wolf can emerge more powerful."

"The advantage is to have the power of both—a victory claimed," argued Magnar. Shifting his stance he swiped at blood instead of sweat this time. "You allow the wolf to rule in this challenge. And there will be nae winner."

Ivar's eyes shifted to darkened orbs with silver edging the rims.

"You refuse to listen?"

"I believe the time has passed for words, *MacAlpin*."

The wolf within Magnar clawed at him to be released. The lack of respect was an act of defiance—a total disregard of respect for his alpha. In one swift move, he gave the wolf partial rein and within seconds had the man flat on his back with his head twisted into the muddy ground.

Magnar clenched his other hand around his throat. "You have *forgotten* your place."

When the man refused to relent, Magnar continued to affirm his authority by squeezing firmly.

He leaned close to his ear. "You are nothing but a thief." The look he gave Ivar would singe the hair from any man or beast as he allowed his eyes to change to those of the wolf.

Ivar sputtered. "You…bar…*barbarian*."

His fury was doused by curiosity as Magnar lifted

his head to the sound of soft feminine laughter. Distracted by the flame-haired beauty walking by the entrance on Rorik's arm resulted in a blow to his nose from Ivar. Blood spurted forth, and Magnar delivered a hard fist to the man's chin, knocking him cold.

Elspeth's gasp surrounded him.

Breathing heavily, Magnar stood slowly. Doing his best to temper the wolf within, his gaze lingered on her before he sought out Rorik. For reasons he could not fathom, Magnar longed to rip the man's limb from his body. He should not be touching the lass. Especially not the *seducer of women*.

Rorik gave a curt nod. "I see you are the victor once again. 'Tis a shame for Ivar."

Magnar spread his arms wide. "Ready to battle another," he challenged.

Elspeth's features paled. She pointed to Ivar. "Is he alive?"

Kicking the man's leg with his boot, Magnar replied, "Aye. His pretty face will be covered with bruises for a few days, but I do not believe the lasses will mind while they tend to his injuries."

Rorik coughed into his hand to hide his mirth. "Never thought the man had a pleasing face."

"You are hurt," remarked Elspeth, removing her hand from Rorik's arm.

As the lass approached, Magnar fought the urge to take a step back. From the moment he stepped into the hall last evening, something primal had emerged—lust, as well as *possession*, and Magnar craved to have her beneath him. Never had he experienced such raw emotions over a female. He simply bedded them hard, swift, and then left.

Control was his shield—his strength.

Elspeth lifted her hand. In one swift movement, Magnar captured her wrist and trailed his thumb over the vein. Her scent surrounded him, and he inhaled sharply. *The fragrance of roses mixed with her female essence.* Even in the gray light, he noted the tiny freckles dotting her nose and cheeks. However, it was those emerald eyes that had him enchanted. Her lips parted, inviting him to take and plunder their soft fullness.

"I was only going to inspect your nose to see if it was broken," she offered softly.

He tilted his head to the side. "Why would it concern you?"

She gave a nervous laugh. "I had to tend to my brother's injuries many a time after sparring in the lists. His nose was in constant need of healing."

Magnar blinked and released his hold. *Harness the lust.* "I thank you, but there is nae need."

Wariness flared briefly within her eyes. She took a step back and nodded.

It took all of Magnar's restraint not to pull her back to him. He quickly stepped around the lass and walked away. The bite of wind slapped at his face as he wiped the blood from his nose on the back of his hand.

When he approached a smiling Rorik, he paused. "You will not bed this lass," he ordered with deadly calm.

Rorik's good humor vanished in an instant. "I have nae—"

He cut the man's words off with a growl. "Remove her from your conquests of women."

Keeping silent, Rorik shoved past him. Magnar

fought the temptation to steal one last look at Elspeth. Instead, he stormed out of the lists, heading for the icy waters of the stream behind the castle.

His blood required cooling—not from sparring in the list, but because of the heady scent of a certain beguiling woman.

****

A dull ache settled behind Magnar's eyes as he continued to drink heavily. The evening spent in the great hall had gone from quiet conversations to loud boasting and fighting over the best plan to attack Castle Steinn and rid the vermin from the lands. The king did little to thwart the heated debates. In truth, he sat back and listened with intent. A ploy Magnar often witnessed from the man.

Some of the thoughts being discussed echoed his own. Magnar should take the guards, slip inside the castle, and slit their throats. With the enemy vanquished, Lady Elspeth and Erik could continue with their lives.

After draining his cup, he reached for a jug next to Rorik. Though the man was sitting next to Elspeth, he refrained in any conversation and kept his hands on the table. In truth, Rorik appeared terrified when the lass took a seat next to him.

Magnar smiled inwardly. *At least you heeded my words.*

Never before had Magnar ordered Rorik—a good friend—to keep away from a female. His command bothered Magnar. Why should he concern himself with the lass? She was a female like any other. Unable to fathom any reasoning, he slammed the door on his thoughts and refilled his cup.

"Does he always drink so much?" she asked Rorik.

Magnar's hand stilled midway to his mouth. With his keen sense of hearing, the question had reached his ears. He turned slightly in his chair and lifted the cup outward to the lass. "Again, why would it concern you?"

Confusion marred those lovely green eyes. "You are mistaken in the question I posed for Rorik. Considering you have emptied two jugs and left none for the rest of us, I grew curious over your consumption."

"Should you confess or shall I?" interjected Rorik, giving him a bold look.

Magnar relented and judged it wiser to remain silent. The pain in his head increased.

Rorik folded his arms over his chest. "Whenever Magnar drinks heavily, 'tis due to a decision he is battling over within his mind. Two jugs, you say? I have seen the man drink a barrel in one night."

"Truly," she responded dryly, seemingly not impressed in the slightest. Pushing a trencher filled with boar's meat and onions toward him, she added, "Considering the beating you had in the lists, you might want to replenish your body with food and leave the wine for another night."

Loki's balls! Her tongue was as sharp as any he had encountered. "My body is none of your concern, unless you have other thoughts on what might fulfill my needs." The words spilled out of his mouth before he could take them back. Worse, he had stated them loud enough for some to halt their conversations.

Red splotches began along her neck and spread to her face. She lifted her chin and gave him a hard look.

"You are correct. Please accept my apology."

Elspeth spoke quietly to Rorik and then rose from her chair. "My king, the hour grows late. With your permission, I will take my leave and go tend to my nephew."

Giving her a smile, he replied, "I thank you for gracing us with your presence at our table tonight."

She never even looked at Magnar as she passed him on her way out of the hall.

The wine soured in Magnar's gut. He required no apology from the lass. He was the one with poor manners and tossing out sharp barbs. By the hounds he required fresh air to rid himself of the uneasiness and pain inside his head. Quickly draining his cup, he pushed away from the table and stood.

"What best plan of attack do you deem the wisest, Magnar?" asked King William.

He narrowed his eyes in thought. There was only one truth to profess to the king. "Let me take the guards, and we shall reclaim Castle Steinn."

"All of them?"

Magnar cast his gaze around the room, counting the number of the elite. "I will take those within the hall—Steinar, Bjorn, Ivar, Gunnar, and Rorik."

The king rubbed a hand through his beard and nodded slowly. "Take your leave from here after sunset tomorrow. Ten of my other guards will accompany you. We shall discuss more in the morning."

Relief coursed through him. Magnar dipped his head toward the king and then made swift strides from the hall. With a quest to plan, there was no time to dwell on anything else. Nevertheless, he yearned for the freedom to clear his mind and body from a certain lass.

When Magnar reached the castle entrance, his beast sensed the approaching shift. Shoving the doors open, he began to cross the bailey and halted. Standing in the middle was Elspeth gazing up at the partial full moon. Moonlight spilled around her tiny body creating a vision for him to feast upon.

The wolf within howled to be released. The man agreed.

Continuing on his journey out of the bailey and toward the portcullis, her words made him pause.

"Have I offended you in any way?"

He should keep on walking. The battle between his wolf and the man screamed within his mind. Clenching and unclenching his fist, he took a deep breath in and exhaled slowly. Turning to face her, he stared into emerald depths that shimmered in the moon glow.

"Nae, Lady Elspeth. 'Tis I that has offended you with my sharp words."

She chuckled softly. "Do not be so forgiving of my barbs either, Magnar. The nuns at the abbey were constantly chastising me for speaking my mind openly."

Stunned by her declaration, he asked, "You lived with nuns? Why would your brother send you to live with those who do not follow in his beliefs?"

"Aye. My brother sent me there when I was ten. I fought against leaving our home. But I was headstrong, outspoken, and was often found climbing trees or playing with the sheep and goats. He thought the women—nuns would soften my temperament. In many ways, my brother was attempting to make me obedient for marriage."

She lifted her head and pointed to the stars. "I

wanted to learn other things, not what was demanded of me." Blowing out a sigh, she returned her attention to him. "Nevertheless, I am grateful my brother did send me to the abbey. I found great love for our Lord there."

And I am a heathen in your eyes. A part of him saddened at the thought. "Your brother would be proud of you," he stated with sincerity.

Her eyes widened in surprise, and she smiled at him. "You knew him?"

Magnar returned her smile. "Aye, most definitely. I counted him among the few I call friends. He spoke only the one time of you." Clasping his hands behind his back, he lifted his sight to the stars. "Becoming chieftain at a young age after the death of your parents was an honor he accepted. It was the task of having to care for an unruly sister that caused him anguish."

"You do not need to remind me," she responded dryly. "I was a dreadful sister. He used to say my temper matched the color of my hair, stating that nae man would ever want such a rueful wife. Nae wonder he only spoke of me once to you."

Returning his attention to her, Magnar studied her taut features. "I reckon I would be upset if I had a sister who put maggots in my morning gruel."

Elspeth clapped a hand over her chest. "By the saints! I was beyond the threshold of anger with Thomas on that day. He had forbidden me from stepping outside the castle for *one* week. I nearly went mad. I made a vow to seek revenge on the mighty Chieftain Gunn."

"Truly," replied Magnar, doing his best not to laugh out loud. "I am sure he learned his lesson and never punished you again."

She pointed a warning finger in front of him. "I see you are jesting with me."

He held up his hands in surrender. "Do you see me laughing?"

Elspeth snorted. "I can see the mirth showing in your face, especially around your eyes."

Shrugging, he replied, "'Tis a witty tale."

"Aye, *aye*, but soon thereafter he sent me to the abbey," she confessed in a somber tone.

"Perchance Thomas judged it wiser for you to be tutored there. If I may ask, why did you not stay there?"

Sighing heavily, she wrapped her arms around her body. "I came back for the marriage of my brother. Our reunion was mixed with emotions—mine mostly filled with tears. I had not seen him in five years. I pleaded with him to allow me to remain, and he agreed. That was eight years ago. I did love the nuns, but my home was with him. Yet he soon found me challenging his belief in the old ways, and we argued many a night."

Doing the figures in his mind, he concluded the lass' age of three and twenty. "And you have not married?"

As she glanced at him, her expression turned guarded. "It was a constant battle of words between us. I argued against most of the other chieftains—"

"Too old," interrupted Magnar.

She nodded vigorously. "How did he expect me to have any children with them?"

Magnar burst out in laughter. Never had he encountered a woman so forward in her speaking. One moment, he wanted to rip out her tongue, and then the next, he found himself listening with interest.

"Pray forgive my words. I should not have blurted

that one out. I realize I am old to most men for a wife, but I would not settle for anything less than what our parents had." She twisted her hands together in front of her. "They truly loved one another."

"Did he insist on a chieftain?" asked Magnar, attempting to lessen her discomfort. "Surely there were other men offering to take you as their wife."

She shuddered, and Magnar yearned to take her in his arms to bring warmth to her.

Blowing out a breath into the frosty night air, she said softly, "It was one of our last arguments over my marriage. Thomas even suggested one of the Northmen who had graced our table. He argued my age would be against me, thus I should be grateful for any man to take me as his wife."

When she lifted her gaze to meet his, her eyes shimmered with unshed tears. "If I had agreed to a previous marriage, Thomas would not have been killed. 'Tis my stubborn fault that I did not take any of the other offers."

Magnar drew back. "You are not to blame, Lady Elspeth."

"*Aye*." She pounded her chest with her fist. "The guilt will haunt me to my death and beyond, Magnar. He sought out the Northmen to trade and to discuss marriage plans. Word had reached him of how they had great wealth in furs, amber, and mead. And I was the wealth he was going to bargain for in obtaining those goods. When I found out, I threatened to leave. And he vowed to send me to the abbey for the rest of my days. There are many moments when I wished I had returned to the safety of those holy walls." She lowered her head on a sigh. "I carry his death on my soul."

The battle to seek vengeance rooted within Magnar—not only for his friend, but for the lass standing before him.

An abbey is not a place for you to hide, Elspeth Gunn. Nor are you matched to become a nun.

Chapter Eight

After giving one final inspection to the supplies and weapons secured on his horse, Magnar reached for his cloak and sword off a nearby bench and departed the stables. Early morning light shimmered off the treetops as he made his way to meet with King William. He nodded to those in passing, and skirted out of the way of a passing dog intent on wreaking harm on the rabbits that wandered inside the castle gates to feast on the garden greens.

Rorik met him halfway across the bailey with a look that did not bode well. "The king received a message before dawn from Castle Steinn."

His steps slowed. "From whom?"

The man nodded in the direction away from the castle entrance and other folk.

Magnar followed after Rorik as he led them toward the lists and away from any others. A tremor of unease settled within him. When the man turned a corner, he continued down along the wall of the south-facing castle. Coming to a halt near a secluded area and sheltered by trees, Rorik turned around.

Arching a brow, Magnar asked, "Why are we hiding here?"

"You ken there are ears everywhere, even inside Lord Sutherland's castle."

"Speak, Rorik," he demanded, his patience waning.

The man leaned against the stone wall. "Halvard Baardsen."

Fisting his hands on his hips, Magnar glared up at the sunlight. "I have not heard of him."

"He claims to be the leader of his men and has made demands from the king."

"Demands?"

Rorik shrugged. "I was not privy to the particular details. I wanted to give you the news *before* you entered the king's chambers. His temper is foul now, to the extent of cursing and crumbling the missive in his hand."

Wiping a hand down the back of his neck, Magnar began to pace. "Nae matter. I shall have the head of this bastard soon. Or I will take my time in slicing certain limbs from his body."

Rorik pushed away from the wall. "Our plans have changed."

Halting abruptly, he asked, "*Why?*"

"Unsure. But the king is expecting you." The man gestured him forward.

Making quick strides back to the castle and up the stairs, Magnar slowed his steps. Curiosity battled with anger—*anger* that he had to halt his attack against this Baardsen. When he reached the king's chambers, he found the door ajar. Pushing it open, he stepped inside.

Rorik stood at the entrance. "I shall inform the other guards we are not leaving."

King William moved away from the blazing hearth. "Nae. I require a witness. Come inside and close the door."

A chill of foreboding swept through Magnar as he exchanged glances with Rorik. Clasping his hands behind his back, he waited for the king to speak.

When the door was closed, the king went to his desk and waved a hand over the wrinkled missive. "I misjudged this man, Halvard Baardsen who has taken over Castle Steinn." He rubbed a hand through his beard and leaned against the desk. "He has requested his *future* bride to be restored to him at once. There was an agreement between Thomas and this man in front of many witnesses. If needed, he will present names upon her return. In addition, Thomas withdrew his sword *first* in a drunken rage."

Stunned by this news, Magnar blurted out, "*Elspeth*? How did he ken she was here?"

"Uncertain," replied the king, tapping a finger to the missive. "Is she a spy? Did she plot to kill her brother and then flee realizing her mistake?"

"Nae!" Magnar slashed the air with his hand. "I heard her account of her brother's death. She spoke the truth. I will rip out the tongue—"

William held up his hand. "Aye. But Halvard claims those within the Gunn clan witnessed this pact. Strange you would come quickly to her defense. Do you find a connection with the lass?"

Confusion settled within Magnar. "If I may be so bold to ask, what are you trying to say, *my king*?"

"According to the verbal agreement between Thomas and Halvard, Elspeth was promised to him. 'Tis an ancient law in the Gunn family. Any *verbal* contracts pertaining to marriage are binding, even if the clans resort to war. The written word is not required."

"Even if you murder your host?" snapped Magnar. "It should be without value. Perchance Thomas judged this man a poor husband and took back his offer. Aye,

Thomas enjoyed his ale, but he always remained courteous with his guests. 'Tis this bastard's word over our dead friend's. What about those within the clan? Surely they were forced to speak falsehoods."

A sour look passed over the king's features. "I agree. As the current chieftain is far too young to make any decision regarding his aunt, I as their king, have taken control. Aye, I can send you to slit his throat, *or* we can thwart their plan with another."

The king picked up the missive and crossed the chamber. Standing in front of Magnar, he crumpled the note in his fist. "*You* shall wed Elspeth Gunn and return to Castle Steinn with your wife and the new chieftain. Not only will you take the elite guards, but some of my own guards, as well. I want this man removed, but I also want to abide by the edicts of the Gunn clan. In the end, we can tell this man that you had fallen under the lass' charm and agreed to wed her. We can profess that this missive came too late."

Magnar took a step back. "Marriage? *To me*?" He pointed a finger in Rorik's direction. "Why not him?" Yet the idea of his friend bedding Elspeth twisted his gut like a pit of snakes.

"Nae, *nae*!" The man shook his head. "You fancy her, not I."

Giving the man a scathing look, Magnar uttered softly, "Hold your tongue."

"Enough!" ordered King William. He clamped a firm hand on Magnar's shoulder. "Would it be so awful to take a wife?"

Returning his attention to the king, he responded, "Aye! You ken I must share what I am. It would only serve to have her see me as a heathen. And in our ancient bylaws, I cannot wed until I have shared our ways with her."

The flames from the fire snapped, echoing the mood within Magnar. Marriage to a woman who followed the new religion would only end in biting words between them. Elspeth would come to despise him, and the thought left him unsteady.

William blew out a frustrated curse and released his hold on Magnar. "Castle Steinn requires a strong leader to guide the new earl, and he must return to his home. Marriage to Elspeth and taking over Castle Steinn will ensure continued support for my kingdom—*without* a bloody war."

"Why not wipe out the bastard and then find a suitable match for Elspeth?" suggested Magnar.

"Again, you are forgetting the agreement between Thomas and this man. I am certain he proclaimed it to all within hearing. Aye, you can storm into the castle and take control, but another might present himself from this band of warriors, and I need to quell the source."

Magnar crossed the room and drew back the partially open wooden shutters. Crisp air slashed across his face, and he inhaled deeply. His gaze roamed over the landscape as he leaned against the ledge of the arched window. Freedom beckoned him beyond the hills and over the sea to *Orkneyjar*. Even so, he was honor-bound to his king and to an ancient code of edicts. Duty always above personal needs. Exhaling slowly, he said, "She will learn to hate me."

William approached and stood by his side. "Again, I ask, do you have a bond with Elspeth?"

Ignoring the question, Magnar challenged, "And

my duties as the leader of the wolves? Will they be stripped and given to another? What about the search for my brother? Must I cease in finding Thorfinn?"

"Nae," replied the king. "This will add more to your duties when you take on this additional responsibility."

To oppose his king would only result in another stepping forth to take on the burden of the marriage. *Could it be a union in name only?* His mind agreed, but his body betrayed him. And if in name only, the marriage would be left open for opposition for any others to challenge Magnar.

Pushing away from the ledge, he turned toward the king. "Then I shall take Elspeth to be my wife. Before we are wed, I must share my lineage." He paused and returned his gaze once more to the sun-drenched land. "Have you considered the lass might not be agreeable to your proposition?"

The door to the chamber opened, and Magnar glanced over his shoulder.

The king glared back at him from the entrance. "Convince her, Magnar. She will either marry you, *or* I can return her to Halvard Baardsen."

****

Pacing back and forth in front of an oak tree, Magnar tried to settle the battle of emotions within him. Marriage was something he had avoided for years, and his mother would agree with him. Although she'd wanted him to take a wife, she would not be pleased the intended bride was not from where he was born.

Why hadn't he taken a wife from one of the *Orkneyjar Isles*? He scrubbed a hand vigorously over his face. "Because they would bore me."

And Elspeth stirs the blood like nae other.

Magnar stilled his movement. Her floral scent drifted past him as he heard her footsteps approaching.

"Who is bored, Magnar?" asked Elspeth, coming alongside him.

"Does it matter?" he responded taking in her appearance. Lush curves that had enticed and lured the lustful man within. Her full rosy lips tempted him beyond reason. Would the fiery red-haired lass be a temptress in bed or a timid mouse? He shook his head to rid himself of her naked image, straddling his cock.

Turning away from her, Magnar went to the edge of the stream.

"What troubles you?" She moved to his side, staring outward. "The king stated you had wanted to discuss an important matter—one that concerns Erik."

He clasped his hands behind his back. "King William received a missive this morning from Halvard Baardsen. He has requested his future wife be returned to Castle Steinn."

Elspeth gasped, but made no comment.

Magnar kept his focus on the soothing water. "We are uncertain how he came upon the knowledge you are here. His account was Thomas drew his blade on him in a drunken rage, and Halvard defended himself. By ancient Gunn law—"

"Bastard," hissed Elspeth. "How *dare* he accuse my brother of such a vile act!"

Glancing sideways at her, he arched a brow. "Continue."

"My brother realized too late the monster he had invited to Castle Steinn." Wiping a shaky hand over her forehead, she added, "An argument broke out after my brother refused to side against King William. He renounced the entire agreement in the hall that evening. I witnessed the anger and fear in my brother's eyes. When I rose from the table and started to make my way to leave, Thomas met me at the doors. He told me to find Erik and one of the guards and flee from Steinn. It all happened quickly. One moment he was whispering his demand and the next, a blade was thrust through his back. The hall erupted into chaos, and I ran out of there."

"Halvard claims to have witnesses to the contrary."

"He lies!" she spat out in defense. "He's as low as a snake with venom." She slashed the air with her hand. "He most likely used threats, or worse." Elspeth trembled, and she wrapped her arms around her body. "Those are good people we left behind. Now they are suffering."

Moved by her sorrow, Magnar drew her to him. When she didn't stiffen or object, he placed his arms around her. "We can thwart their plan with another," he uttered softly, her scent filling him.

Elspeth lifted her head as a long tear trickled down her cheek. "Then there is hope?"

"Aye. You shall marry me. The king desires this union."

Her mouth dropped open as she gaped at him like a forlorn fish. Quickly snapping it shut, she struggled to be free from his hold. "Nae!"

Magnar released her, and she stumbled back. *She sees you as a loathsome heathen.* Ignoring her denial, he continued, "With this marriage, we shall return to Steinn as a united front with King William's blessing. The elite guard will accompany us—"

She shook her head. "'Tis *not* happening."

"—along with some of the king's guards." He paused and added, "Once there, Halvard will acknowledge the marriage and the new chieftain. Then I will request his departure. If not, I'll challenge the man in the lists."

Elspeth snorted and folded her arms over her full breasts. "'Tis not your right."

"To which? Marriage or slaying Baardsen?"

"Both. I shall return to the abbey, and when Erik is of age, he can seek his vengeance for the death of his father," she answered in a rush.

Magnar stormed to her side, glaring down at her. "You would allow him to carry this burden until the deed was done? The lad is only seven. It will harden him to a shell of violence, and he cannot rule without counsel."

She grimaced from his words but kept her chin held high. "I won't let him be hardened."

"You ken *nothing* of the responsibility," he snapped. Turning from her censure, Magnar went back to the stream. "I understand I am not a husband you favor. Nevertheless, as marriage to me, we can undo this pact your brother made."

She stomped the ground with her foot. "I will not be forced to marry a...*a heathen*!"

He gritted his teeth—her words sparked outrage from his inner beast. Glancing over his shoulder, he offered, "Then which would you prefer? Halvard *or* me? Make your choice, Elspeth. Did you not consider I do not favor this union either?"

Confusion marred her features. She fisted her hands on her hips and glanced upward. "Did you argue against this marriage with King William?"

"Aye."

"Yet he convinced you?"

"*Aye*."

When she returned her gaze to him again, resolve and a bit of stubbornness filled them. "Why, Magnar?"

"The king will permit me to continue with my duties with the elite guard, including an important task which requires my attention after our marriage."

Chewing on her bottom lip, she nodded slowly. "Then you will be absent most months from Steinn?"

"Most assuredly, and when I am there, Erik will be my focus."

Her face softened as she moved slowly toward Magnar. "Therefore this marriage is in name only for Erik's protection, aye?"

Annoyed with the direction of his thoughts, he looked away. How Magnar longed to tell the lie on the tip of his tongue. The word ached to be released. He turned and stared into her jeweled eyes in an attempt to offer her any hope of what she wanted to hear.

When she placed a hand on his arm, she whispered, "Tell me honestly, Magnar."

He swallowed and removed her hand from his arm. Placing it securely over his heart, he stated, "Our marriage will be binding in all ways, Elspeth—in name *and* body. You may worship your God and I shall do so with mine, but ken this, you will be *mine* completely."

The battle of emotions splayed across her face. She stepped closer and pulled her hand free from his. "Then you understand this, Magnar MacAlpin, you can have my body on my terms. The time of *my* choosing. I am tired of having men telling me what to do. Will you accept my terms?"

By the hounds! Her words sparked his lust further. Magnar concluded he did not want a simpering wife by his side. For the first time, he yearned to have one challenging him—in mind and body.

Grasping her around the waist, he ignored her gasp and cupped her chin. Her eyes widened as he slowly lowered his head. "Agreed." He breathed the word against her cheek.

When he drew back, Magnar was the one perplexed. Lust shimmered back at him from those emerald eyes. Her full lips parted, and he required no invitation.

Instantly, he took fiery possession of her mouth, devouring its softness. The kiss shattered his senses and tossed him into a stormy sea of pleasure. Her lips were warm and moist, and when she moaned, Magnar thrust his tongue into the velvet warmth of her mouth. Unable to be gentle, his kiss became demanding—burning with need. Especially when Elspeth wrapped her arms around his neck, urging him onward.

Skimming his hand upward from her waist, he found her breast and squeezed the taut pebble through her gown. The roar of desire to strip the material from her body and feast on her honeyed rose-scented skin sent him spiraling. She whimpered as he trailed a path with his tongue from the soft spot below her ear to along her neck. He pressed his lips to her throat and felt the wild beat of her pulse.

"Magnar, *Magnar.*"

His lips recaptured hers, more demanding this time. The tempest of desire swirled around them.

Finally, a small whisper in the back of his mind

clawed at him to stop this madness, or he'd strip her gown from her body and take her maidenhood here on the ground.

Withdrawing from her luscious mouth, he stared at her. Her gaze—both hungry and confused—tore him apart. Never had a woman stirred such a passion so violently in him. Her lips were already swollen from his kisses.

Her chest rose and fell with each breath she took. "Remember our deal, Magnar." Turning quickly, she darted away through the trees.

In that quiet moment as the air cooled around him, Magnar had left out one declaration to share with Elspeth—the wolf within him. And the beast gnashed his teeth.

The thought soured inside his gut.

"You will *never* come to my bed willingly, Elspeth."

Chapter Nine

Elspeth paced back and forth in front of the arched window. Her nerves were a jumbled mess ever since her conversation with Magnar. Two long days had passed, and she refused to take any of her meals in the hall. She sent her regrets on the first day to the king with a note stating she required time alone. And he responded with his own missive stating he would give her this time to prepare for the marriage—in three days' time.

Several of the women came earlier in the morning with gowns for her to look over. The thought of choosing one for her marriage to the MacAlpin only added to her distressing senses. In the end she relented and chose a gown in a deep shade of blue.

She hated to be forced into this situation. Even so, she had no one to blame but herself. All because she refused to take any of the other men her brother had presented to her.

Elspeth wiped a hand over her brow. Guilt continued to torment her. "Why was I so stubborn, Thomas? You should have asserted your power and forced me to marry." She snorted, realizing her brother could never make her do anything. "How I miss you, my brother."

The flames from the fire snapped, and she jumped, only adding more to her misery.

However, it was more than the approaching marriage to Magnar MacAlpin that bothered her. Brushing her fingers across her lips, she sighed, recalling his kisses. They left her with a burning ache for something more. A dizzy spark of pleasure she was unable to fathom.

She should not want him. Should not crave his touch. Though it was difficult to deny, Elspeth desired Magnar.

"You confound me," she murmured, placing a cool hand on her cheek.

Startled by the soft knocking on her door, Elspeth turned suddenly. "Enter."

Erik pushed open the door and ran inside. Reaching for her hand, he asked, "Are you still feeling unwell?"

Guilt plagued Elspeth as she knelt down in front of the lad. "Forgive me for being absent, even from you. I had much to think upon." Giving him a reassuring smile, she added, "I have some news to share with you."

His face lit up. "I ken the *good* news!"

"Do you?"

His head bobbed up and down. "You are to marry the MacAlpin tomorrow."

Elspeth's smiled faded. This was not how she wanted her nephew to hear the news. Was Magnar taking pride by rejoicing in this union with everyone who would listen? Before she would pass judgment on the man, she asked, "Who gave you the account?"

"King William."

Her shoulders sagged in relief. "Of course." *It was the king's plan anyway.*

His brow furrowed. "Are you not pleased?"

Elspeth released his hand and stood. *Stunned is the word I would have chosen.* She glanced over her shoulder at the fading sunlight. "I do not ken the man."

Erik pulled on her gown. "He is a great leader amongst his men."

She huffed out a breath and returned her gaze to the lad. Uncertainty warred with her other emotions. *Being a great leader does not make for a good husband.* Curious, she asked, "Have you spoken with Magnar?"

The boy swallowed. "Only once when the king wished to tell me the news in his chamber."

"He was there?"

"Aye. Man to man, Magnar spoke with me."

Elspeth's mouth twitched in humor. "And what did he say?"

Erik pointed to his chest. "He made an oath to protect you and me. Always. Nae harm would ever befall you after you married him."

"'Tis a vow easily broken if he is working for the king and not at Steinn," she uttered with dismay.

"He told me that in his absence, one elite guard would always watch over us until I can wield a strong sword-arm." Erik withdrew his small dirk in a show of display. "Magnar is going to train me. He is powerful."

"Most likely many already fear him. He towers over most men. The man is as tall and wide as some of the trees," she stated.

Erik ignored her as he continued to wield his sword about. This was no longer about her needs. Her nephew required guidance and leadership, which she was unable to provide. With the king's blessing, Magnar and the other guards would offer a stable foundation and future for Erik, and the people under Gunn protection.

Elspeth went and retrieved her cloak. She was tired of hiding in her chambers. Determined to be brave in the face of any storm, she crossed the room and stood at the entrance. "One of my maids stated you are taking lessons from one of the guards called Gunnar? I heard he is teaching you the lessons of our Lord. Have you finished for today?"

Erik halted his actions and cast his gaze at the floor.

"By your silence I can presume this to mean you have fled your studies?"

"He makes me state *his* prayers in *Latin*," complained Erik. "And he made me take Sir Mouse out of the chamber."

She would not be dismayed by his sullen behavior. "And this poses a problem? Even King William speaks Latin, and I believe those are the king's prayers, as well. As for Sir Mouse, I deem 'tis time for him to find a new home."

Raising his head slowly, he frowned in obvious thought. "Aye. I did hear the king give the blessing before we ate. Do you think the king will like me more if I say his prayers?"

Elspeth held out her hand as her heart softened. "You already have gained his favor."

Tucking his dirk back into the sheath on the belt at his side, he rushed to take her hand. "Do you think Father would mind if I learned the new prayers?"

She brushed a lock of hair out of his eye. Smiling, she answered, "A good leader should always learn as much as he can. What harm would it be to learn the prayers our king recites? And if you find your tongue refuses to move, then utter the ones your father taught you in Latin."

Giving her a broad smile, he nodded. "Aye, *aye*."

"Good. You shall strive to learn your lessons from Gunnar, and I'll resolve to embrace this marriage to Magnar."

As they departed her chambers, Erik said, "I ken Magnar to be a good man."

Her nephew had an uncommon ability to sense others' inner self. Curiosity spurred her to ask, "What makes you sense the man to be good?"

He shrugged. "'Tis his eyes. They shine like a wolf. And wolves are loyal."

Elspeth regretted even asking the lad the question. His belief in the old religion had him spouting questionable tales. Holding back any further questions, she continued along the corridor. Yet a troubling thought raced through her mind. Did not her grandmother speak of men who roamed the land on the *Orkneyjar Isles*? She offered the same account—men with eyes that mirrored the soul of a wolf. They worshipped the old Gods and guarded the land.

I nae longer believe in the old tales, Grandmother. Forgive me.

****

"A wedding day should be one of joy *and* in a church," whispered Elspeth, doing her best to compose herself.

She fingered the blue stone around her neck to steady the knots within her. The pendant was the only item she retrieved when she fetched her cloak on that fateful night of her brother's death. A notable gift from her grandmother on her twentieth birthday. The old woman made one dying request—to wear the jewel on her wedding day. She had forgotten about the jewel, having stuffed the pendant deep within the pocket of her cloak. Never did she consider marriage when she took it with her.

"You are a vision of rare beauty," uttered the familiar male voice behind her.

Elspeth's skin tingled with awareness and a longing for his touch. The stone grew warm within her palm, and she dropped her hand. She cast Magnar a sideways glance. "Are you not supposed to be waiting in the great hall?"

His smile came slowly. "Aye, but here we both are."

Elspeth fought the smile forming on her own mouth. The man was splendid in his ivory tunic and dark blue trews. She did not even mind that he was wearing his torc. He made her insides flip in the most wondrous ways. "Should not the king be present?"

Magnar shifted his focus to the closed doors and then quickly returned his attention to her. "He awaits us." His good humor transformed to a more somber tone. "I must speak with you, first."

"By the hounds, Magnar!" Rorik came charging down the stairs. "Get yourself into the hall. You can speak with Lady Elspeth after the formal vows."

Magnar gave the man a scowl. "'Tis important." As he made to take hold of her arm, he stilled his movements. He lifted his hand as if to touch her pendant. His eyes darkened, and he blinked several times.

Elspeth took a step back in wariness. "We can speak later, Magnar."

The man continued to stare at the stone.

When Rorik approached by his side, his mouth gaped open. "Sweet Goddess," he muttered. "Can it be?" asked a stunned Rorik.

Magnar shook his head at the man, silencing any further outburst.

Grimacing at Rorik's choice of heathen words, Elspeth started forward.

"Where did you get the pendant?"

Magnar's question halted her progress. She again clutched the stone around her neck. "A gift from my grandmother. Generations of women have passed this down to the oldest daughter. Since my mother died when I was young, it was gifted to me." Lifting her chin, she added, "Its only value is to our kin."

Magnar moved slowly toward her. "You are wrong, Elspeth. The stone you possess is far more valuable than you can ever imagine."

"And how do you ken this?" she snapped.

"It shimmers with magic," he admitted. Taking her hand, he placed it in the crook of his arm. "I plan on discussing more with you, but for now, our king awaits."

The man confounded her with his irritating beliefs. "You might be getting a marriage, Magnar MacAlpin, but you are not staking claim to this pendant." Shoving aside her unrest, she tried to pull free from his steely grip.

He leaned closer. "There is only one thing I desire to claim, Elspeth."

A tremor coursed through her body. "You are a brute, Magnar."

His breath was hot against her cheek as he added,

"Agreed." He glanced at Rorik. "Will you be so kind as to open the doors?"

The man gave Magnar a bewildered look, but swiftly complied.

Immediately, the scent of wildflowers and fresh green rushes filled Elspeth's senses. People stood on both sides of the hall—from the elite guards and those within the castle. Her mood shifted between uneasiness, sorrow, irritation, and fear. Nowhere within her was the spark of joy that should attend a woman on her wedding day. Tears smarted her eyes, and she blinked them back.

As Magnar moved them steadily down the center of the Great Hall, she cast her gaze over the crowd searching for the lone person who could bring forth a smile. When she spotted Erik standing next to Lord Sutherland, she smiled fully. And her nephew returned the gesture with one of his own.

I am doing this for you, Erik. Magnar and I shall keep you safe.

Despite the consequences, who would keep her safe from Magnar? Aye, she trusted the man. But not enough to allow him into her bed chamber. Thankfully, he had agreed to her terms.

Her mind was firm. Her body was sorely another matter.

When the priest stepped around Lord Sutherland, Elspeth gave a sigh of relief. At least the ceremony would be blessed by God.

Elspeth's heart pounded fiercely against her chest the closer they approached. Standing before the priest, she found herself trembling and dug her nails into Magnar's arm. Lights spun in an arc around her, while the priest professed his words of wisdom over the sacred vows of marriage. His somber tone matched her mood. Only when Magnar nudged her did Elspeth grasp they were waiting for her to recite her promise to obey and serve her husband.

Quickly giving her acknowledgement, though grudgingly, she attempted to finish the vows and let out a long sigh when it was completed.

Half-listening to Magnar's vows, she waited for the priest to give his final blessing and closed her eyes.

"By the power that Christ brought from heaven, may his love bind you both forever," intoned the priest.

Her eyes fluttered open, and she watched as Magnar drew forth a ring from the outstretched hand of the king. Placing it on her third finger, he whispered, "The ring belonged to my mother. Will you accept this ring?"

Smiling weakly, Elspeth nodded. "Thank you." The cool silver ring fit snug on her finger, and she longed to find out more about his kin.

He brushed a kiss across her knuckles and then wrapped his arm around her waist. "A kiss to seal our vows?"

Giving her no time to respond, Magnar took possession of her mouth in a passionate kiss. The kiss sang through her veins, igniting a pleasurable sensation from the top of her head to the tips of Elspeth's toes.

When the hall erupted into unruly shouts, clapping, and cheers, Magnar broke the contact. He tasted of ale, wheat, and his own male scent. His kiss was one of promises yet to be fulfilled—promises she vowed not to take part in. But never in all her life had Elspeth yearn as much for a man as she did for Magnar. Yet he was nothing of what she wanted in a husband. Their beliefs were completely opposite. Only he set her body humming with desire.

Nevertheless, until she learned everything about this brute of a man, Elspeth could ill afford to share any more enjoyable kisses with him.

Chapter Ten

Magnar watched the first star of the evening dust the sky with its twinkling glow. He drew in a long breath and released it slowly. Lifting his cup outward, he whispered, "You can rest easy, Mother. Your son has taken a wife."

After draining the last of the ale in his cup, he wiped his mouth with the back of his hand and crossed the room to the table. Retrieving a jug of wine and another cup, he deemed he had given Elspeth enough time to prepare for his return to their chamber.

Despite Magnar's beliefs, the bed in his chamber had been blessed with holy water from the priest. While the man spoke in a dull tone about the sanctity of the marriage bed, he studied his wife, noting her strained features. As soon as the man concluded his prayers and left, the women of the keep went to the task of helping his wife out of her gown.

And Magnar retreated to another chamber for some solitude. His thoughts drifted back to the stone around Elspeth's neck. His wife had no idea the power she had in her possession. It stunned him and his friend when they stood outside the great hall. Neither Rorik nor he had the ability to touch the powerful relic. It belonged to Elspeth. And to her alone. Until she presented the stone to another.

"The lost stone of Odin." He laughed at the

recklessness of her owning the stone. "If you knew the power, Elspeth, you could rule the wolves."

His inner beast snarled.

Magnar glanced sharply at the door, sensing the approaching footsteps of Rorik. Placing the cups and wine back onto the table, he waited for the man to enter.

A frown marred his friend's face as he stepped inside. Closing the door, Rorik approached. "What are you going to do about the stone?"

Magnar folded his arms over his chest and leaned against the table. "What do you suggest?"

"'Tis the lost stone of Odin! As leader of the Wolves of Clan Sutherland, 'tis yours by right. You are now wed to the woman." His mouth pulled into a sour grin. "I find it difficult to fathom that women have controlled the power for years."

"Nae," he snapped, furious over his own doubt. "The stone has been lost since the second Alpin wolf," countered Magnar. "If Odin judged it necessary for the relic to remain with women, then I cannot argue with the wisdom of All Father."

"Can you not sense the magic?" asked Rorik, coming closer.

Nodding slowly, he replied, "Aye. But there is nothing I can do. To touch the stone without permission will weaken and possibly destroy the wolf within me."

Rorik blew out a frustrated breath and reached for the jug of wine.

Blocking the man's progress with an outstretched arm, he scolded, "Nae. 'Tis for my bride."

The man backed away. "Forgive me." He arched a brow in amusement. "Should you not be tending to your *duties*?"

He winced. *First, I must confess the truth about who and what I am.* Clamping a hand on his friend's shoulder, he ordered, "As my second in command, I bid you to watch over the others tonight. Assure them that all is under control. At least we have found the magical relic. Until I can delve further into the history and its connection to Elspeth, we tread carefully."

Rorik rubbed a hand over his chin. "Are we forbidden to celebrate the marriage of our leader?"

Chuckling softly, Magnar pushed away from the table. Reclaiming the wine and two cups, he strode out of the chamber. "We leave after the first light of dawn touches the treetops. I will not have you falling off your horse from too much drink and bedding women," he spouted over his shoulder.

"You wound me, Magnar, with your lack of faith in me!"

"Heed my words, Rorik MacNeil, one day a woman will steal and crush your heart."

"Never! Do you hear me, Magnar? *Never*!"

****

As Magnar's steps led him closer to the chamber, uneasiness clawed at him. Would Elspeth remain true to her terms? Could he woo her with kisses, tempting her to surrender her body to him? By rights, Elspeth was his. Any other man might take and seal the marriage by force.

Even so, Magnar was not any man. He must confess all to his wife.

He halted before the oak door. "Aye, you called me a brute, Elspeth. But I will not take you forcibly."

Tucking the mugs under his other arm, he knocked

softly on the door. When he heard no response or stirrings within the chamber, Magnar knocked louder. Did the lass mean to bar him completely from his chamber? If he found the door bolted, he'd remove it from its hinges.

Unrest settled like bees inside his gut as his hand pulled on the iron handle. Stunned and relieved when the door opened, he swiftly stepped inside and closed the door. His heart hammered inside his chest at the vision of his sleeping wife in a large chair by the hearth. Her beauty stole the breath from his lungs.

Only an ivory chemise adorned her body. Elspeth's red hair tumbled free past her full breasts and down to her narrow waist. Soft snores escaped her every so often. With her feet tucked under her, she appeared peaceful, and Magnar pondered if he should leave the chamber and seek rest elsewhere.

"I barely ken you, Elspeth. And yet, you are now my wife," he whispered into the quiet chamber.

He glanced at the items in his hands. Releasing a sigh, he went to the table and put them down. Crossing the room, he went to the bed and sat. He swiftly removed his boots and tunic. Tossing the garment aside, he stood.

As he approached his sleeping wife, he bent and scooped her into his arms. She mumbled words of protest and then surprised him by wrapping her arms around his neck. Nuzzling his neck, she continued to torment his lustful beast with her scent and lips. He could feel her lush body within the thin material, and his swollen cock fought to be free from his trews. Yet when she whispered his name, he halted his progress.

"Aye, Elspeth?"

Dark eyelashes fluttered open, and he stared into her emerald depths. "Magnar?" She grimaced as if coming out of a deep sleep. "Wha…*what* are you doing?"

"Taking you to your bed, wife."

She stiffened in his arms. "Put me down!"

Magnar promptly complied.

Elspeth glanced in all directions and took a step back.

"Where will you go, wife?"

She fisted her hands on her hips. "Stop calling me that. And we had an agreement."

He arched a brow. "I see I must clarify two things with you. First, you are my *wife*." Magnar took a step toward her. "Second, I honor *all* my vows."

Elspeth dared to push at his chest. "Then why was I in your arms?"

"For the love of Odin, you were sleeping in a chair! I solely wanted to place you in the bed for your comfort."

Her nose wrinkled, and she turned away. "Forgive me," she muttered.

"Apology accepted."

She peered over her shoulder, beguiling him further by biting on her lower lip. "I grew tired of waiting."

A tiny spark of hope flared within him. Reaching for her hand, he brushed a kiss on the vein along her wrist. "I wanted to give you time. Would you care for some wine?"

She sighed. "There is none here."

He gestured toward the table where he had placed the jug.

Giving him a radiant smile, she sauntered to the table.

Did the lass not ken the view she presented? The gossamer material revealed a heart-shaped bottom he craved to touch and feast upon. Raking a hand over his face, he glanced around the room until he spied a wrap on the trunk. Quickly retrieving the garment, he went to her side.

As Elspeth handed him a cup, he draped the wrap around her shoulders.

"I am not cold, Magnar."

He tipped her chin up with his finger. Brushing a chaste kiss over her lips, he explained, "The view you present is trying my patience *and* my vow to you. I can see your pleasing body through this sheer gown."

Elspeth's eyes widened. "*Oh.*" She breathed out the word on a gasp and glanced down at him.

His cock swelled even more. Magnar immediately drained the contents of his cup and stepped around her. Refilling it with more wine, he said quietly, "I need to speak with you on an important matter."

"Does this message come from the king or you?"

"There is something I must share about myself, Elspeth. My intention was to speak with you prior to our marriage."

A concerned look passed over her features. After taking a sip of wine, she went to the chair by the hearth and sat. "Continue." She motioned for him to take a seat across from her.

Magnar shook his head and went to stand by the arched window. Drawing back one of the wooden shutters, he stared out at the night sky. "How much do you ken of the Wolves of Clan Sutherland?"

"Only that they are the elite guards for King William, and what my brother told me. Of course, you are their leader."

He swirled the wine within his cup. "What do you ken about the whispered *legends* of the wolves?"

When Elspeth didn't answer, he glanced over his shoulder and saw the confirmation. Fear showed in those beguiling eyes. *You have heard about the real wolves.*

"They're purely stories told to frighten the people and our enemies," she blurted out.

"Men who were able to become the wolf," he added.

She let out a nervous laugh and waved her hand about. "Even my grandmother was held captive by the tales of these animals doing heroic deeds for king and country. I heard them often enough during the long winter nights. But they were only fables."

"Your grandmother was a wise woman."

"Wise, yes. Flawed, because she believed in the old ways."

"You are quick to pass judgment on those who do not follow your belief."

She shook her head slowly. "And now you are judging me? Do not mistake my meaning, Magnar. I loved her fiercely. When she passed from this world, I mourned for almost a year. Furthermore, the stories she told were part of an ancient line of tales passed down from one generation to the next. After I went to the abbey, I tossed aside the folly nonsense."

"'Tis a shame," Magnar scolded.

"Are you seriously trying to say that you—the Wolves of Sutherland—are part man *and* wolf? Our

110

king is a devout man. Are you telling me he surrounds himself with ancient superstitions?" She shook her lovely head. "I think not."

Magnar studied her over the rim of his cup. "You are incorrect. The wolves do exist, Elspeth. And they serve our king. He has accepted the brotherhood, as the kings before him have done so for many years."

She took a long draw from her cup. "They are men who *behave* like wolves. Nothing more."

After guzzling the rest of his wine, he stormed to the table and slammed the cup down. Going to her side, Magnar glared at her. Elspeth's indrawn breath surrounded him as he loomed over her. Placing his hands on the arms of the chair, he lowered his head. "Do you require proof?"

"You are scaring me, Magnar," she whispered.

His eyes bore into hers. "Do not fear me, Elspeth. The wolf and man will *never* harm you. I pledged my vow to you for always. Once again, do you require proof?" His patience grew thin. This was why he fought against marriage to this woman. She was not from the *Orkneyjar Isles* where the women honored the wolves.

Anger surfaced swiftly in her eyes. "Move away from me."

Magnar straightened and yielded to her demand.

Elspeth stood slowly and brushed past him. Her hand shook as she deposited her cup next to his. He watched as she went to the bed and withdrew a *sgian dubh* from under one of the pillows. Drawing her wrap more securely around her body, she turned and faced him.

"Show me your inner wolf, Magnar, but be warned, I will not tolerate any abuse from you. I have seen the

111

fear in my brother's eyes when he spoke of the elite guards."

It took all his control not to unleash the fury in him. Did he not profess he would do her nae harm? Did she not listen to his vows? Aye, she was scared, but she scoffed him with her words and actions.

She was not ready to witness his wolf. Respect must first be earned.

Magnar quietly crossed the room. In one swift move, he removed the blade from her hand.

Rendered speechless, she took a step back and tumbled onto the furs.

"Pull back the coverings," he ordered with steely calm.

She swallowed and scooted to the far side of the bed. Yanking with all her might on the furs, she snapped them back.

"When you learn to trust me, *wife*, I will let you see the beast who resides within me. Until then, you are not worthy."

Holding his hand outward, he slashed across his palm with the blade. He ignored her gasp and watched as the blood pooled within his palm. Stepping near the bed, he let the blood drip onto the thin sheet. When he judged enough had stained the material, he fisted his hand closed. He tossed the *sgian dubh* onto the bed. "To prove to everyone that I have taken your maidenhead. Now get some rest. We leave at dawn."

As he made his way back to the table, he heard Elspeth crawl under the covers. Letting out the breath he had been holding, he picked up the jug and went to the hearth. The fire had burned low. After tossing in more wood, Magnar settled down on the wooden floor and surveyed the growing fire. Guzzling more of the wine, he waited for the ache and fury to subside within him.

What did he truly expect from Elspeth? Did he truly believe her to be willing to accept his other side? A small part of him hoped—*prayed* she would.

How was it possible to build a life together when they shared nothing in common, save one?

Erik.

And as the night waned into early morning, Magnar considered the consequences of this decision to wed the beguiling woman who was now his wife.

His mind found only one solution.

Even if you asked me to your bed, Elspeth, I would refuse—until you accept the beast within me.

Chapter Eleven

Elspeth yawned and stretched her arms overhead. She tried to ease the tension that still lingered within her body. Dreams of Magnar had haunted her throughout her fitful sleep, especially ones of her new husband fighting against the razor-sharp teeth of a wolf. She opened her eyes, and the cruel light of dawn smacked her with the reality of her current situation.

"I am married to a man who believes he is part wolf," she uttered into the cold, empty chamber.

She tossed aside the fur coverings and sat up. Massaging her temples, she tried to bring forth the stories her grandmother had told her about these ancient wolves. Often held spellbound by the woman's tales, Elspeth once believed in them. But the passing of time and being sent to the abbey altered everything.

Confusion settled like an unwelcome companion. What if the tales were true? A small thread of certainty wove itself within her. Even her grandmother had confessed to seeing a wolf once in the forest behind their home. She said it was nae ordinary wolf. Nae. He actually had winked at the old woman.

Elspeth had thought her grandmother daft, considering the amount of ale she consumed on a daily basis.

Hugging her arms around her body, she rocked back and forth. "Could it be possible?" she mumbled.

I should have given you permission to show me, Magnar, before you denied me.

Letting out a snort of nervous laughter, she stepped onto the cold, stone floor. Pushing aside the doubts and fears, Elspeth transferred her attention to the current dilemma. Returning to Steinn.

Making her way to the table, she quickly poured water from a large jug into a basin. After scrubbing the sleep from her face, she retrieved her clothing. Her stomach protested at the lack of food within her, and she chastised herself for not sampling some of the fine fare last evening. "You could not even take one bite at your own wedding feast."

After hastily dressing, she glanced out the window. A sliver of light dusted the treetops in the distance. She knew her husband was most likely waiting on his horse. "Well the man can wait."

His bark of orders to his men carried upward, and she jumped. Narrowing her eyes, Elspeth went to the window and glanced at the scene below. *Sweet Mother Mary.* Her instincts were correct. He was already on his horse. A great battle axe was strapped to his mount's side, and a sword was sheathed behind Magnar's back. Power and raw strength surrounded the man, and she found herself drawn to him.

She darted a glance at her nephew, who was already mounted and guiding his horse toward the men. Magnar shifted on his horse and smiled at Erik.

"Though you are feared by many, Magnar, I shall be forever grateful for the compassion and guidance you have shown my nephew."

As if he heard her words, Magnar lifted his head. Their eyes locked, and she was held captive. When a soft knock sounded on the door, Elspeth broke the connection and moved away from the window.

One of the maids entered with a trencher. "You must quickly break your fast, Lady Elspeth. Would you like me to fix your bindings on your gown, and what about your hair?"

"Bless you, Neala," exclaimed Elspeth. "Aye. As for my hair, put the mass in one braid. I feared I would have to start the journey without any food. I see my husband and his men are waiting for me."

After Neala placed the trencher on the table, she picked up a comb. "Do not fret. Your husband has stated he will wait until you have eaten. You must regain your strength after last night."

Elspeth almost choked on her first bite of bread, cheese, and berries. "Truly?" Reaching for a cup, she poured herself some ale.

When the girl remained silent, Elspeth pondered if she told a lie. Surely her husband would not discuss their marriage bed with others. Or would he?

As soon as Neala finished the task of braiding her hair, she collected the rest of Elspeth's clothing and folded the garments. Two bright roses stained her cheeks. She kept darting looks at the bed.

"What troubles you, Neala?" asked Elspeth, taking a sip of the ale.

The girl snapped her attention to Elspeth. "Why nothing." She swallowed and started to fidget with a lock of her hair.

Ever so slowly, Elspeth returned her gaze to the rumpled furs and pillows. She placed her cup back onto the table. Heat crept up her neck, and she stood. Clasping her hands together, she turned back toward the girl. "Are you here to collect the wedding sheets?"

The maid's cheeks bloomed brighter with color, and she nodded.

"Did my husband speak with you regarding them?"

"Aye," she mumbled. "He wanted to let everyone ken you were now his wife completely."

And to save my honor. Elspeth gave the girl a weak smile. "Thank you for my meal. Will you tell my husband I shall join him shortly? Then you can return for the bedding."

The maid gave a quick nod and darted out of the chamber.

Elspeth slumped down in her chair. Her husband was stirring a mix of emotions within her.

"*Husband?*" She smacked the table with her palm. "I do not ken you."

A bark of laughter from Magnar floated up on the breeze, and she lifted her head. The sound made her heart skip a beat. She smiled and closed the door on her troubling thoughts.

After taking a few more bites of her meal, Elspeth gathered the remainder of the food and wrapped everything in a cloth. Securing the ends firmly, she placed it inside a satchel. She had nae desire to spend one more night here.

Steinn called out to her. *Home.* There she would seek her answers.

****

Warm sunshine stayed with them on the first day of their journey, helping to ease the strain within Elspeth's mind and body. Yet the night unsettled her. She continued to dream about Magnar and wolves. When he positioned himself next to her on the ground, she fought the urge to scoot away. Did she think he was going to ravish her with more kisses? In front of his men and her nephew? Nae. In truth, Elspeth was ashamed of wanting his touch.

Thus, she spent another distressing night unable to get the rest she required for the long journey.

When Elspeth opened her bleary eyes, the new day had begun to streak across the treetops. Erik continued to snore softly, curled up near Rorik. She smiled at the scene, recalling the fit of anger he gave her last night. He refused to bring his wrap and sleep next to her, stating she was now married to Magnar, and he was a warrior.

As she attempted to sit, she winced from the pain. Her feet were numb and stiff. Part of her cloak was bunched up around her legs, adding more to her misery. Stretching her feet out, she tried to bring some warmth to her toes. A trickle of awareness brushed over Elspeth. She stole a glance to her right.

Magnar was on his side staring at her. The look he gave her singed the coldness from her body. She allowed her gaze to roam his features—from the arched brow, broad nose that had suffered from one too many a fist, and the dimple in his strong chin. Nevertheless, it was those full lips that sparked images of their heated kisses. There was nothing soft about her husband, and she pondered the thought of his body beneath the clothing.

Tempted to touch the stubble of hair on his face, she clenched her hands. *Nae!*

"Good morn." She struggled to keep her voice level. His eyes glittered like the blue sky on a sparkling summer day.

He rose up and scooted behind her. "You ken there are a few more days on our journey to Steinn?"

Elspeth transferred her focus to the trees in front of her. She would not dare glance over her shoulder. The man was far too close. "Aye."

She stiffened when she felt his fingers trail across her back. "You are not sleeping well."

"'Tis not your concern. I shall manage."

"*All* who ride with me are my concern." He leaned forward against her back. "Do you wish to hinder our journey?"

"Goodness, nae!" she answered in a rush. "Simply allow me to stretch out the tightness."

His breath was hot against the side of her neck. "Allow me to knead the stiffness from your limbs."

Elspeth fought the desire to relax into him. She simply nodded her consent.

"Bend your head forward," he instructed.

Slowly complying, she held her breath until his fingers pressed along her shoulders. Elspeth let out a moan and closed her eyes. Delicious prickles of heat seeped into her weary body as he continued to work his way down her back and up to her neck. The heady mixture of pain and relief made her sigh, and her body relaxed.

Too soon, he finished and moved away. Elspeth slowly lifted her head. "Thank you."

He stood and reached for her hand.

Accepting his strength once again, she grasped his hand. She was on her feet instantly with his arm wrapped around her waist. In awe of the man's strength, Elspeth leaned into him. Standing on her tiptoes, she placed a kiss on his cheek. "You might have to knead my shoulders every morning."

When she drew back, she studied his confused expression.

Cupping her chin, Magnar bent his head near her ear. "I shall strive to give my wife anything she desires."

Loud coughing behind them ceased all conversation, and Magnar released her.

Rorik, Erik, and the rest of the men sat staring at them. Each with their own varying smiles.

Elspeth glanced down and shook out the leaves from her cloak. "Give me a few private moments, and then I shall be ready to leave."

"I hear water nearby, Gunnar. 'Tis the stream. Do you think you can catch us some fish to break our fast?" asked Magnar.

"Depends on how many?" The man chuckled.

"Is that a challenge?" shouted Bjorn. "I say you can fetch only three."

Joy infused Elspeth as she stepped away and into the trees. The men were each offering their own thoughts on how many Gunnar could strip from the stream. Though she was eager to return home, a good morning meal of fish brought a smile to her face. The thought of tucking the moist pieces between the bread she brought had her licking her lips in anticipation.

After she finished taking care of her personal business, Elspeth emerged from the trees. Removing her cloak, she hoped to wash the grime from her hands and face. Reaching for a water skin, she did the best she could without any of the rose-scented soap she favored. She shook her hands to rid them of the water.

Eager to join the others, she followed the sounds of

unruly talk and laughter. When she made her way along a narrow path to the stream, Elspeth's steps faltered.

Standing in the middle of the stream was Erik, minus his trews. The water came almost to his knees, and she pressed a fist to her chest. *Do not fall, dear nephew.*

Swallowing the fear within, she crossed to Magnar's side. "Did Erik mention he cannot swim?"

Magnar fisted his hands on his hips. "Nae. Is he not a lad of seven? Was he not taught?"

Elspeth gave an exasperated snort. "Forgive my brother in failing to teach him. He thought it best to see to his training with the horses and lessons. In truth, he had plans on giving him lessons this summer."

He narrowed his eyes. "Even if he falls, the lad is surrounded by many. If I may propose, allow me to give him his first lesson after we have control of Steinn."

Shielding her eyes from the morning sun, Elspeth replied, "I am certain you will have nae argument from Erik. You do not require my consent, Magnar. After Thomas' death, my nephew has had to learn to be stronger."

"I am certain Erik will be a great leader among his people," praised Magnar.

"My only hope is that he treads carefully. He seems not to fear anything."

Magnar chuckled softly. "Do not be deceived by the confidence and chatter of the lad. There is fear behind those eyes. Nevertheless, he pushes through— making for a strong leader."

Dropping her hand, she turned and faced Magnar. "You can see this in his eyes?"

He shrugged. "Even now I can smell the fear of him within the water."

Stunned, she asked, "How?"

Humor softened his hardened features. "I am part wolf."

Elspeth bit her lower lip and looked away. Exhaling softly, she shook her head. "You must understand how difficult this is for me to understand."

"I sense you are now open to the possibility."

She slid a glance at him. She had to choose her words carefully. "Let me affirm that I am open to discussing this subject further."

He gestured outward. "I suggest speaking with Gunnar."

"Erik's tutor?" She swept her gaze to the man.

Magnar reached for her hand and placed a kiss across her knuckles. "Aye. He follows your God, and he is part wolf. Would your God condemn such a man?" Releasing her hand, he moved away.

Laughter bubbled out of Erik as he brought forth his first fish from the stream. The other men surrounded him in triumph, sending out their praises for the fine catch. Elspeth watched her husband cheer Erik. In one motion, Magnar lifted the lad out of the water and onto his broad shoulders.

Erik held the fish high. "I did it, Aunt Elspeth!"

Smiling, she pushed away Magnar's words, and blew her nephew a kiss. But she planned to have words with Gunnar, once the time presented itself.

Several hours later, Elspeth continued to ride on her horse behind Magnar and Erik's mounts as they followed the path of the stream. The conversation between the two continued to be muffled, broken occasionally by a chuckle from her nephew.

The water twisted through the lush trees like a silver ribbon. Wild bluebells and clover dotted the land. Inhaling the fresh scents, Elspeth allowed her mind to settle and enjoy the passing scenery. With her stomach now content with a delicious meal of fish, cheese, bread, and berries, she offered a silent prayer the rest of their journey would remain peaceful.

And as the day turned to gloaming, Magnar led them north away from the stream.

She stifled a yawn as he brought them beneath a cluster of aging oak trees. She marveled at the ease of his movements off his horse. When he approached, he held out his hands.

"I must confess I am too weary to lift my leg."

He never said a word. Big, strong hands grasped her firmly and pulled her off the animal. Her feet never touched the ground as Magnar cradled her into his arms.

Resting her head on his shoulder, she uttered softly, "I pray sleep will come tonight."

"Eat and drink, first," he suggested.

"I nibbled on cheese while riding," she admitted.

In the fading light, Elspeth saw his mouth twitch.

She placed her arms around his neck. "You should eat," she urged.

He gently placed her at the base of a tree. "My wife's needs come first on this journey."

Touched by his kindness, she grasped his hand. "I am strong, Magnar, but I thank you."

Glancing down at their joined hands, he rubbed his thumb over her skin. "So soft."

"Yours are rough and strong." The words tumbled

out of her before she could take them back.

He dropped down in front of her. His guarded look eased slightly. "And you are not afraid?"

A renewed sense of honesty and interest spurred Elspeth onward. "Of the wolf, perchance." She swallowed, unable to explain further her meaning.

After giving her hand a squeeze, he released his hold and stood. "You should fear the man more than the wolf. Wolves are always honorable."

Elspeth watched as her husband made his way to his men. Startled by his declaration, she had to consider there was so much she needed to learn about this barbarian.

Chapter Twelve

When Magnar approached his wife with a portion of dried meat, cheese, ale, and a wrap, he shook his head in resignation. The sharp-tongue beauty was fast asleep. Light from the fire danced off her hair and face, transforming her into a delicate vision that continued to steal the breath from his lungs. Often times, he found himself unable to speak, preferring to hear the musical lilt in her voice, or watch the way her face would transform into fury when anger overcame her.

He found his wife unable to shutter her emotions. And Magnar enjoyed watching the display of feelings. His world was one of order, control, and authority. With Elspeth, she brought a balance to his life. Admiration for her grew with each passing day.

Quietly, he went to her side and sat. He draped the wrap over her sleeping form and proceeded to eat part of the meal. Guilt plagued him as he stared into the fire. Images tumbled forth—flame by flickering flame.

His life as a warrior remained untarnished. His life as a son and now as a husband—unsettled.

He had sought to offer a prayer to the Gods and Goddesses for his failure to his mother before he left *Orkneyjar,* in hopes they would carry his plea on the winds across the void. Yet in all his preparations, the single act was left undone. And the start of his union with Elspeth had begun tersely.

The cheese and meat soured in his gut. He reached for the ale skin and drank deeply. The flames snapped, and he watched the embers drift into the night sky.

I shall make amends when I return, Odin. Forgive me.

A gentle breeze touched his face, scented by fire smoke and the woman asleep next to him.

His thoughts drifted to the possession she wore around her neck—a powerful one. Did she not ken the importance of the stone she carried? How it could command all within the brotherhood with its power? Strange how this woman from the Gunn clan had not listened more keenly to the stories told to her. They became fables after she found her new belief, and Magnar pondered if the knowledge of Odin's stone was left unsaid by Elspeth's kin.

Enough! He could ponder these questions another time. Protecting his wife and the magical stone would be enough until a time of his choosing.

The wolf inside clawed at him to be set free, if only for an hour.

Wiping his mouth with the back of his hand, he reasoned it was time to allow the animal to roam the surrounding hills. First, he would charge Gunnar with keeping a watch on his wife until he returned.

As he placed the ale skin on the ground, he started to leave.

"Have you eaten everything?" asked Elspeth softly.

Turning to face her, he handed her the package of food. "Nae."

She struggled to sit more fully and took a few bites of cheese. "How much longer until we reach Steinn?"

Magnar braced his arms over his bent knees. "With

126

the Gods favoring good weather, we should be there in two days. When we reach the last hill before Steinn, I am sending a few of my men to announce our arrival."

Elspeth's mouth narrowed. "Do you fear a battle?"

"Since I am unable to discern this Baardsen, I cannot say for certain."

"He's worse than a snake," she bit out tersely.

"This is why you will not proceed inside the keep until my men and I reason it safe for you and Erik."

Dropping the cheese, she snapped, "You cannot expect us to stay behind like timid mice."

He arched a brow. "I admire your courage, Elspeth, but ken this—I am your husband, your sword, *and* your shield. If there is a battle, I must maintain my focus." Magnar tapped a finger to his chest. "The wolf within would rip apart any who thought to harm you. There is much you do not ken about the animal. I do control him, but I've never had a wife to protect. Furthermore, there is much I need to learn, as well."

"Two days, you say?" She pursed her lips and resumed eating.

"Aye," he reaffirmed quietly.

She held out her hand. "May I have a drink?"

After complying with her demand, he watched as she drank deeply. His fingers itched to wipe the crumbs and droplets of ale near her lips.

"Then teach me about your wolf, Magnar. If you refuse to bring forth the animal, you might as well tell me about him. My memory of the stories my grandmother told me are unclear and scattered within my mind." She turned toward him. "Will you share your knowledge?"

Taken aback by her words, Magnar tipped her chin

up with his finger. "If I do, will you listen with an open heart? Or will you judge and damn me in front of your God?"

Her gaze roamed over his face. "I have nae desire to damn my husband, despite his beliefs. Your soul shall be judged by God at the end of your days, not by me." Elspeth grasped his hand and then released her fingers slowly.

"As with the judgment from my God as well," he added and took the ale skin from her.

Taking a sip, he glanced upward at the twinkling stars. "Foremost, the wolves protect and defend our king. It is a duty deep within our souls. My father used to say that when I take a wife, a shift happens with the wolf. His keen sense of loyalty splits in two—duty to king *and* the wife. Once, when my mother was threatened by another man, my father was unable to control the beast, and the wolf instantly came forth."

Elspeth touched his shoulder. "Did the wolf kill the man?"

Magnar lowered his head. "Almost. My father swiftly recaptured control and transformed back into a man. Yet the man the wolf injured along the side of his neck remained scarred for the rest of his life. It was a lesson my father realized too late. *His* father had died before he had a chance to counsel him on the ways of the wolf. Therefore, my father started my studies early on wolf lore."

"A wise man," commented Elspeth.

"Wise *and* foolish."

Elspeth handed him a portion of dried meat. "Is your father still alive? Your mother? What would they think of our marriage?"

After taking the food, he paused in thought. "Nae. He died many years ago from a fever that scourged our village. He was one of the strongest leaders ever. Nae one believed it until they witnessed his body on the funeral bonfire. Grief stricken, my mother left Scotland soon thereafter for their second home on *Orkneyjar Isles.* She died earlier this year." He pressed a fist over his heart. "My mother followed the old beliefs but honored the new religion. I reckon she would have favored our union, since she yearned for me to take a wife."

"I am sorry for your loss, Magnar," she offered softly. "If I may ask, why was your father foolish? Was he not a good and kind man?"

Magnar almost choked on the piece of dried meat. "Good *and* kind are not words I would choose for my father. Stern, fair, and loyal." He returned his attention to Elspeth. "My parents left out mentioning one important detail to me. I had a brother—a *twin.*"

Elspeth drew back, her eyes growing wide. "Sweet Mother Mary. What happened? Why did they leave that out? Did he die at birth?"

He pinched the bridge of his nose. "Only the first-born male can become a wolf." Magnar hesitated on how to proceed with the telling. How could he make Elspeth understand? She followed a different path—one where magic was considered evil.

She nudged him gently. "Continue. I shall keep silent. Remember, I will not judge you."

When he glanced at her, he noted tenderness in her eyes and smile. Her courage to listen spurred him onward with the tale.

"We are bound with magic from long ago,"

Magnar paused, fearing a reaction. When none was given, he continued, "There can be only one elder male wolf. Any other children do not carry the magic. Yet my brother, Thorfinn, was born a wolf and lives. My parents feared we would rip each other apart and sent Thorfinn to live in the northern isles. My mother told me of him last year. I became angry and lashed out with bitter words. Soon thereafter, I left."

Elspeth touched his cheek with her fingers.

Magnar grasped her hand and placed it over his heart. "I never had a chance to offer amends for my harsh words."

"You must find your brother," she affirmed.

He chuckled low. "'Tis my important task, *once* we have control of Steinn. I intend to find and bring him into the brotherhood of the wolves."

Worry creased her features. "Surely you will allow him to choose?"

"A lone wolf can do harm to many, including himself." Magnar considered it best to not reveal the possibility his brother might be raiding across Scottish lands with other Northmen.

"If I may suggest, you can always offer your amends in a prayer. A mother's love is all-forgiving."

His hardened shield cracked, and Magnar allowed the healing balm of her words to settle inside him.

Leaning her head on his shoulder, she yawned. "Thank you for giving me my first lesson on the wolf."

He wrapped an arm around her shoulders. "If you give me a few moments, I shall prepare a bed of pine branches. Some of the men have gathered them for you. The ground is much harder here."

She lifted her head and gave him a radiant smile.

"How wonderful *and* kind."

"Furthermore, I shall use my body as a shield from the coldness, if you will consent."

Even in the glow of firelight, Magnar noticed the bright red splotches forming on her cheeks.

Swallowing visibly, she whispered, "Aye."

Placing his forehead onto hers, he whispered, "I have nae intention of ravaging your body out in the woods, especially around so many. But with two bodies tucked close together, we shall keep warm."

"Thank you."

Magnar withdrew his hold and stood. Giving a short whistle, he pointed to Ivar and Bjorn. Within moments, the men had gathered the collected pine branches and crossed to him. They worked quietly to make the ground into a comfortable bed for Elspeth. Each gave a curt nod to him after their chore was completed.

Going to his horse, Magnar removed another smaller wrap and returned to Elspeth. After placing the wrap over the branches, he took her chilled hand. "Lay down. You must find rest this night."

Elspeth squeezed his hand. "I fear there isn't enough room for us both."

He smiled slowly. "The ground will fit my needs."

Drawing her cloak more firmly around her body, she settled onto the bedding.

When he reckoned she was finished finding a comfortable position, Magnar joined her on the ground. He wrapped his arm and cloak around her waist, drawing her against his body. The fresh scent of pine and Elspeth had his head spinning, and he let out a groan.

She stiffened.

"Relax," he urged, but found it difficult to do so himself.

Giggling, she replied, "You are warm and making noises."

"And you find humor in this?"

"Simply...*nervous*."

Curious, he asked, "Why, Elspeth?"

"I can't explain what I do not understand," she confessed quietly, relaxing more into him.

Her body tempted him beyond reason—lush breasts to savor and round hips to plunder and slake his need. Magnar fought the growing lust. He nuzzled her neck. "Would you feel better if I shared that I am nervous as well?"

"You? A strong warrior? Of what?"

Did he dare share his inner torment with her? If he did, would he appear weak? Banishing the thought, he said, "Never has another female stirred me so, *wife*."

Exhaling softly, she muttered, "I ken there have been many who have warmed your bed, Magnar. I am certain they were lovely."

He scowled. Aye, he had bedded many, but Elspeth was wrong. None made him a thorny mix of feelings, leaving his gut twisted like gnarled vines. "You are far more a beauty than any of those other women."

Twisting around, she gazed into his eyes. "Truly? Freckles mar my nose and cheeks. I have unruly hair and a color not favored by many. Furthermore, I have nae wisdom on—" She swallowed and looked away.

"*Wisdom*?" he echoed.

"On the ways of pleasing a man," she blurted out.

His wife misjudged her enchanting qualities.

"When you are ready, I shall show you how to please me, Elspeth. In return, you must tell me what you favor. I want to give you pleasure."

"I find your kisses pleasing," she whispered. "I...I enjoy being in your arms."

She squirmed against him, and Magnar fought the urge to slip his hand under her gown and stroke the soft flesh. His cock swelled to an unbearable ache with the need to sink into her heated core.

Clenching his jaw, Magnar attempted to dwell on other thoughts—fighting in the lists with the other men, an icy swim in the waters off *Orkneyjar Isles* where the water would slash at your skin like tiny blades, anything but the enticing woman in his arms.

"You are quiet. Have I offended you with my words?"

"Nae." He growled out the word. "I ache to bury myself into your womanly folds." Not prone to soft words or actions, he also found himself unskilled when it came to control around Elspeth.

She gasped. "Should I move away?"

"Do not even think of removing your lush body from mine, *wife*. I'll snatch you into my arms and take you deep into the woods. There I will give you pleasure and quench my needs."

"Magnar MacAlpin, did you not give me your word?" she chastised, though there was a hint of teasing in her tone.

"Aye, that I did. Will you consent to a favor?"

Her delicate fingers began to trace slow circles over the top of his hand. "A kiss for my husband?"

Blowing out a sigh, he gazed upward into the night sky. "I fear one kiss will not be enough. Nae. My request is simple. Quit your stirrings and get some rest. It will ease my burning desire to claim you."

She remained silent for several heartbeats and then whispered, "An easy request. Granted." Elspeth ceased her movements and removed her fingers from his skin.

Nevertheless, Magnar continued to be tormented by her body. His hand burned from where she stroked the skin. Images of her straddling his rigid cock had him clenching his jaw so tightly he feared it would snap.

The ever-growing moon cast her milky white glow against the velvet night, but this did not deter his purpose.

Drawing upon his training, Magnar banished all thoughts of the woman he held close. With the stars twinkling down at him, he brought forth the names and shapes of the beasts that watched over all warriors. One by one, he silently uttered their names and offered a prayer for continued support over this journey and those that would follow.

He sought out the mighty Thor in his grand chariot streaking across the cosmos. When his gaze touched on Freyja's Dress, and the belt and sword on her girdle, his inner anguish resumed again, and his thoughts returned to the woman within his arms.

Was he enchanted because Elspeth refused him? Was this the reason he found himself out of control and unable to harness his desires? She had called him husband earlier. A word he thought never to hear from those lips. At least not so soon.

Magnar closed his eyes. His lust for his wife consumed him.

Control. Bind. Dismiss.

Slowly releasing the tension that drummed in his veins, Magnar centered himself. Nocturnal animals skittered in the silence. The flap of wings swept in a breeze over him, and his wolf lifted his head.

The night called to all beasts. His was no exception.

Until Steinn was under his control, Magnar required the utmost concentration. His wife proved to be a heady distraction, and he could ill afford to be swept into a lustful tempest to claim and devour what she had to offer.

Even so, the words he ordered into his body and mind seemed to slip into the mists that hugged the mountaintops. And when the first rose-light of dawn streaked the sky, Magnar had found no rest.

Chapter Thirteen

When the sound of laughter touched her ears, Elspeth twisted around. Frustration seethed inside of her. "'Tis unfair," she complained.

After breaking their fast earlier that morning, Magnar led them back toward the stream. He instructed some of his men to cleanse their bodies in the cool water. If they were going into battle, they should enjoy some pleasures before death sought to claim them.

The other guards gaped at these Northmen but finally relented and joined them. Of course, Erik jumped in glee and was the first to be rid of his clothing.

Magnar announced this would be her nephew's first lesson on how to swim.

Ever so delicately, her husband took her elbow and steered her into a safe enclosure with the horses and one of his guards. Did he not think she would overhear his order to Gunnar to keep her tucked securely within the trees? Or did her husband not consider she required some time to bathe as well?

Elspeth waited until her husband retreated. She would not be dismissed so easily and promptly informed Gunnar she required some time alone for private matters. In truth, she understood their conditions, but the grime of their travels had her itching constantly.

Elspeth shielded her eyes from the intense glare of the sun. Light shimmered off the water in front of her—inviting *and* tormenting her. Though the nights were chilled, the days had proven to be warm, and she longed to strip her clothes and swim in the cool waters of the stream.

She swatted away the flying vermin attempting to nip the exposed skin along her neck. "Be gone. I am not your feast!"

Her gown clung to her skin like sap on a tree—sticky and moist. She tugged at her bindings yearning to be free from the material.

Grumbling a curse, she slipped off her boots and went to the water. Squatting by the edge of the stream, she splashed the cool water over her face and behind her neck. "Rules! Can we alter some for women? If I have a daughter—" She paused and cupped a hand over her mouth, her eyes growing wide in delight.

First, you must permit your husband into your bed.

Fits of laughter spilled forth from Elspeth, and she tumbled back on the rocks bordering the stream. Her guard stormed through the thick copse. She glared up at him. "I am in nae need of saving, Gunnar."

The man brushed a hand down the back of his neck. "You ken my life would be forfeit if Magnar found you in danger?"

Shocked by his words, she gaped at the large man. "As you can see, I am not in any danger, but please explain your meaning."

Gunnar gestured toward the water. "Have you completed your *private matters*?"

Guilt assailed her for the previous lie. "Aye. I simply wished to take advantage of the cool water."

He held out his hand. "Will you accept my aid?"

After allowing the man to help her stand, Elspeth brushed out the bits of dirt and pebbles from her gown. "Thank you."

Gunnar clasped his hands behind his back. "You ken Magnar is our leader, aye?"

"King William told me."

"And he is part wolf?"

"Aye," she responded hesitantly.

"Those who are under his leadership must obey him. I was given an order—*one* important task to watch over his wife. If I fail, my life is his to end."

"I meant nae harm, Gunnar," she lamented and turned away. Crossing her arms over her chest, she steadied her voice. "Not only am I having a difficult time believing my husband is a wolf, but also the restraints of being wed. 'Tis a wonder Magnar agreed to marry me. I am not like other women who are meek, submissive, *and* obedient."

"You are wrong, Lady Elspeth."

She stole a glance at Gunnar in surprise. A smile curved his stern features. "What Magnar *requires* is a strong woman to stand by his side and honor the ways of the land, Gods, Goddesses, and most of all—his wolf. You have all these qualities."

Dropping her hands, she turned and faced him. "But therein lies the one thorn of truth. I do not believe in his Gods and Goddesses. Once, aye, but nae more."

A twinkle of mischief creased the corners of his eyes. "I can understand your hardship. 'Tis one I battle with daily after my morning prayers." He slipped his hand beneath his tunic and drew forth a wooden cross.

Elspeth shook her head. "I had heard you follow

my faith in the one true God, but how can you find any peace living amongst those who do not?"

Gunnar's humor was replaced by sadness. "Because I believe our Lord refuses to damn my soul. I deem he has given me this honor of spreading his good news to all. Aye, I am part wolf, but I ken there is a purpose for me within the brotherhood. Cannot I speak about our Lord at a table honoring Odin?" He nodded slowly. "Your husband allows me to say a blessing before meals, all battles, and when we bury the dead."

"Then there is hope Magnar will accept the new religion?" Elspeth was moved by the man's words.

Narrowing his eyes, he answered, "Sadly, nae. Magnar is rooted in ancient beliefs. He only gives respect to our beliefs. If I may ask, can you live with a man—"

"A heathen?" she interjected.

The man grimaced but added nothing further.

Elspeth returned her gaze to the water, allowing the gentle rhythm to ease her disquiet. Her mind continued to battle with her heart, and she suspected it would always be thus. "I married him. Pledged my vows in front of King William and the brotherhood. Nae matter our beliefs, I ken he is a good man. I sensed it after witnessing how he took charge of my nephew." She drew in a breath and released it slowly. "I can live with Magnar, because I *chose* to be with him. In the beginning, I fought against it, but I listened to Magnar's words and made a choice. Though this marriage was thrust upon me—*us*, I shall continue to stand with my husband."

Gunnar surprised her by placing a hand on her shoulder. "You might have been born in Scotland, but on the *Orkneyjar Isles*, our people would call you a shield-maiden."

Giving the man a radiant smile, Elspeth said, "You honor me with your kind words. Thank you for sharing. It has brought me comfort."

He shrugged. "I spoke the truth." He waved his hand outward. "Follow the path of the water around the bend of trees. There you will find your husband. His lesson with Erik has ended."

Elspeth stood on her tiptoes and glanced down the stream and then back at him. "How do you ken he's out there?"

The man tapped a finger to his nose. "I can smell him. Let him ken his time in the water has ended. 'Tis time we continue on our journey."

"Are you giving him an order?" she scolded.

He chuckled and moved away from her. "Most assuredly. One of my duties is making certain we keep to our schedule."

After retrieving her boots, Elspeth wandered along the edge of the stream. Approaching the bend, she was caught unaware by the sudden dip in the land and almost slipped. Recovering quickly, she continued on the narrow pebble path until the view opened up.

Her breath caught, and she dropped her boots. Mesmerized by the scene in front of her, Elspeth took in Magnar's mighty form stretched out on his stomach atop a boulder. Not a stitch of clothing covered the man. Words failed her as she continued to rest her gaze on his powerful body. She noted the blue markings across his back, and her fingers itched to trace the interesting patterns. Would he share their meaning? Lowering her gaze farther, heat crept up her neck and flamed her cheeks. Unable to move from her spot, she placed a cool hand on her face to squelch the fire.

The man tempted her beyond reason. Teased her to touch, taste, and take her fill. Her body ached in places she could not fathom the meaning. Was it wrong to crave her husband? He had been patient, not forceful. Days ago, she thought never to welcome the man to her bed. Yet now?

"Let us first return to Steinn," she whispered into the soft summer breeze.

"Do you find my body pleasing, *wife*?" asked Magnar.

Embarrassed she was caught gaping at her husband, Elspeth averted her gaze. Should she even ask how he knew it was her studying him under the branches of the tree? She needed to know. "You can smell me, aye?"

He laughed boldly.

Elspeth bit the inside of her cheek to stifle her own laughter.

When she heard him approaching, she slid him a glance. Wearing only a tunic, the man looked as if he meant to devour her. She steadied her breathing as he came to stand mere inches in front of her. His damp hair was pulled back, and Elspeth noted a scar marring his right temple. Curious, she lifted her hand and traced a path over the jagged rough patch of skin.

He flinched from her touch but made no effort to move away.

Slowly, Elspeth's fingers traveled through the light shadow of beard until they settled on his bottom lip. His tongue slipped out and teased her fingertips.

Without warning, he grasped her around the waist

and pressed her body against his. "You tempt me to undo my vow."

"Out here?" she asked, uncertain of his meaning.

Magnar's other hand cupped her breast. "Many pleasures can be found in the water, once you are free from clothing."

She regarded his features—intense and compelling. Granted she understood part of what her husband was referring to—she found herself gritty from the weather, and Magnar refreshed. "'Tis not fair," she declared and quickly added, "You were able to swim without any clothing. Whereas, I was kept to the trees."

He lowered his head and nipped her lower lip with his teeth. "Why did you not say you wished to bathe? With me?"

His finger made lazy circles over her breast, and she fought the moan bubbling forth. "I...I believe 'tis time we keep to our schedule," she mumbled.

"Agreed." He lifted his head and smiled.

Unable to stop herself, Elspeth grasped his tunic and pulled him toward her. Her lips brushed against his as she spoke. "One kiss."

His groan swelled all around her as he took her mouth in a fiery blaze of a kiss that curled her toes. She wrapped her arms around his body, opening fully to him. When his tongue delved inside her mouth, Elspeth was shocked at her own eager response. The kiss sent the pit of her stomach into a swirl of pleasure. Magnar smelled like the land and his own male scent, causing her to become dizzy.

When he broke free from the kiss, he swiftly lifted her into his arms.

Dazed, Elspeth clung to his shoulders and stared at

his rugged face. "What are you doing?"

His jaw clenched. "One of us needs to be set free."

"Gunnar will not be pleased with you breaking the schedule."

The growl rumbled low in Magnar's throat, and a muscle twitched in his jaw. "A word of warning, Elspeth. When you are in my arms, *never* mention the name of another wolf."

Curious, she dared to ask, "Why?"

"You belong to me—nae other. Even my wolf kens this."

As he carried her into the dense pine trees, cool air brushed against Elspeth's cheeks, soothing the fire on her skin. Birds darted out from tree limbs, shrieking their displeasure at being invaded.

His steps slowed, and he gently lowered them both to the ground. Magnar leaned against a huge pine and cradled her body on his lap.

"Why are we here?" she uttered softly.

His fingers skimmed under her gown and touched her leg. "Do you trust me, Elspeth? To give you pleasure without taking your body?"

Even though she felt his hard length under her, Elspeth trusted her husband to keep his promise. "Aye," she affirmed.

"Keep your focus on my eyes, *kærr*."

Her heart skipped a beat when he called her *beloved*. Tingling ripples traveled up her body, followed by an ache of longing as his rough fingers trailed a path up her leg. She squirmed, not understanding the feelings coursing through her body.

Eager to know, she asked, "Wh…what are you doing?"

His smile came slowly, but he remained silent.

His warm touch left her breathing heavily, and when his finger swept across her sensitive core, Elspeth arched in pure pleasure and closed her eyes. "*Magnar*." She whispered his name on a plea for more.

"Look at me," he demanded in a rough voice.

Her eyes fluttered open to gaze into his. The look of raw need in his eyes should have frightened Elspeth, but she trusted her husband.

When his finger delved inside her, her grip on his shoulders tightened. A gasp of pleasure fell from her lips, and her nails bit deeper into his tunic. He continued to torment her body in ways she had never imagined. The fever of desire grew and spread throughout her.

"You are soft, my *kærr*. Does this please you?"

Elspeth whimpered, not understanding what was happening to her. She tried to grasp the elusive flame. "More," she pleaded in desperation.

With a fierce growl, he took possession of her mouth. His tongue sought entry, and she surrendered to the kiss. A pulse of need thrummed between her legs, and she rocked against his hand. When the tide of passion swept across her skin, Elspeth soared on the wave, and uttered a guttural cry as the tremors shook her body. The pleasure lifted her higher as she clung to Magnar.

Finally spent, Elspeth collapsed against her husband's chest. Her breathing was ragged as he slowly removed his fingers from her body. She was blissfully contented being held in his massive arms.

"Are you pleased?" His breath was hot between the curve of her neck and shoulder.

Slowly, she lifted her head. Staring into his heated gaze, Elspeth felt as weak as a newborn lamb. "Will it always be thus between us?"

Magnar settled his hands on her hips. "Aye, but you have barely sampled a brief amount of the pleasure I can bring you."

She shuddered, aching to learn from him. Did Magnar understand how his touch ignited a powerful need for more? No longer did Elspeth battle against having him in her marriage bed. In truth, she yearned to have him teach her the ways of being a wife—completely.

The man had awakened the woman in her. There was no going back on her decision—one she was allowed to make.

Placing her hands on his chest, she started to move against him.

"Nae," he ordered in a ragged breath. "My need for you is fierce." Rubbing his cheek against hers, he whispered, "Unless you want me to claim you swiftly, do not grind into me."

Brushing a soft kiss against his skin, she replied, "Once Steinn is under our control, will you teach me more, Magnar?"

Leaning back, he stared at her for several heartbeats. Cupping her chin, he asked, "You want me in your bed?"

Removing his hand from her skin, Elspeth placed a kiss inside his palm. *Would he think me too brazen?* Banishing the thought, she responded, "Aye, *husband.* Furthermore, I wish you to show me how to pleasure you, too. Tell me your desires."

His eyes widened in surprise. Reclaiming her lips,

he crushed her to him. The kiss sent her body into a wild swirl all over again, and she let out a moan.

Abruptly breaking free, he blew out a curse and removed Elspeth from his lap. He stood and turned away. Placing his hands on his hips, he glanced upward. "I shall give you some time to bathe in the water."

Her body trembled as she made to stand. "What about our schedule?"

He raked a hand through his damp locks. "Since we have prolonged our time here, I am positive Gunnar will not cease his grumbling for days." Shrugging, he added, "Therefore, another hour will not matter."

"Will you help me to undress?"

Magnar chuckled softly.

Elspeth moved to his side. "I trust you."

He reached for her braid and wrapped the end around his fist. "You might. But I do not. I will help you with the outer garment only. 'Tis best if I not look at your bare skin until you are covered by the water."

This time, Elspeth was the one who laughed. She knew her husband would not be able to resist a peek at her naked form once he heard a splash of water.

Chapter Fourteen

As foretold, Gunnar continued with his relentless
objections over Magnar wasting costly travel time. The
man snapped, cursed, and gave scathing looks at him at
each opportunity. Thankfully, he directed his
grumblings toward Magnar and not within hearing of
Elspeth. When Gunnar pointed to the setting sun, he
raised his fist at him for not reaching the first hill before
Steinn.

Magnar ignored the man completely.

His thoughts kept returning to his flame-haired
wife—images that had him hard all over again. He
dared not glance over his shoulder at her. She would
only incite his lustful beast further.

He licked his lips, recalling her ivory, smooth
curves entering the stream. Aye, he made a vow not to
take her, but that did not mean he would not spare a
glance at his wife's naked form whenever he could. It
had taken his utmost control not to step into the water
and join her. And more restraint not to watch and bring
himself to pleasure. Especially when she'd bent over
and splashed water over her taut skin.

Scrubbing a hand vigorously over his face, he
attempted to banish the lustful images.

A gentle breeze blew past him, sweeping the leaves
around the travelers. His wolf sensed the intruder first
and lifted his head. Magnar slowed his horse and

sniffed the air. With deft skill, he removed his axe from the sheath attached to the side of his horse and brought it across his thighs.

Rorik flanked his left and kept a slow and steady stride with him. "You ken there is *another* out there."

"Aye." A tremor of unease settled within Magnar. There was only one wolf not within the brotherhood. *Thorfinn!*

"Are you worried?" asked Rorik quietly.

Magnar shrugged, attempting to ease the tension across his shoulders. "This makes my quest to find my brother much easier. He has come to us."

His other men slowed their pace but remained silent. Magnar understood they had sensed this new wolf. Each lifted their heads and inhaled deeply. Ivar let out a low growl.

They continued on their subdued, easy gallop across the landscape.

Rorik rubbed a hand over his chin. "You ken what this means?"

Curling his lip in disgust, Magnar glanced sharply at his friend. "He is a *spy* for Baardsen."

"Or he is with others," suggested Rorik, scanning the dense trees that hugged the hillside.

"Nae," argued Magnar, his fingers tightening on his axe. "Clearly, Thorfinn was the one who followed Elspeth to us—at Castle Vargr. 'Tis what makes sense. He spies in his wolf form for the enemy."

"What do you propose we do?" asked Rorik, returning his gaze to Magnar.

Frustration seethed inside Magnar. Unprepared for this latest interruption on their journey, he spat out a curse and surveyed the region south of Steinn. If they traveled another path, they would be delayed one more day. He kept his sight fixed on their original path. "We shall continue to the first hill. Inform Ivar and Gunnar that they will leave at midnight for Steinn with my terms and those of King William's to surrender the castle and leave."

Smiling slowly, Rorik nodded. "You send the peacemaker *and* a strong arm."

Magnar arched a brow. "Would you have me send Bjorn?"

Rorik grimaced and scratched behind his ear. "Nae. Most likely blades would be drawn before the man uttered a word. Ivar is nae better, though."

"His tongue will remain silent. Ivar can observe the strength, number, *and* weaknesses within the keep and surrounding area."

"What of Thorfinn?"

Narrowing his eyes, Magnar replied, "Until Steinn is under our control, my brother is the king's enemy. We must move forward with *our* plans. Until I ken the true nature of my brother's actions, I cannot abide his decision to stay with the enemy."

Rorik tilted his head to the side and drew in a breath. On the exhale, he said, "The wolf has retreated."

"Aye, I sensed his departure as well." Magnar brought his horse to a halt.

Soon the others gathered around him. His gaze landed on each of his warriors. "Despite the fact that this other wolf is my brother, you shall consider him the enemy. Our task is to secure Steinn for our king." He settled his gaze on Erik, adding, "For the new chieftain."

"Aye," responded his warriors in unison.

After Magnar returned his axe to the side of his horse, he gestured for Rorik to take the lead. "Let us move swiftly away from here."

Magnar regarded the frown marring his wife's features as she drew near him. She waited until the others had moved onward and then reached out to touch his arm. "Your brother rides with Halvard?"

"I fear 'tis the truth. Can you recall seeing anyone—"

"Resembling you?" she blurted out. "Nae!" Elspeth dropped her hand and gaped at him. "I would have remembered."

Magnar studied his men through the dimming light. "It nae longer matters. We must get to Steinn. I deem Halvard presented your brother with only a few of his men when he entered the keep. Most likely he had other men—including Thorfinn—hiding within and around Steinn. He thought to offer himself in a humble fashion. Your brother was wise in witnessing his true nature."

Elspeth leaned forward. "What if there is a battle? What if you must fight Thorfinn?"

Magnar snorted. The light was fading swiftly, and his men were getting farther ahead. "A plan I have yet to solve, wife. Now off with you." Giving a smack to her horse, he watched as animal and rider galloped away. He knew one of the wolves would fall back and wait for his wife. And he needed a moment to himself.

"What shall I do with the traitor, Thor?" he muttered. "Especially one who is my brother?"

The God of Thunder did not respond.

Slamming the door on his troubling thoughts, Magnar sped his horse onward.

****

Castle Steinn

"You call this wine, you foul wench?" demanded Halvard.

"Aye," she offered meekly, twisting her fingers into the folds of her gown.

Thorfinn shifted his stance within the great hall. He had given his account, waiting for the information to settle within the man. He clenched his fist repeatedly, noting how Halvard's fury was now directed toward the thrall serving him wine.

Tossing the contents of the wine into her face, he raged, "Nothing more than piss! When I find the remainder of the barrels, I will slit your throat and let the ravens drink your blood. Get out and do not return until you have brought me the best Steinn has to offer!"

Clasping a hand over her throat, the woman paled and scurried out of the hall.

Halvard glared at him. "Tell me again how many?"

"Sixteen men, one child, and a woman," responded Thorfinn in a calm tone, and he relaxed his fist.

In another display of anger, Halvard slammed the mug against the stone wall, splintering the wood into bits that embedded themselves in his hand and the wall. As blood pooled within his palm, the man clenched his hand. "How many *wolves*?"

"Six, including their leader."

Halvard stepped near him and studied him.

Thorfinn knew the man well and remained silent. He would not challenge his leader until his anger had simmered.

Malice reflected within Halvard's eyes. "Therefore, you have seen your brother?"

"He is *not* my brother," argued Thorfinn,

tempering his growing ire.

The man shoved past him, leaving bloodstains on Thorfinn's tunic. Halvard paced in front of the hearth. Giving him a scathing look, he spat out, "You are blood kin, do not forget. Are you prepared to fight him?"

The flames snapped and hissed, echoing the mood within the hall.

Clasping his hands behind his back, Thorfinn glared at the man. "As I have stated, I owe you my life. I have journeyed from *Orkneyjar* to Scotland with you. I seek to take back this land and any riches we can attain for our people. The time for King William's reign is over."

Halvard snarled and ceased his motions. "You have not answered my question."

Why must he always challenge my loyalty?

"If I must put a blade in Magnar MacAlpin, then I shall make it a clean strike. We may have claim to the same woman who birthed us, but I owe nae loyalty to the man."

Pointing a bloodied finger at him, Halvard shook his head. "Nae, *nae*. You must fight each as wolves." Rubbing his hands together, he resumed his pacing. "Once the leader is slain, you can take your role and bring down the mighty Wolves of Clan Sutherland. By the ancient edicts, 'tis your right. They will do your bidding or enter into Valhalla."

Thorfinn had nae desire to become a leader of anything. He regarded giving his account but held back. Halvard appeared intent on moving forward with his plans. Any who argued against him found themselves beaten, thrown into whatever dungeon they came upon, or made to swim the icy North Sea to rid them of any opinions, where most died.

"What of the woman and child?" asked Thorfinn.

Halvard shrugged. "I will take the woman as my wife, and you can kill the child. Her escape has hindered our plans."

Wary of this plan to end a child's life, Thorfinn offered another solution. "Why not make him a thrall?"

Halvard dismissed him with a wave of his hand. "He poses a threat. His life is mine to end."

"Nae," a low voice uttered from a corner of the hall. Stepping out of the shadows, the Seer came forth. He fingered the strand of eagle talons around his neck as he strode toward Halvard. "You shall not end the life of Magnar MacAlpin, nor take the woman as your wife, *or* slay the boy."

Halvard fisted his hands on his hips. "Explain, Ketil!"

The Seer closed his eyes. "If you continue on this reckless path, death will come to many, including you."

"You have seen a vision? A great battle to be fought here?" Halvard's tone was guarded.

Ketil opened his eyes. "A murky one. Filled with violence and power."

"Power?" echoed Thorfinn, unclasping his hands, curious to learn more.

The Seer tilted his head to the side and lifted his gnarled finger at Thorfinn. "They bring an *ancient* power with them." He paused and closed his eyes again. "We are not prepared. We must flee Steinn, and then wait for the Gods to show us a plan."

"Can you not reveal more, Ketil?" demanded Halvard, leaning against the table.

"Do you seek to thwart the Gods' plans?" snapped

Ketil, opening his eyes. He reached for the leather pouch secured at his waist and tossed the item onto the table. "If you can read the runes, then go forth with your plan."

Halvard gave him a horrified expression and pushed away from the table. "I do not wish to offend the Gods."

"Then refrain from questioning me further. Order your men to make ready." Brushing past Thorfinn, the Seer left as quietly as he entered.

Unease settled within Thorfinn. The Seer had spoken to him directly. His subtle message was unclear, though. What ancient power? As part wolf, he already possessed many magical qualities. Thankfully, his leader remained unaware of the Seer's underlying message to Thorfinn.

Your perception is addled from too much drink, Halvard.

If not bound by honor and loyalty to his leader, Thorfinn would be tempted to remove the head from the man's shoulders in one blow. His reckless actions caused undue harm to many of their men after the untimely death of Thomas Gunn. His leader often times presented an unstable thought, along with his actions.

"You are quiet, Thorfinn," observed Halvard, moving past him. He snatched a cloth off the table and bound his hand to stanch the flow of blood.

"Considering the Seer's words." In truth, he had no desire to lie to his leader.

The man grunted a curse and cast a steely look around the hall. "Pity he did not offer his insight earlier, aye?"

Reaching for the pouch of runes, Thorfinn

considered his reply. *Depends on which Gods the Seer favors*. He slid a glance at Halvard. "Even so, who are we to question a Seer?"

The man's shoulders sagged in resignation. "Aye, we must follow his sage wisdom. Our plans were thwarted long ago when two were allowed to escape."

They fled due to your hasty decision to slay the chieftain in front of too many witnesses. You should have listened to me.

"Where shall I tell the men to retreat to?" asked Thorfinn in an attempt to sway the conversation. If not, he'd be forced to listen to the endless rants spouting forth from his leader.

Blood seeped through the cloth as Halvard continued to squeeze his hand into a fist. "*Retreat?*" Spittle flew from his mouth. "Are we meek rats to scurry away from the onslaught of wolves?" Pounding his fist against his chest, he shouted, "Nae! The might of the Gods favors us! Loki will show us another way to *destroy* this pack of animals. They should all cease to exist."

Fury surfaced within Thorfinn. His wolf growled in contempt over the man's choice of words and urged him to take vengeance. Clenching his jaw, he fought the desire to shift. With great effort he forced his wolf to withdraw.

Thorfinn dared to take a step toward the man. "Might I remind you, I am a wolf."

Wariness passed briefly over the man's features, yet he made no move to step away. "A wolf that is loyal *and* obedient to me."

A low warning growl escaped from Thorfinn. "Loyal to you, aye. Obedient to the Gods!"

The man took a step back. "Are you challenging me?"

Thorfinn laughed bitterly.

The color drained from Halvard's face, and he placed a hand on the dirk at his side. "You find humor in my words? You, who I have saved from bondage on *Orkneyjar*, dare to mock me?"

Thorfinn relented. This constant arguing of words had no place here. "Forgive me. Your words inflamed my wolf."

"Then your wolf should understand the enemy and my meaning." Halvard dismissed him with a wave of his hand. "Go prepare the men and horses."

Giving the man a curt nod, Thorfinn steadily made his way out of the hall.

"One more order," added Halvard.

Halting his steps, he glanced over his shoulder.

"If I ever see your eyes shift to those of the wolf again, I will have my men bind you to a stake, and I will personally burn them out of your head," warned Halvard in a fierce tone that did not bode well for Thorfinn.

Without acknowledging the man, Thorfinn swiftly departed the hall.

Chapter Fifteen

In an effort to calm the growing restlessness of his wolf, Magnar dismounted from his horse and bent down on one knee near the base of a hill. Damp, cool morning air refreshed his body. Placing his palm on the soft ground, he let the soothing power of the land ease the animal. Many weeks had passed without allowing the wolf to wander across any landscape. With all that had occurred, he sensed the growing displeasure of the animal.

Seek the moist earth, my friend. Find comfort in the scent of the land and richness of the soil.

Magnar brought a fistful of dirt to his face. Inhaling deeply, he sought to ease the anguish within his beast.

Settle into the realm of Asgard, you who were created from magic with Odin's approval. Temper the disquiet, especially as we prepare for battle.

His wolf ceased his pacing.

He tossed the dirt outward and stood. Magnar's gaze sought and found the path leading up the side of the hill. Making quick strides over the rocky incline, he observed the dawn of a new day.

When the first glow of sunlight creased the morning sky, he placed a fist over his heart. "Protect my body with your shield and hammer, mighty Thor. Let my enemies' death by my hand be swift and just.

All Father, if any of my men are taken by death's hand, permit them to enter into the Hall of Valhalla. They are all honorable warriors."

He scanned the landscape. Many hours had passed since Gunnar and Ivar had departed after midnight to reach Steinn. Did he anticipate their swift return with good news to proclaim? Nae. Halvard had nae intention of surrendering the keep and lands. The battle was forthcoming, and he prayed for a swift resolve.

Magnar's thoughts drifted to his wife. "I may not have bedded you, Elspeth, but you are mine." His heart hammered with a fierce need to protect her. Once again, his night had been filled with torment. Each hour she spent curled up against him caused him agony.

He clenched his fist. The struggle to serve his king *and* guard his wife grew with each passing hour. *You must maintain your focus.*

Unable to dwell on Elspeth for too long, fearing he'd abandon his men—if it came to a battle, and seek to guard her himself. Magnar sought out a prayer. *Goddess Freyja, if war comes to my wife and I cannot be by her side, I pray you protect her with your shield and cloak. Let the falcon be a warning to her to be on guard for any foe.*

The sun rose higher in the sky, spreading its light across the land below. Just beyond the valley stood the massive castle shrouded by dense trees. With a heavy sigh, he turned to leave and make ready with his men.

A faint tremor of awareness alerted him of the oncoming wolves. He knew the scent of his men, but Magnar took cover behind a thick pine tree and waited. The riders moved steadily forward, and he looked beyond them. Once he made certain no one followed his men, he emerged forth.

He allowed his taut stance to relax just a bit, but Magnar itched to take hold of his axe.

When the laughter and unruly bantering of Gunnar and Ivar reached his hearing, Magnar rested his hands on his hips. Neither was prone to outbursts, especially before a battle. Confused over the mirth, he sought to contain his fury.

Unless his men were overjoyed for another reason?

As they approached, Magnar stepped back to grant them entrance within the protection of the trees.

Elation covered their features. Gunnar dismounted first and drew near him.

"What news?" Magnar demanded.

"The castle and grounds are vacant of Halvard and his men," replied Gunnar. "We found a few servants hiding in the cellar. Many of Steinn's clan were killed by Halvard or fled to the hills, taking as many of the children who had survived with them. Those who were forced to become thralls were treated dreadfully. One of the servants witnessed the Northmen and their leader's departure to the north yesterday morn."

"Why would they leave?" Magnar glanced over their shoulders, half expecting the enemy to be out there.

Ivar shrugged and spat on the ground. "Pity. I yearned for a good fight."

Gunnar gave the man an annoyed look. "They departed the keep, realizing there was nothing to gain by staying. The fear of King William took hold. Can you not take this as a blessing?"

"From Odin, aye!"

"Enough!" ordered Magnar and stepped around

them. Rubbing a hand over his chin, he pondered this news. Did the threat of so many wolves cause Halvard to run in fear? Even so, he could ill afford to let his guard down. Steinn was now his to take control of, but he would ensure its safety from future enemies as well.

An easy victory, and I thank you, Thor.

Magnar went and clamped a hand on each man's shoulder. "Return to Steinn and prepare for our appearance. Have the servants find the others and let them know this joyous news. Furthermore, continue to be on guard. I have nae desire to step into a trap."

Releasing his hold, he added, "We shall arrive soon."

Both gave a curt nod.

As soon as they departed, Magnar hastily returned to his horse. His shoulders eased as he urged his mount onward along the path to the others.

Bjorn was the first to approach him with some of the king's men not far behind. "They have returned? You have heard news?" The man's question was laced with worry as he clutched his sword.

Magnar swiftly dismounted and gave a gentle pat to his horse. "There will be nae battle. They have fled north from Steinn."

The man sheathed his sword. "Loki's balls! Wished I could have skewered one of the vermin."

"Exactly what Ivar said," admitted Magnar, searching for Elspeth among the group of men. "Another time, perchance. For now, we claim victory. Where is Steinar?"

"Behind you," announced the man, coming forth. "Heard everything. Sharpened my blade this morn in anticipation of drenching the steel with their blood."

Lifting his long blade to the light, he added, "'Tis a shame."

Out of all the wolves in the brotherhood, Steinar proved to be the most silent—in words and movement, making him an elite mercenary for the king. His cunning skills outmatched all, including Magnar's. If a battle had been fought, he'd have sent Steinar in the lead.

"Take the news to King William. Tell him Steinn Castle is in our control. Until I am confident there is not a threat of the enemy returning, I will keep all the men secured at Steinn. I will nae take this man lightly again."

Steinar shifted his stance. "And after I deliver the message?"

"Return to Steinn. I intend on maintaining control surrounding the keep."

"Good plan," acknowledged Steinar and slipped away.

Scanning the area once again, Magnar was determined to give the good news to Elspeth. Yet Rorik hailed him from across the trees with Erik following closely behind him. He let out a frustrated sigh.

"'Tis true?" Rorik continued to maintain his grip on his blade.

"Aye. Confirmed by Gunnar and Ivar. They have returned to assist the others who are left."

Erik narrowed his eyes in thought. "I was ready for the battle—to take down those who killed my father."

Magnar crouched down next to the lad. "Your orders were to protect my wife. Forsooth, the battle would have been fought far away from you and your aunt."

The young chieftain swallowed visibly. He leaned near him. "You ken *your wife* would have disobeyed your order to stay hidden."

By the hounds! Magnar wanted to shout. Instead, he let his inner wolf growl his displeasure.

Erik's face paled, and he took a step back.

"When I give an order, *all* must obey. Do you ken my meaning, Erik?"

Pounding his chest with his fist, Erik confessed, "If I had to, I would have seen her injured to keep her safe."

"A feat I would have liked to have witnessed, Nephew."

Magnar stood slowly, noting the fury within the depths of Elspeth's eyes. "Leave, Rorik, and take the *young* chieftain with you," he ordered.

Rorik grabbed Erik by the tunic and pushed him forward.

Magnar's wife stood rooted to the ground with her arms crossed over her ample breasts.

With his fury barely contained, Magnar remained in his position for fear he'd take her over his knee for a proper punishment. Did he not explain to Elspeth what would happen during a battle? He thought she understood. Clearly not only was his wife mocking him, but she gave no regard to his beast. He clenched and then slowly unclenched his hand.

"Does Erik speak truthfully? Were you planning on following us to Steinn?" His tone held a note of warning.

She lifted her chin. "Aye," she challenged. "But I had only planned—"

He waved his hand in dismissal. "Nae! My orders

were precise, Elspeth!" He dared to take a step forward. "And what about Rorik? Did you not consider him in your plot?"

When she averted her gaze from his glare, Magnar thought he understood her plan. "Either harm would befall Rorik or you sought to appease him with your plan."

She snorted. "Neither. Escape from your guard was the plan." Pointing a finger at him, she added, "Only to the top of the hill. I couldn't endure not being able to witness anything. Not knowing if something happened…*to you*."

He clasped his hands behind his back. Her concern for him lessened some of the anger. Did Elspeth care for him? Magnar banished the thought. "Nevertheless, you engaged your nephew, your chieftain. Even the stench of a battle not fought was on his skin—eager for the kill. You could have put him in danger."

Elspeth dropped her hands by her sides. "Waiting is the hardest, Magnar." She peered around him. "I shall go take my place with Erik and Rorik. Perchance in time you will forgive my inclination for disobedience."

Apparently, his wife was the last not to hear the good news. "Nae battle shall be fought," he declared.

Her mouth gaped open and then snapped shut. "What are you saying?"

"Halvard and his men have fled Steinn. Gunnar and Ivar seek to bring back the others who escaped into the hills."

On a choked sob, she lunged at Magnar and wrapped her arms around his neck. Stunned by her reaction to his news, he was unable to offer her any words of comfort. Instead, he allowed her to weep her tears as he brought his arms around her body.

After several moments, she released her hold. "Sorry," she mumbled against his chest.

Magnar lifted her chin with his finger. For the first time, he noted the dark smudges under her eyes. Little sleep and worry had taken its toll on his brave wife. "You were overcome by the news. Nae need for regret," he reassured.

When a lone tear trickled down her cheek, he brushed it aside with the pad of his thumb.

Elspeth grasped his hand and leaned her warm cheek into his palm. "Thank you."

Magnar brushed a gentle kiss across her lips. "Allow me to assist you onto your horse. Steinn awaits."

"I would welcome your aid," she whispered.

He placed her hand in the crook of his arm. Walking slowly through the trees, they soon came upon her mount. Even the animal appeared tired and strained. He gave a gentle pat to the horse. "You have served us well."

Elspeth smiled and stroked the horse's mane. "Indeed, husband."

How Magnar enjoyed hearing her calling him thus. "Give me your foot."

Instead, she faced him, placing her hands on his chest. "From this day forward, I give you my word I shall obey your orders, if we go into any battles."

Magnar arched a brow in question.

"*Or* if there is a threat," she added hastily.

His hand skimmed down her waist and settled on her lush bottom. "Therefore, you will obey only if there are battles or threats?"

"'Tis a start, aye?"

His hand squeezed. "Do you want to hear what I shall do to you if you disobey another order—one that could put you in harm, again?"

With a gasp, she tried to wrest free of his hold. "You would not dare?" Though her tone betrayed shock, her eyes danced with mischief.

He gripped her bottom more firmly. "A challenge that I accept."

She dared to lean against him. "Show me."

By the Gods how you tempt me, Elspeth.

He rubbed his face against her cheek, inhaling her womanly scent. "Nae, wife. Not here. For your *punishment*, I might have to consider removing your clothes and tossing your naked body over my knees—"

"Will it bring me pleasure?" she interrupted on a moan.

He stilled his progress. Did she not understand how her words inflamed his desire? "Depends…"

Lifting her head, she regarded him. "On what?"

Smiling, he answered, "How hard or soft you wish me to stroke your bottom."

She shuddered, but desire reflected in those emerald eyes. "Hmm…"

Magnar released his hold. "Best we get to Steinn. Your foot, *wife*."

Red splotches stained her cheeks and neck as she complied. After settling her firmly on the horse's back, Magnar gave a short whistle.

His horse emerged from the trees, trotting toward him. Swiftly getting onto the animal, he reached for the reins, and they slowly made their way onward to the hillside. When they reached the top, Elspeth brought her horse to a halt and Magnar approached beside her.

Wariness marred her face while she scanned the valley below. "Magnar?"

Concerned, he reached for her hand. "Aye. What troubles you? Steinn is truly under our control. You should be happy to return to your home."

She bit her lower lip. Darting him a furtive glance, she explained, "You...*you* do not think me brazen?" Fidgeting with the reins, Elspeth continued, "For wanting to learn about what happens between a wife and husband?"

Magnar cupped her chin. "Contrary to what you may have been told, pleasure within a marriage is considered important. 'Tis what I hoped and *yearned* for with you."

"Then you do not mind if I talk thus with you?" Again, her cheeks were stained with a becoming rosy hue he loved seeing.

He brushed his fingers lightly over her cheek. "Nae. In fact, I encourage you to share more of what you desire, *my kærr*."

Averting her gaze from his, Elspeth shielded her eyes from the morning light. "Good."

"Ready to enter Steinn?" he asked softly.

She turned and gave him a radiant smile. "Lead the way, *husband*."

Chapter Sixteen

Laughter and song filled the great hall while Elspeth watched from the entrance. So many emotions swirled within her. Joy and sorrow battled for control. Aye, she was grateful for returning, and 'twas a joyous reunion, yet the sadness of what she'd witnessed lingered within her memories. Earlier when they entered Steinn, there were less than fifteen to greet them. Tears streamed down her face as she embraced each of them, praising them on their brave fortitude.

When she announced that Magnar was her husband, they all shouted their approval. The women embraced him, while the men gave their vow of loyalty and appreciation for returning their chieftain and his aunt safely to them.

Never in all her life had Elspeth witnessed such affection. Although, to be fair, their home had never suffered an attack like the one they'd endured.

Gunnar and Ivar took more guards in an effort to bring back any others who had fled. They left with a reassurance to restore as many as possible to Steinn.

Elspeth's gratitude to Magnar and his men was immense.

She scanned the hall, seeking out her nephew. Barely making out his small form among the other guards, she smiled, allowing the tension to ease from her shoulders. Though the hour was late, she knew the importance of this small feasting. The people needed to be with their new chieftain. And for the first time, Erik listened to their woes, remaining silent about his quest.

"You are a great leader to our people, Erik. Your father would be proud," she uttered quietly. Elspeth drew in a shaky breath, and unshed tears burned her eyes once again.

Magnar approached by her side. He handed her a cup. "Wine."

She bit back the curse as she took the offering. "I am surprised there are any barrels left." Fury rose unbidden, recalling the earlier image of an almost empty larder. The bastards had left nothing for her people.

Magnar nudged her. "You can thank the older woman and man by the hearth. They hid what was left of the good wine in a separate room."

"They are Emer and Dougal." After taking a sip of the wine, Elspeth let the fruity liquid warm her. She laughed softly. "They saved..." She paused and took another sip to steady her nerves. "This is my brother's finest wine."

"Even when the woman was threatened by Halvard, she refused to disclose the location of the barrels."

Elspeth stiffened. "Goodness. Emer should not have been so brave. If the man gave nae regard for my brother, he certainly would not have an issue with putting a blade into an old woman."

Taking her elbow, her husband steered Elspeth inside the hall.

"I would rather stay outside," she protested, trying to halt her steps, but failing miserably under his brute strength.

The warrior expression that graced her husband's face most of the time relaxed a bit. "You must eat."

She shook her head vigorously. "Nae. These people require food." Lifting her cup, she declared, "Wine will suffice."

Magnar blew out a curse and pulled out a wooden chair for her. He waited patiently for her to sit. "Since you have busied yourself with searching the castle for any of your people who may have been hiding, I made sure the food supplies we had, although limited, were distributed among your people. Furthermore, some have secured berries, nuts, and cheese. In the morn, a group of men are planning a hunt."

Elspeth sat in the chair Magnar offered. She placed a hand over her stomach in an attempt to squelch its persistent grumblings.

He bent and brushed a kiss across her lips. "I will return shortly."

Elspeth studied her husband over the rim of her cup. He crossed the expanse of the hall as if he were their leader. She marveled at his ease with her people. Women came up to the giant with smiles and nods, once again giving thanks for bringing peace to their home.

Even after everything they had been through, they gave these Northmen their respect. Her admiration continued to grow for Magnar, along with another emotion. Did she dare to hope for more?

Can I love this man? The word was elusive as a feather blowing in the summer breeze. The feeling blossomed, but fear stayed its approach.

Settling back in her chair, she allowed the murmur

of voices and the wine to soothe her weary body. Erik's laughter floated above the din, and Elspeth yawned. On a sigh, she closed her eyes.

****

As Magnar approached the table with a trencher of food for his wife, he noted the soft snores escaping from her lips while she slept. With only wine for sustenance, Elspeth had surrendered to the strain of their journey. "Once again, I find you asleep before I can offer you some food." His concern for Elspeth grew even more.

Setting the trencher on the table, he went in search of aid for his wife.

Placing a gentle hand on Emer's shoulder, he asked, "Would you show me Elspeth's chambers?"

The woman looked around him and grinned. "'Tis a wonder she did not seek rest the moment she returned." Rising from her chair, she reached for a jug of wine and crossed to his wife.

Magnar followed her. Gently, he lifted Elspeth into his arms. She let out a small cry of protest, dropping the cup onto the floor, and then curled up against him.

"I shall bring the food as well," suggested Emer.

Steadily, they made their way out of the hall and down a corridor to the stairs. After adjusting her in his arms, he traveled at a quiet pace. The torches along the stone walls cast eerie shapes and shadows in passing.

The dead still lingered. Warriors who sought revenge for battles not won.

Approaching the chambers, Magnar slowed his progress.

Emer placed the jug on the floor and opened the wooden door. "Take the lass to her bed. Forgive me…umm…*your* bed." Seemingly flustered, she reached for the jug of wine and went to deposit everything on a table by the window.

Magnar grinned and entered the chamber. Though the day had been warm, a chill infused the room, as if the ghosts from the past had entered with them. The shutters by the arched window were open, and he watched the sun slip behind the trees. "Day enters night," he whispered.

"Shall I send for someone to light a fire? Or tend to the candles?"

"Nae. I thank you for your kindness, Emer. Go seek your rest."

The woman gave him a smile and slipped silently from the chambers.

After carefully placing Elspeth on the furs of the bed, Magnar regarded his sleeping wife. With deft skill, he eased the shoes from her feet and wrapped part of the fur over her body. His fingers brushed a curl that had escaped from her braid. "You are lovely."

Magnar craved her beyond a primal need, and this frightened him. He shrugged it aside, believing it was the lustful beast and nothing more. Once he bedded Elspeth, the feeling would wane. Yet in their brief time together, he found himself yearning for more than just her body—he wanted her mind and soul as well.

Enough!

The blue stone shimmered in the darkened room. Sorely tempting him to fondle the pendant for a sense of its power. Magnar raised his hand over the gem. Instantly, his wolf snapped to attention and gnashed his teeth in warning. Even this close, the force pulsed across his skin. To touch the stone would not bring harm to him, only the act of trying to possess what was not his to control. He knew the legend. Nevertheless, the power was undeniable and his wife unaware.

I am nae fool to risk your death, my friend. I cannot take what is not mine to possess.

His wolf receded.

Scrubbing a hand over his face, he attempted to banish his thoughts—from lust to power within the stone. He swept his gaze around the room and noted the wood by the hearth. Even though he preferred the open window, he was eager to rid the cold dampness lingering in the chamber for his wife's sake. Magnar squatted and started a fire in the hearth. Within moments, the wood and kindling snapped to life. Flames flickered to glorious heat, and he rolled his shoulders to ease the tension.

After ridding himself of his boots and trews, he welcomed the warmth of the fire as it soothed his body.

Going to the table to retrieve the jug of wine and a lone cup, Magnar returned to a chair by the hearth. Pouring a hefty amount of wine into his cup, he swirled the dark liquid. He dipped two fingers into the wine and leaned forward, sprinkling the liquid on the hearth. "Hail, All Father. Welcome, Warrior. Come sit by the fire with me. Allow peace to reside here for these people." He guzzled deeply.

Leaning back in the chair, he stretched out his legs and glanced out the window.

"You made a good wine, Thomas." He lifted his cup to the first star gracing the sky. "May you enter Valhalla, my friend."

For the first time in many moons, Magnar allowed his body to relax. Tonight was for rest. Tomorrow he would let his wolf roam the hills.

"Do you find the chair a comfortable bed?" asked Elspeth, stifling a yawn.

His heated gaze locked with hers over the rim of his cup. "Where would you have me sleep, wife?"

She patted the space next to her. "Here."

"Not enough room," he argued, furious with himself for not accepting her offer.

She rose up on her elbow. "I am inviting you to my *bed*, Magnar."

Desire burned within his veins. More than anything, he ached to join her on the furs.

She tossed the covering aside. "Stubborn as a boar, you are, Magnar MacAlpin!"

Affronted by her words, his brow furrowed. "For wanting my wife to get her rest?"

Clucking her tongue in obvious disapproval, Elspeth turned away from him and started to unravel the braid of hair. Bewitched, he watched the way her fingers unbound the silken mass. When she was finished, she shook out her hair, letting it tumble down her back.

He gripped the cup tightly as his breathing became labored. He wanted those locks across his chest, even lower, to brush against his throbbing cock.

She stole a beguiling look over her shoulder at him. "Tempted yet?"

"Nae," he lied, realizing fully the enticing game she was playing. However, his wife required rest, not bedding.

Elspeth turned and scooted across the covers. Removing a *sgian dubh* from under the pillows, she held the blade in front of her.

He cocked a brow. "Do you always keep a blade under your pillows? This is not the first time you have presented one before me in our chamber."

"I have nae desire to sleep in this soiled, tattered gown." With a tug and slice, Elspeth slit the side of her gown. Dropping the blade to the floor, she managed to strip most of the gown from her upper body, where it pooled around her waist.

Her pert nipples reminded Magnar of ripe cherries, begging to be suckled and savored. He found his control slipping severely and drained the remainder of wine.

Elspeth clutched the furs. "Now will you share *our* bed?" she asked softly, biting her lower lip.

His resolve shattered completely.

After wiping his mouth with the back of his hand, Magnar flung the cup out the window, heedless of its direction.

Abruptly standing, he tore his tunic from his body. Fisting his hands on his hips, he let her take her fill of him. He stood rooted to the floor, giving her the time she needed. When her gaze lingered on his thick cock, he let out a groan.

"Help me out of this gown," she ordered, coming to stand on the floor.

Magnar stormed across the chamber to her side. His hands shook as he ripped the garment from her body and tossed it aside.

Grasping her firmly around the waist with one hand, he took her mouth in swift possession— demanding and forceful. No longer could he be tender. The blood pounded in his veins in a way he had never known. She had pushed past his barriers of steely control. He feared if she ordered him to stop, he would not be able to comply.

Her moan resonated within him, and he deepened the kiss, thrusting his tongue into her velvet softness. He fondled her breast and pinched the pert nipple. Elspeth splayed her fingers in his hair, urging him onward with her movements.

He broke free from her mouth and traced a path along the vein of her neck with his tongue. Her skin was as sweet as wine—heady and filling a need he wasn't able to fathom. Nipping on her shoulder, he continued to slake his passion on her supple body. With his free hand, Magnar cupped her other breast and drew his tongue over the pert nipple he had fantasized about, before taking it between his teeth.

"Sweet goodness," she gasped.

"Aye," he agreed, unable to say any more.

Reclaiming her lips, Magnar crushed her to him. His hand skimmed down her waist until he sought her womanly folds. She was hot and moist, and he knew her to be ready to take him into her body. His fingers brushed over her sensitive core, and her scent filled him. He teased her with each stroke, building the fire within her body.

She squirmed and whimpered. "Aye, *more*," she pleaded, arching against his hand.

Grasping her intent, Magnar paused. He wanted her to feel the yearning with him inside her. Despite the fact she was a virgin, conflict tore at him. His body battled against his mind to take his wife slowly.

Her legs began to tremble, and he lifted her into his arms. "You are very warm." She breathed the words against his neck.

"I fear I am unable to be gentle with you, Elspeth," he said, his voice gruff.

Raw desire glittered in those emerald eyes as she leaned back. "I have heard there will be pain, but only briefly."

He choked on a laugh and eased her back on the furs.

Elspeth smacked at his arm. "You find humor in what little understanding I have between a man and a woman?" she asked, her voice unsteady.

Magnar cupped her chin. "I confess I have never bedded a virgin. Especially one who is as brazen as my wife."

She started to protest, and Magnar silenced her by placing his thumb over her lips. "You continue to surprise me in the most tempting ways, my *kærr*."

Her smile speared straight to his heart.

"Will you grant me a favor?" he asked softly.

"Anything, husband."

He winked at her. "I shall remember your words. For now, please remove the pendant. You can tuck it safely under the pillows. All will be explained later."

She frowned slightly, but then complied.

Magnar swept his gaze over her body. "You are a beauty." One hand slid down her taut stomach to the swell of her hips and then across her thigh. "Open your legs for me, *Elspeth*."

"Touch me there again," she pleaded, reaching for his cock.

He nearly spilled his seed into her hand.

Grasping both her hands, he held them above her head. Raw, blinding possession and desire raged through him. Nudging her legs farther apart with his

176

knee, he guided his swollen cock to her entrance. Relentlessly, he rubbed over her nub, stroking her passion. Her moans became tearful, and she begged him for more. Always more.

When he knew her to be near her release, his lustful beast drove fully inside her. When she let out a sob, he let go his hold on her hands and recaptured her lips. Magnar withdrew and sank deeper. With each thrust, the storm within him grew. He thought he'd died when he entered her, so tight and hot.

Magnar slid his hand under her bottom and squeezed. When she slipped her leg around him, he lost all sense of control. His mouth sought hers in a frenzy of kisses. He continued his loving assault on her body until she screamed his name as the swell of desire swept through her.

And with his name still on her lips, the liquid fire exploded forth from Magnar. A guttural roar tore from his throat, echoing off the stones, and he emptied his passion into the woman he had claimed. A woman who eased the loneliness and anguish from his soul.

While cradling her quaking body, Magnar rolled over, and she snuggled against him. He trailed a hand down her back.

"That was amazing, *my husband*," she murmured, her breath warm on his chest.

When she lifted her head and searched his face, he became mute from the emotions swirling in a tempest within him. Magnar found he was unable to say anything in return for fear she might use it against him one day. Love was a weakness, not a defense.

Yet for the first time in his life, Magnar desired to profess his love for another.

Chapter Seventeen

"*More* wildflowers?" complained Magnar, stepping around her and yanking a fistful from the moist ground.

Elspeth approached by his side and held the basket toward her husband, doing her best not to scold him for damaging the delicate flowers. "Aye. And if you have nae wish to help, then I give you permission to find Erik for another lesson in the stream."

He deposited the wildflowers inside. "Your chieftain is currently down by the water with Ivar and Bjorn. He nae longer requires my teaching. I desire to be with my wife. I have not seen you in eight days."

Her mouth twitched in humor while she turned away from his stormy glare. Since Magnar was determined to take up the lead in searching for Halvard and his men, their time together had been brief. He'd return each week without any news, merely adding to his ire. Then they would spend one glorious night making love. Come dawn, he'd gather his men and depart. Though Elspeth kept busy with her tasks at restoring Steinn, she grew restless. Her nights were spent in fitful dreams of longing for her husband. He stirred emotions in her she had yet to fathom herself.

She yearned to learn more from this man who was now her husband. A man who had yet to show her his wolf. *Have I not given you my trust and respect, Magnar?*

"Are you leaving in the morn?" she asked, trying to keep her voice steady.

"Unsure."

Fingering a delicate foxglove, Elspeth debated on pulling it free. "Surely the threat of Halvard is nae longer a concern."

"Men like Halvard are not prone to retreating so easily," he admitted.

"Then you will continue to search for him," she stated flatly, reaching for a dainty flower. *This will never end. Perchance your wish is simply to seek your pleasures in bed and then resume your duties. I mean nothing more.*

"What would you suggest I do?" he asked, coming to stand in front of her.

Elspeth regarded him for several moments. There was no censure within his eyes. Merely a search for an answer.

Stunned, she blinked several times. She had to be certain. Dropping her basket, she asked, "You seek *my* counsel?"

He tilted his head to one side, a smile softening his rugged features. "Aye."

The laughter bubbled up inside her. She fought to control its escape but failed. Her husband narrowed his eyes. A sure sign his behavior was reverting back to one of a caged wolf.

When she finished, Elspeth wiped a hand over her forehead. "Forgive me, Magnar. Not one man has ever asked for my counsel on anything."

Crossing his arms over his chest, he glared at her. "And you find humor in this?"

Elspeth placed her hands on his rough face. "Aye

and nae. In truth, I am overjoyed you asked." She bit her lower lip and quickly added, "You honor me, husband."

Grasping her wrists, he brought them down to her sides. "Then give me your wisdom on this situation. 'Tis your home at Steinn."

"Ours," she corrected.

He shrugged. "Mainly, 'tis Erik's."

"Until he is of age, we are his guardians," she clarified.

"Nevertheless, you have not answered my question."

Elspeth moved away from him and wandered to a nearby tree. Leaning against its rough bark, she sought to give him a reply. "How many weeks have you searched for Halvard and his men?"

"Seven," he acknowledged.

"And have you found any trace they have hidden nearby or in the caves along the hills?"

"Nae."

She tapped a finger to her chin. "Did you not consider they might have fled north for the coast and back to their home?"

"*Orkneyjar*?"

Smiling, Elspeth arched a brow. "Aye. You did state north, so perchance they went there to gather more men."

Magnar folded his arms over his chest. "Aye," he responded slowly. "After the first skirmish in the hall they might have lost men—"

"And the fire," interrupted Elspeth.

"Who is to say how many of Halvard's men were injured *or* slain?"

"Aye!" She smacked her fist into her palm. "They have gone in search of more men. Or to threaten others for their cause."

Magnar's lips thinned, and he rubbed a thumb over his torc. "Which means they will surely return."

Elspeth's shoulders sagged, comprehending her husband's journey across the lands would never end until he sought his own vengeance. *This is not his home. Not for the leader of the elite guards. Your quests are varied, Magnar, and this is one in a hundred.*

She watched him steadily approach. While Elspeth hated where her thoughts were leading, she spoke them out loud. "You must leave in the morn and go north to the coast."

Her husband loomed over her. He placed a hand above her head on the bark of the tree, trapping her with his body. "This is your advice?"

Elspeth sighed, resigned to a life where her husband made short appearances. He would never be content here. Magnar was a warrior.

Lowering his head, he nipped along her neck. "Speak from your heart, *kærr*."

He was too close. Too male. A tingling feeling danced along her skin, and she swallowed. How could she express what was in her heart, if he didn't feel the same? Did he think to mock her? Did he not ask for her counsel, only to scold her by asking what was in her heart? Confusion battled within her like a storm on a summer day.

By pushing with all her might against his massive chest, Elspeth persuaded him to halt his movements. Attempting to dislodge her body from his hold was another matter entirely.

"I cannot breathe," she lied. She managed a small, tentative smile.

Magnar took a step back. "Forgive me." After giving her a curt nod, he turned and started for the path along the stream.

Elspeth thought she knew stubborn, boar-headed men. She was wrong. Her husband towered above them all.

She stomped her foot in protest. "Why does it matter what is in my heart? The advice I gave you was sound."

He halted his stride and gave her a scathing look over his shoulder.

Determined to match his stubbornness with her own, she lifted her chin and fisted her hands on her hips. "If I am to speak my heart, you must give me a reason."

Lifting his head to the sky, he muttered words Elspeth did not understand.

"'Tis important," she urged in a gentler tone.

Thunder rolled in the distance, causing Elspeth to flinch. Rain would soon follow. The conversation with her husband made her head ache. Dropping her hands, she turned to leave.

"Would you rather I stay for a while? Or do you desire to have me continue onward with my men?"

Elspeth clutched a hand to her chest and dared not look at him. "My *heart* wants you to stay, Magnar, but only if you desire it as well."

Suddenly, she was lifted into his arms. On an indrawn breath, she clutched at his shoulders. Elspeth never heard his approach. "You move silently—"

"As a wolf?" After giving her a sly grin, he

proceeded forward.

Studying his rugged profile, she asked, "Where are you taking me?"

"To *our* chambers?"

"In the middle of the afternoon? I am not tired."

His lips twitched. "You will be after I am done with you."

Heat blossomed between her legs and rushed up her body to her face. She trailed a finger over the cool metal of his torc. "Do you ever take this off?"

"Nae."

"And the markings on your back? You have never spoken about them."

He chuckled low. "You have never asked me."

He nuzzled her neck while keeping his stride across the landscape.

When the first drop of rain splattered against her cheek, Elspeth glanced upward. "My flowers. We must return and fetch the basket."

"Do not fret. I shall help you gather more tomorrow."

By the time they reached Steinn, the sky had opened, drenching the land along with them. In an attempt to move out of the way of a passing goat, Magnar slipped on the muddy path inside the bailey. With a resounding thud, they both landed in the murky mud-filled water. Magnar smacked his fists into the ground, uttering a string of curses. And Elspeth burst out in fits of laughter.

Clutching a hand to her stomach, she blurted out, "Does this mean our afternoon plans are cancelled?"

With one smoldering look, his eyes seemed to undress her.

Her husband swiftly got to his feet. Shouting an order for any of his men within hearing, he waited. Soon, all the men under his command—mostly wolves—appeared. He gave orders to them while thunder and lightning shattered the afternoon sky.

Rolling to her side, Elspeth attempted to stand in her sodden gown. Strong arms circled around her waist, bringing her to stand upright. She lifted her gaze to her husband. "Thank you. I believe I can manage on my own."

Her words seem to amuse him. "Not without my help."

Even with mud splattered on his face and in his hair, Magnar made her insides go weak. "Give me your plan."

He held his palm outward to the rain. "We can stand here until we are cleansed from the mud."

Water dripped from her hair down her cheeks, and Elspeth blinked.

He pressed her against his body. "Are you thinking? Again?"

"Now you are jesting with me," she scolded, smacking at his wet tunic. "I found myself at a loss of words over your kind offer."

Magnar's laughter echoed all around her, drowning out the continual thunder. Without giving her time to react, he scooped her into his arms and marched across the bailey. When they entered the keep, he shouted, "You best have that tub filled and ready for my wife!"

Elspeth rolled her eyes at the thought of all his men doing a simple task for her. "You had your men filling my tub."

"Our tub, *my kærr*."

Her cheeks grew hot. "You...*you* are joining me?"

"Aye. My body needs tending to as well."

Once inside their chambers, he placed her beside a chair near the hearth. Bjorn and Rorik had started the task of bringing in the hot buckets of water and filling the tub. She stood rooted to the floor in a drenched mess observing their swift movements. Other men soon followed with steaming buckets of water, and she almost swooned at the sight, anticipating her body sinking into the glorious heat. Several buckets remained near the fire, and she deemed these would be used to wash the grime from her hair.

Her fingers were numb as she tried to undo her braided mass of hair. After several failed attempts, she gave up.

Her husband came to her side and tugged on the braid. "Allow me...later."

She nodded her consent.

"They are taking too long," he grumbled. In his quest to see the task of filling the tub completed, Magnar took up a bucket and bestirred himself to aid his men. When the last bucket was emptied, she bid them all her thanks and watched while her husband closed and bolted the wooden door.

In two strides, he was at her side. Her legs trembled as she gripped his shoulders. With deft skill, he withdrew his *sgian dubh* from his boot.

"Nae," she protested, understanding his intent with the blade. "Do you ken how many gowns you have ripped from my body?" Removing her pendant, she placed it on the wooden table by the tub.

"Do you prefer remaining in this wretched condition?"

185

She sighed in resignation and lifted her arms out to the side. "Do what you must. But Muir will not be happy tending to another torn garment in less than a month."

Her husband ignored her complaints and sliced through the gown as if it were butter. He then peeled the soaked material from her skin, letting it pool at the bottom of her feet.

Elspeth shivered but not from the cold or absence of clothing. Nae. It had to do with the searing heated glare Magnar gave her. The man didn't even have to touch her to give her pleasure.

Swiftly, he rid himself of his boots, soiled tunic, and trews. His desire for her was evident, but before she could reach out and touch him, he lifted her into the tub. Warmth invaded her skin, and Elspeth sighed in pleasure.

Magnar reached for the soap and cloth from a side table and joined her in the tub.

Hugging her arms around her stomach, she protested, "I do not believe there is room for both of us. I cannot even sit with you inside the tub."

When her husband smiled, he disarmed every thought and argument within her.

"There is plenty of room to clean and warm you," he stated, dunking the cloth and soap in the water. "And by standing I can tend to every inch of your skin."

She became mute as he started on her shoulders, lathering the soap in gentle motions across her skin and down to her breasts. Watching in a lust-filled haze, Elspeth became captivated with his attention to her body. When his hand delved farther down, he nudged her legs apart with his knee.

Her breathing became labored, complying to his unspoken demand, and Elspeth opened to him. His hand teased her around her intimate area, stroking ever so lightly. When one finger entered her, she let out a moan while watching him give her pleasure. "Need more," she begged.

His hooded gaze never left her body as he grasped her waist and turned her around in the tub. "You are tormenting me, Magnar."

He nibbled on her shoulder. "Torment can be pleasurable."

The tight knot within her begged for release, especially when his hand traveled down to her bottom. Again, he nudged her legs apart and caressed her between her thighs. His movements were steady and driving her to the edge. She gave no care when water sloshed over the edge of the tub. After giving her bottom a smack, he dropped the soap into the water and placed the cloth on the side of the tub.

"Bloody hell," she blurted out, frustrated, and aching for more.

Magnar twisted her braid around his fist and yanked hard. He pulled her head back toward him. "Cursing, are you?" He bit the side of her neck—his breath hot against her skin.

"Your time shall come, Magnar MacAlpin," she avowed. "I shall tease you without mercy."

He smacked her bottom again, this time much harder. "I *accept* your challenge. Stay still while I undo your hair."

She tried not to fidget as he tugged and loosened the hair from its braid.

"Now dunk your head into the water so I can wash

your hair," he ordered.

Pleasurable sensations danced up her spine, and she shivered. Her husband was driving her mad. Ideas swarmed in her mind, forming a plan of attack on her husband's body.

Quickly kneeling down, she doused her locks in the water and then stood. He worked up a good head of suds with his hands. And with tender care, his fingers splayed throughout her hair, massaging her scalp, and she closed her eyes. Minutes ticked by and her body relaxed.

She heard the soap drop back into the water and realized what was coming next. Turning around, she lowered herself into the water and bent her head forward. Magnar poured the clean bucket of water slowly over her head.

Magnar kissed the top of her head. "My wife is now clean."

"Ahh…wonderful," she mumbled.

Opening her eyes, she gazed upon his enlarged manhood. A smiled curved her mouth as she reached for the cloth and soap. "My turn."

His steady gaze bore into hers with silent expectation.

Elspeth took her time rubbing the soapy cloth around his upper thighs. Ignoring the main source of his desire, she stood. With the cloth, she traveled a path up his powerful body and across his chest. With purpose, she brushed her breasts against him and was rewarded with an indrawn hiss. Onward she continued to clean and study his body. Tapping him once on the shoulder, she motioned for him to turn around. The crisscross of small scars and markings on his back fascinated her.

She lowered her hand down to his bottom—taut and firm.

He clenched his fist, and she watched him unfurl the hand slowly.

Standing on her tiptoes, she traced a finger along the side of his neck. "Dunk your head, husband."

She smiled as he swiftly did as ordered. Elspeth took her time in washing and kneading his head and scalp with the soap. When she judged she had made him wait long enough, she reached for the other bucket.

Bending on one knee in the tub, he waited for her to dump the water over his head.

Elspeth deposited the bucket onto the floor.

Raking a hand through his damp hair, he bit out, "About bloody time."

"I am not finished," she announced and knelt down in the water in front of him.

Before he had a chance to move, Elspeth grasped the outside of his thighs.

"*Elspeth*," he rasped out in warning.

She would not be forestalled.

Her husband made her feel wanted—*a woman*. She tried to slow the dizzying current racing through her veins. How she had been tempted in their time together to touch and taste her husband. He had tormented her once with his tongue, and now she pondered what it would be like to do the same. Willing to try something new, she moved forward.

Yet first, she yearned to feel his hardened length. When her hand took hold of him, he let out a low moan. She stroked him in a leisurely fashion. And when her lips lowered over the top of his heat, Magnar growled and began to move in a steady rhythm.

The power she had over him filled her, making her eager to please him as well.

Elspeth continued to give her husband pleasure with her mouth and hand. His hands covered her head, urging her along. A ripple of desire grew within her each time Magnar groaned. She wanted all of him—to take him totally inside her. No longer shy with her husband, she became brazen.

"I can...*cannot* hold back," he rasped out.

The heady sensation of passion overtook Elspeth. Giving Magnar pleasure stoked her fiery desire.

With a guttural cry, Magnar bellowed her name within their chambers and emptied himself into her.

As she slowly withdrew, Magnar lifted her to standing. His gaze roamed her face as if he wanted to make a declaration. Her heart pounded fiercely against her chest, waiting, pondering his thoughts. He drew in a ragged breath and released it slowly. Yet, he remained silent.

One day you will share your thoughts—your feelings with me, Magnar, and I shall do the same. But this is not the day, my warrior wolf.

And in an instant of clarity, Elspeth knew her heart had opened to love this man. She did not ken when it happened or the exact moment, but she knew and allowed the feeling to blossom. She banished her concern that he believed in the old Gods and Goddesses. Had he not asked for her opinion, taken care of Erik, and not once did he object or complain about her beliefs.

Honorable, loyal, and noble. Trust will come, Magnar. You must learn to trust and love as I have learned to trust in God's plan for us.

She brushed a stray lock of hair from his eyes. "Make love to me, *husband*."

Chapter Eighteen

Magnar cradled his wife close while his fingers trailed through her flame-red locks. Earlier she had caught him by surprise with her eagerness to pleasure him. When her lips covered him, he thought the world had shattered around him. Each time they made love, it seemed like the first, and his wife's desire to learn certain pleasures enchanted him.

He lifted a curly strand. "You have the most stunning hair, Elspeth."

"Thank you, but 'tis a matted mess," she murmured against his chest.

"Nevertheless, I am fond of your hair," he confessed, dropping the silken tress.

Lifting her head, she stared at him. "You are the first."

He scowled. "And the *last*."

Resting her chin on his chest, she reached out and traced a finger over his torc. "Tell me about your home on the *Orkneyjar Isles*. Where did you live?"

Magnar tensed. He had nae desire to speak of his other home.

"I want to learn more about you, husband," she pleaded.

Tucking his arm under his head, Magnar glanced upward before giving into her request. "For the first ten years of my life, I lived on *Orkneyjar* to train—learn the ways of the wolf in a town near the coast called *Kirkjuvágr*. That is where I was born. My father, the former leader, often in his duties visited Scotland. He left most of my training in the care of another man and wolf called Berulf. Upon my ten-year completion, I was sent to live in Scotland with my parents. I furthered my training and studies at the Sutherland keep with my father. We are a vital part of the Sutherland clan and a stronghold for King William."

"And your mother," asked Elspeth. "Did she not stay with you?"

He grinned. "Nae. She preferred to stay away from the conflict intense training can bring to us and sought out a smaller keep deeper in the forest. We would return to her every other sennight and stay for a few days."

Magnar noted her expression stilled and grew serious. He dared to pose the question and feared her response. "What are your concerns, Elspeth?"

She tapped his torc. "Must our first-born son live on *Orkneyjar* for his training?"

With his wife's beliefs, this is what frightened him the most. Would she easily banish the child into the care of another because he was part wolf? From the moment the king demanded he take Elspeth as his wife, he knew the day would come when they would be forced to have this discussion.

He kept his gaze steady with hers. "Aye."

She blinked and lowered her head.

Sorrow filled him. *So…you would hate our son.*

When Magnar felt moisture on his chest, he gripped her chin. Stunned, he wiped the tears from her cheek with his fingers. "Why do you weep?"

Her lips trembled. "How can you expect me to give away my child to someone in a land far away? Given I ken *nothing* about the ways of the wolves and traditions—I ache at having to relinquish my son. Is this what you want as well?"

Relief coursed through his veins, and Magnar wrapped his arms around his wife. "*My kærr,* I am happy to hear you would not send our son away. I feared—" Magnar paused, unsure how to continue with the conversation. Had she not called him a heathen on several occasions? He winced at the memory. Even so, the time to speak about their gnawing concerns had to be done.

Easing her gently from his body, he scooted back against the pillows. From his new position, this advantage roused his lust as he viewed her naked form. He patted the spot next to him. "Come sit next to me."

She smiled warily. Moving to his side, she brought the fur covering up to her chest.

"Since you have spouted about my heathen ways, I *feared* you would not love the child, and would be eager to banish him from you."

Her eyes widened in alarm. "Sweet Mother Mary and all the saints! How can you think so foul of me? Any babe I bring into this world is one I shall love with my whole heart." Determination echoed in her words. "We can choose to live with him together in *Kirkjuvágr* or here in Scotland. I will not be parted from my son. *Ever.*" She jabbed him in the chest. "Nor should you think of doing so, unless you have a task for the king."

His heart swelled at her declaration. Elspeth repeatedly stunned him, and he ached to confess what was in his heart.

But his fickle tongue twisted and remained silent.

Reaching for her hand, he placed a kiss against the vein along her wrist. "Thank you," he whispered. "I have nae ambition of having another train my son. However, Berulf was an excellent tutor and loyal friend to my father." He shook his head solemnly, recalling his time spent on the *Orkneyjar Isles*. "In truth, I yearned to be in Scotland with my family. The people fear and respect the wolves on *Orkneyjar*, but there is jealousy as well. Here in Scotland we are spoken of as legends around the fire. Tales to frighten the young. Few believe we truly exist."

On a choked sob, she lowered her head onto his chest. "My heart is happy to ken you feel the same, Magnar. You must understand how difficult this is for me to fathom."

He cradled her gently. "Aye, *aye*. From this day forward, you will learn all about the Wolves of Clan Sutherland."

"Magnar?"

"Aye, wife."

"Tell me about my pendant—the blue stone."

Unsure how to explain its meaning, he sought only one recourse. The truth.

"The Blue Stone of Odin was given to the second leader of the wolves many moons ago. Legend recorded by an ancient *skald*—"

"Bard," she interrupted on a yawn. "My grandmother used to teach me some of the words."

He smiled at her knowledge of his other language. "You are correct. The *skald* spoke of a bright, burning summer day. Though not a cloud showed in the sky, fierce lightning slashed across the land. As the leader grew concerned, he ordered the other wolves to protect the people and all were ushered indoors. The leader traveled down from the hilltop to the valley floor. Fearing he had displeased one of the Gods, he knelt and begged for mercy for his people. The sky split in half and Odin appeared, holding out the blue stone. Sensing a division among the other Gods, Odin judged it wise to bestow a secondary gift of power to the wolves and placed the pendant around the neck of their leader. Never could another man attempt to remove the stone for fear of death or weakening a wolf."

Elspeth lifted her head. "But how did *my* grandmother come into possession of the pendant? By her account, the stone has been in our family for hundreds of years. She was adamant I wear it on my wedding day."

Magnar blew out a frustrated breath. "I do not ken the answer. Only a reference by a *Scottish* bard who spoke of the stone being lost after its power was misused. You can imagine my shock at seeing you had in your possession one of our most powerful stones. By rights, 'tis mine."

She swallowed visibly. "Is it that important to you?"

He regarded her for several heartbeats. "Immensely."

"What can it do?"

"Not only can it control the wolf in each of my men, but all the beasts of the earth. One must ken the ancient words to bring forth the power."

Her eyes widened in horror. "*Nae.*"

Each time Magnar sensed they were coming to an understanding, another problem presented itself. "Do you see me as a demon, Elspeth?"

Her features softened, and she cupped his cheek. "Nae, husband." She lowered her head against his chest. "You must give me time to pray on this new predicament."

"Good. And remember, as long as you possess the blue stone, nae one can take it from you without your consent."

"Thank you."

Watching as the setting sun bled into the sky toward gloaming, Magnar allowed the warmth of his wife to fill and soothe him. On a sigh, he closed his eyes.

"Have I earned your respect to see your wolf?" asked Elspeth softly.

His wolf lifted his head. A sure sign that the animal had heard his wife's plea. The bond between the two was important—one he had not envisioned on witnessing so soon in their marriage. Perchance the Gods and Goddesses favored this union? His wolf rose to a sitting position.

"When the moon shines fully in the night sky this evening, I shall take you to the forest and introduce you to my wolf."

"Finally," she whispered.

****

As her husband bent down on one knee, Elspeth watched him scoop up a clump of moist dirt near the base of a yew tree. Moonlight filtered through the tree limbs, dusting the forest floor with its gleaming beauty around him. He inhaled the rich scent, and on the exhale, tossed it outward.

Standing, Magnar asked, "Do you fear what I am

about to show you?"

Elspeth told him earlier she had nae indecision within her, but she understood Magnar required hearing her consent out loud, once again.

Elspeth reached for his hand. "*Nae.* Are you not one and the same?"

"The beast and I are one, yet I am in control. I shall allow the wolf to appear in the ancient way of calling, instead of simply giving him free rein to shift."

She dropped his hand and took a step back. "I am ready."

After giving her a swift nod, Magnar removed his boots and clothing. "All that will remain is my torc, which shall be transferred to the animal. He turned away from Elspeth and lifted his arms and head to the sky. Digging his feet into the ground, Magnar spoke the ancient words.

"From this veil to the next. From my skin to his fur. From my blood and bones to his. With my heartbeat to the heart of the wolf. Hail the Gods of Asgard. Bring forth the beast."

Tendrils of cool mists swirled around her. Clutching a hand to her chest, Elspeth watched in awe as her husband shimmered into a gray mist and into the form of a huge gray wolf.

Sweet Mother Mary.

The animal sniffed his surroundings and turned to face her. Regarding Elspeth for several moments, he padded near and sat in front of her. Gone were the blue eyes she loved. What stared back at her were glassy orbs as black as the night sky, flecked with silver. The animal tilted its head to one side as if waiting for something.

Should she acknowledge him in a matter fitting to wolf and man? Her husband had not given her instructions on what was to happen after he transformed into the wolf.

Elspeth uttered a silent prayer, and a sense of calm settled inside of her. Bringing her cloak more firmly around her body, she took her place beside the wolf on the ground. "You are mighty handsome."

Her hand shook as she reached out to stroke the smooth fur on his back. When her fingers brushed across his fur, the animal imparted a low groan, causing Elspeth to grin. She remained focused on the animal, noting the darker gray on the tips of his ears, and the solid black patch in the middle of his brow. Unusual darker coloring dotted the back of his thick coat as well.

On a deep sigh, the wolf stretched fully out on the ground and rested his head on his legs. The animal's warmth surrounded her, and she scooted closer to him. After scratching behind one of his ears, she placed her hands in her lap and lifted her gaze to the moon.

"You were correct, Grandmother. The tales you told me were true." Smiling longingly, she added, "Oh, for you to see me married to one, aye? I can hear you boasting to all the elders."

Joy filled her at the trust Magnar gave her this night. Elspeth doubted he would hear her words, but threw caution aside, yearning to profess a part of her heart. Foolishly, she believed she must speak with her husband regarding these matters and not to his wolf. Yet in the quiet forest under a moonlit night, she found the words tumbling free.

"Will you ever learn to accept all that I am? Can we find more in this marriage?" Twisting the folds of her cloak, she added hesitantly, "I desire more, but if you can only give your friendship, then I shall not complain."

The wolf lifted his head and licked Elspeth's hand.

Surprised by the animal's tenderness, she burst out in laughter. "Pray tell, who am I speaking to—the man or animal? Perchance both can understand me?"

This time she tilted her head to the side, waiting patiently for any sign from the wolf.

Exhaling softly, he lowered his head back onto his outstretched legs.

When a nocturnal animal skittered past them, the wolf rose from his position.

"Goodness! Pray tell me you do not stalk and eat other animals?" Horrified, Elspeth never considered the wolf might want to roam the hills for his meal.

The animal let out a low growl and padded away from her.

She shrugged. "Forgive me, but I do not ken your ways. If you can understand my words, *Magnar*, then give me the added particulars, so I do not offend your wolf."

Elspeth could have sworn the wolf smirked. She extended her arm outward, and then waved her hand in a circle. She prayed he'd understand her meaning. "I give you consent to leave, if that is what you wish."

This time the wolf snapped his teeth in obvious anger and took off running.

"Wonderful. I have been left all alone in the forest. Why am I not surprised? You are simply an animal in search of your next meal."

Giving out an unlady-like snort, Elspeth attempted to stand, only to be shoved back onto the ground by a snarling wolf. In less than a heartbeat, the animal shimmered into her naked husband.

Trapping her with his body, he leaned near her ear. "For one, the wolf does not require meals to sustain him. He receives his sustenance from me. Second, the wolf is your protector. To believe he would wander away and leave you—*my wife*—undefended is madness."

Smiling broadly, Elspeth wrapped her arms around her husband's neck. "'Tis good to ken I am protected, *and* your wolf does not need to kill for his meals. I would loathe having him present his recent kill in my lap."

Magnar threw back his head and roared with laughter. "Will you ever cease to amaze me, wife?"

Shoving aside her sudden turmoil, she waited until his humor lessened. "I pray to never bore you, husband."

"*Elspeth MacAlpin*, you have nothing to fear. You have enchanted me since the moment I saw you in the hall at Vargr."

She gasped. Her heart skipped more than a beat at the mention of her name and his confession. "Truly? But—"

Magnar silenced her with a scorching kiss, leaving her senses reeling.

Chapter Nineteen

Shifting his stance from the afternoon sunlight, Magnar studied the group of men wandering across the expanse of the meadow toward him. Rain had drenched the ground earlier in the morn, and he smiled. His keen observation detected those who would not remain standing after a few blows. Too much drink from the night before had many already stumbling over their feet.

"Again, what is the name of this game?" asked Elspeth in a guarded tone.

Giving her a quick glance, he replied, "'Tis called *Skinnleikr*—a skin throwing game. Usually we play indoors—inside the hall." He gestured outward with his hand. "Many of my men suggested we take the game out in the open to show everyone how 'tis played. We judged it wiser outdoors, since we do not want to cause further damage to Steinn."

She tapped a finger against her chin. "And 'tis made from the skin of a bear?"

"Aye. You take the skin and roll it into a ball."

"Procured from your home in *Kirkjuvágr*."

He smiled. "You are correct. 'Tis a good game to test your balance and strength, along with swiftness of feet."

Elspeth stepped in front of him. "I overheard Rorik mention that bones are often broken in this game. Are you sure Erik should be permitted to join this vigorous, rough sport? Are the king's men aware they may become injured?"

Shrugging, he explained, "He is the chieftain, and he asked to join in the game. He seeks to gain knowledge of what we—*Northmen*—enjoy. He has boasted of learning certain board games, and I have challenged him later with one called *hnefatafl*. As for King William's men, they have played this sport many a time."

Narrowing her eyes, she protested, "Erik is a kindling stick compared to you...and *your* boulder-sized men! He will be crushed!"

Magnar fought the smile forming on his mouth. As a rule, he would never jest with his wife in regard to her nephew. However, he enjoyed seeing his wife teem with fury. Her face took on a coloring to rival her locks. Reaching outward, he tugged on a curl that had escaped from her braid. "You have a healer, aye?"

She gave him a glare that would singe the skin from any hardened warrior.

Unable to contain himself, he belted out in laughter.

"You brute," she scolded, shoving at his chest. "I honestly believed you would let him play the game."

Recovering quickly, he added, "But we are. Erik is to toss out the skin, and then retreat."

"You ken my meaning, Magnar."

He swiftly reached for her before she could leave. Grasping her around the waist, he nuzzled the soft skin below her ear. "Forgive me, Elspeth. I could not resist the temptation to tease you."

Turning her face toward his lips, she smiled fully.

"You must now pay the price for causing me distress."

He arched a brow and drew back. All thoughts of joining his men in a game were tossed aside in favor of spending time alone with his wife. "Does this involve forms of enticement? One where I allow you to do anything to me?"

Her laugh was low, throaty, and beguiling. Standing on her tip-toes, she leaned close to his ear and whispered, "Banishment from my bed for *two* nights."

Horrified, he complained, "You would not dare."

She flicked a piece of flint from the sleeve of her gown. "You can seek a bed with some of the men in the hall."

His grip tightened around her waist. "'Tis *our* chambers. And I have nae desire to sleep near any of my men, especially when my wife is conveniently nearby."

Casting her gaze behind him, she responded, "There is a sturdy bolt on the door I can use."

"I will smash the door to shards of wood with my axe!" he thundered, determined to let her know that she should never attempt to keep him from her bed.

Her eyes widened. "Goodness, you are a brute."

Magnar grimaced and dropped his hands. "On that we are in agreement, *wife*."

"Perchance I should return to the abbey for a time," she suggested, returning her sight to him.

Magnar's heart clenched. *Would she truly leave him?* And then he noted a flash of humor cross her face. "Loki's balls," he hissed out.

Elspeth cupped his cheeks. "Two can play the jesting game." Kissing him soundly, she released him. "Your men are waiting."

He eyed her skeptically. "I am allowed in our chambers?"

"*Aye*," she reassured. "Do you honestly believe I would keep you away? Besides, I have nae plans on adding an oak door to the repairs already needed."

He rubbed a hand down the back of his neck. "Good to hear."

Magnar turned to leave, yet Elspeth stayed his progress by grasping his hand.

Her smile was as radiant as the sun when she declared, "I love the brute in you, husband, *particularly* in our chambers."

Stunned into silence, he brought her hand to his lips and placed a kiss along her knuckles. When her hand slipped free, Magnar watched as she ambled toward the group of women.

"Are you done ravishing your wife?" complained Bjorn.

"I say we cease our proposed activity," recommended Rorik, tossing the bear skin ball within his hands. "An afternoon spent ravishing a woman sounds wiser."

"The request from the *charmer* of women is denied," proclaimed Magnar, reaching for the ball.

"I thought it a wise plan," admitted Rorik, stumbling back.

Magnar gave his friend a stern look. "Too much drink has addled your thoughts *and* body."

"I have had none this morn."

"Liar."

Rorik arched a brow in challenge. "Two mugs do not make many."

Magnar was keenly aware of the man's scrutiny.

Ever since they had arrived at Steinn, Rorik's habit of drinking and bedding any woman who caught his interest had become unbridled. Several times, he'd attempted to discuss this with the man, but Rorik dismissed any conversation. He sensed concealed frustration within his friend, and until the warrior was ready to talk, Magnar could do nothing.

"Then are you ready?" asked Magnar, scanning the group for the lad.

"We have been ready, unlike our leader," admitted Rorik.

Ignoring the scornful remark, Magnar shouted, "Come forth, Erik!"

The mass of men parted as the young chieftain dashed forward. "Gunnar was telling me the rules of the game, though he did remark that most do not abide by them."

"You are correct," muttered Rorik, scratching behind his ear.

Magnar tossed the ball to the lad. "You can pitch it out into the group of men."

"Who is the middleman? The one who must attempt to retrieve the ball without any aid?" asked Erik, excitedly.

Regarding each of the men, Magnar's gaze landed on Rorik.

"Nae," his friend warned.

Stripping his tunic from his body, Bjorn proposed, "Let another be chosen."

"Agreed. I shall be the middleman," stated Magnar.

A combined groan echoed within the group, and Magnar stepped away from the men. Swiftly removing his tunic, he rolled it up and flung the garment toward

Elspeth. Stretching his arms overhead, he waited for the barbs about his strength to start. Magnar did not have to wait long, and he smiled inwardly.

"Savage," shouted one man.

"Beast without a heart! I look forward to making your face so hideous, your wife will turn away while you bed her," claimed Ivar.

Magnar's inner beast came to attention. After rolling his shoulders several times, he turned to face the mighty force of men. They continued to fling out their curses and boast who would draw first blood.

Let us take down the weakest first, aye, my friend? Then we'll break the face of those who made the crudest remarks.

His wolf snarled in agreement.

Erik tossed the ball into the group of men.

After giving partial rein to his wolf, Magnar sprinted at full speed toward them. Instantly, the unruly crowd spurred into action by giving looks of contempt. Magnar knew his eyes had changed to dark shards of ebony. Determined to eliminate each foe, his first blow landed on Rorik's jaw. The man swayed into Bjorn but remained standing.

Shouts and curses spewed forth as the ball was pitched high to another.

In one swift move, Magnar clipped Ivar in the back of the legs and reached for the ball.

Gunnar rammed into his side, causing Magnar to stumble into Gilmore, one of the king's guards and miss the catch. The man turned and leveled a blow to Magnar's nose. Indifferent to the blood gushing forth, he slammed his forehead against the man's face.

Seeing Rorik fast approaching, Magnar used the

dazed man as a shield and barely avoided Rorik's fist. He then shoved the weakened man against his friend.

"Bastard," hissed Rorik, his inner wolf showing within his eyes as well. He let Gilmore crumple to the ground and stepped over him without giving him a passing glance.

Magnar hunched down, keenly aware of who had the ball. "Awake now, are you?"

The rumble of Rorik's growl surrounded Magnar, but he gave no care. He lunged past his friend, avoiding any further conflict.

Sensing another wolf approach, Magnar reacted swiftly and landed a blow to his foe's abdomen.

A howl of displeasure left Gunnar gasping on the ground as he fought for air.

He pointed a warning finger at Gunnar. "Better for you to stay down or the next time it might be your ribs you hear cracking."

Stepping over him, Magnar continued his relentless pursuit in not only taking down all the men, but eager to claim victory by capturing the ball. He succeeded in knocking out Bjorn—a mighty feat in itself, considering the man boasted he'd be the first to draw blood from Magnar.

More men continued to be cut down with his mighty blows. With only a couple men left standing, Magnar studied each—Ivar and Rorik. Both who were intent on doing severe harm to him.

Each displayed a sense of assurance they had won by tossing the ball back and forth to one another.

"You do see your predicament, Magnar, aye?" Rorik smirked with confidence.

Wiping the blood from his nose, he responded, "Do

clarify."

Ivar laughed.

Rorik shifted his stance. "If you take one of us down, the other claims victory. You are unable to win without procuring the ball."

Ivar nudged Rorik. "We should walk away and claim success."

Your over-confidence at victory is your downfall. The game has yet to be concluded. With a loud roar, Magnar lunged at both men. Neither had time to thwart his assault. In two consecutive blows, he leveled them flat on their backs.

Magnar quickly retrieved the ball off the ground. Looming over Rorik and Ivar, he scowled. "You should have distanced yourselves from one another. You posed nae threat standing together and spouting a victory before the game was finished. Did you honestly think I would not attack you both?"

Ivar sputtered a curse and stood. "We should not have allowed you to be the middleman." After spitting out blood onto the ground, he retreated to where the others had gathered.

Rorik made a feeble attempt at moving his jaw. "'Tis broken," he complained.

Magnar kicked him in the leg. "Nae. Only bruised. I am certain you will find a comely lass to kiss away the pain."

His friend made to stand. "I have nae desire to hear the lashing from you, if I do yield to the healing charms of a lass."

Magnar shrugged. "You pay nae heed to what I say."

Rorik eyed him suspiciously. "Speak your words,

Magnar."

"What troubles you?"

Before his friend had a chance to utter a word, Erik came charging toward them.

"You won!" shouted the lad.

Magnar tossed the ball to him. "Aye. The game has been fought and won."

"You cheated, though," stated Rorik.

He nodded slowly. "Aye. But then you were all prepared to show your beasts. I am nae fool."

Erik snickered. "You mean your wolves."

Magnar gaped at the young lad as he scampered away. "Wise for his years."

"You should hear some of the conversations we've had with the young chieftain. Not only does he spout his opinion but listens keenly when others give theirs," acknowledged Rorik.

Magnar fisted his hands on his hips. "He knew we were wolves."

"His father told him about the king's elite guards. Furthermore, Erik asked to see my wolf."

Glancing sharply at his friend, Magnar demanded, "And did you?"

Rorik shook his head. "Nae. But I did tell him on his tenth winter I will take him to the forest and reveal my wolf. It shall be a pledge of protection from both— man *and* wolf."

"Good plan." Placing a firm hand on his friend's shoulder, he offered, "Come to my solar after the gloaming. We will speak further over a jug of mead."

Rorik regarded him hesitantly, and then sighed. "I would welcome the conversation."

Seeing his wife strolling toward them, Magnar

released his hold on his friend.

"Your wife seems displeased with your appearance," teased Rorik as he walked away.

"Aye, aye," he acknowledged, firmly aware his face was now covered in bruises.

Elspeth approached. "You are a wretched sight!"

He winced when she touched his jaw.

"And your nose is broken," she declared.

"Not the first time." He wiped away more blood seeping from the injury.

She handed him his tunic. "You can stanch the flow with this."

"Thank you, wife."

Pursing her lips, she cast her gaze to the other men. "I hear Gilmore may have suffered a broken finger. Everyone else appears to have minor injuries."

"Truly? I thought I did more damage."

Elspeth glared at him. "Henceforth, this game will *never* be played inside the hall. You can pass the message to the other men."

Wrapping an arm around her shoulders, Magnar steered her onward. "Were you concerned for me, wife?"

She jabbed him in the ribs with her elbow, and he grimaced. "Very much, Magnar. From my vantage, the looks they were giving you were deadly. My heart stopped beating many times."

Halting his stride, his gaze roamed her features. "You care for me?"

Elspeth's shoulders relaxed under him. The smile she gave him speared straight through his heart.

"Magnar, I must confess—"

Shouting erupted from the men, and Magnar's

attention fixed on Steinar and another of the king's guards galloping across the meadow. The grim expression on Steinar's face did not bode well, and his gut twisted. Releasing his hold on his wife, Magnar waited for their approach.

He gave a curt nod to the man called Gordon. Yet it was Steinar who dismounted and walked toward him.

"The threat has not been vanquished," announced Steinar.

"Where are they?" demanded Magnar, doing his best to temper the growing unrest.

"At the coast, seeking more men. They barter with amber and coin."

"Coin?" Elspeth took Magnar's hand. "Most certainly from our coffers."

The man remained silent.

Magnar narrowed his eyes. "What else?"

"Their plans are unsure. Unable to secretly gain any information due to another who thwarted my plans to gain inside the inn where they were staying."

"*Thorfinn*," snapped Magnar. "He sensed you were there to spy and told Halvard."

"Agreed. With more men, I fear they will be arriving forthwith."

Magnar dropped his wife's hand. "I require all the wolves, except Gunnar. He shall remain here at Steinn to watch over Erik and my wife, along with some of the other men. Have everyone meet me in the hall. We depart before the first star appears in the night sky."

"An easy kill in a dark forest, if they have begun their journey here," declared Steinar.

"Go gather the others," ordered Magnar.

Hearing his wife's indrawn breath, Magnar turned

toward her. He cupped her chin—warm and soft in his rough hand. "I ken this is not the news we wanted to hear, but trust me, I have nae choice but to end the man's life. He poses a threat to our king *and* the people of this keep and elsewhere. For reasons I cannot fathom, he seeks to make Steinn his stronghold, and I cannot allow this."

Her eyes shone with unshed tears, and she swallowed. "May God keep you safe."

Magnar fought the emotions within him. His focus was now on a battle—one to the death. That she offered a prayer to her God brought a sense of comfort to him.

When he brushed his lips over Elspeth's, he whispered, "Upon my return, you can confess how much you care for me, *my kærr*."

Chapter Twenty

The flames snapped and hissed into the night sky echoing Thorfinn's mood. He tossed another piece of kindling into the fire in contempt for Halvard's new plan.

"You ken what must be done?" asked Ketil, tossing the carcass of a rabbit into the fire. The man studied him from across the flames, wiping his mouth on the sleeve of his tunic.

Thorfinn placed his hands over his bent knees. "'Tis a question that should not be asked." His regard for the Seer ranked somewhat higher than Halvard, though he often pondered the Seer's motives.

"True. You seem...*unsettled*."

"We have coin, goods, why go back? Why not move onward? Seek others who are *not* loyal to King William?"

Ketil brushed away pieces of meat from his tunic. "Your insight serves you well. Have you shared your thoughts with Halvard?"

"For what purpose? He seeks vengeance and power. You and I both ken this. We are bound to follow, unless you can offer another plan of action to him."

Reaching for the ale skin, Ketil guzzled deeply. Afterwards, the man offered it to him.

Thorfinn dismissed the drink with a wave of his

hand.

"You must settle the beast within," observed Ketil, dropping the ale skin beside him.

Thorfinn held back his growl, but he gave the Seer a scathing look. "Your concern for *my wolf* has been noted."

"Then will you find rest if the beast continues to prowl inside you?" A sudden thin chill hung on the edge of his words.

In the brief time Thorfinn had known Ketil, he never defied the Seer. Until now.

"Does the beast bother you, Ketil?"

The man belched but refused to answer the question. Withdrawing a rune from the pouch belted at his side, the Seer studied the bone over the flames. "Do you not long to be a leader?"

Thorfinn refused to be led into a trap by confessing anything to this man. "Of what? I do not crave power."

"The wolves? Have you not considered you might serve Loki in a position by *leading* the wolves to him?"

He gritted his teeth, despising the unstable God. At present, none of the Gods deserved his service. Thorfinn simply kept silent and complied when the others within their group spoke of the great God Loki. "The wolves are loyal to King William and would not seek to follow another who would lead them away from his service."

"You should ponder another plan, if you are not happy with the current direction Halvard foresees."

"Were you not the one that spoke of keeping away from *Magnar* and the wolves?"

"A momentary circumstance."

"What direction do you see, Ketil?" asked

Thorfinn, eager to shift the conversation away from himself.

The Seer held up the rune bone. "Ahh…a question I have waited for someone to ask."

Thorfinn shifted on the ground and stretched out his legs. *Do all seers speak in such confounded riddles?*

After returning the rune bone to his pouch, Ketil settled back against the broken log. "We are drawing near a mighty force of power—one that is difficult to foretell. Even with magic, I am unable to determine its commanding source." He pointed a gnarled finger at Thorfinn. "Within my vision, it is not Halvard who must take possession but you."

The wolf within Thorfinn ceased his pacing.

"With this power, can we thwart King William from taking full control of the north?" Though he was cautious with his question, hope surged within Thorfinn.

Ketil shrugged. "Anything is possible. Perchance we can succeed in capturing all of Scotland."

Thorfinn considered the Seer's words. Did not the warriors of old speak of conquering all of the country? As a young lad he used to listen to the *skalds* recalling the tales of how Scotland was once connected to the *Orkneyjar Isles*. When the great dragon, *Nidhogg* grew angry at the people in the far-off land, he severed the land from the isles by gnawing on the root of the tree that linked them. The Gods spoke of a time when it would take a great warrior to unite the two once again.

However, he would not be lulled into a fool's quest by another, even if Ketil was a Seer.

Reaching for his axe, Thorfinn placed the weapon across his thighs. Drawing in a huge breath, he released it slowly. Temptation to shift and let the wolf roam ahead of Ketil had him smiling. Yet now was not the time to make an enemy of the Seer.

An owl hooted in the tree above him, unaware of the wolf below, and Thorfinn lifted his head. Even in the dark, he could make out the gleam within the bird's eyes.

You are a creature of wisdom. Guide me on my quest.

Returning his attention to the Seer, he stated, "Get some rest. We depart before the last star fades from the sky."

****

Dark clouds hovered over the morning landscape like a blanket of doom, adding more misery to Elspeth's mood. She chastised herself for her sullen behavior when she had broken her fast earlier with Erik. 'Twas nothing more than worry about Magnar. Yet it seemed as if her mood captured others in the keep. Even her nephew had remained silent. Had he, too, sensed the unrest lingering around the keep like the mists snaking the hills?

She rubbed her temples, easing the ache behind her eyes, but it did little to soothe the chill that seeped into her bones. "This is the one time I wished I had your gift of insight, Grandmother, so I can see the path of my husband. I ken it has only been a few days, but this foreboding will not fade."

Releasing a frustrated sigh, Elspeth moved away from the arched window. Thunder rolled in the far distance with the threat of rain to follow. She desperately wanted the unease to leave her thoughts and spirit.

"You cannot stay confined in your chambers all day and night," she chastised with a heaviness that made her spirit weary.

You must cease this madness!

Reaching for her cloak, she sought to keep busy by tending to the herbs in the kitchen garden. Her steps led her quickly from her room and along the quiet corridor. Making her way steadily down the stairs, she paused by the entrance to the great hall. Not a soul dwelled within, but the ghosts long dead reached out to her. Even the silence within the keep was troubling.

She rubbed her hands together and banished the horrible images, especially those of her brother.

When she entered the kitchens, some of the women were tending to the meal for the day. Their grim expressions mirrored her own. In an attempt to shake off the uneasiness, she gave each a small smile in passing.

Grabbing a basket off the table, she paused and reached for an apple.

"Would you like me to fetch you something, Lady Elspeth?" asked Muir from a chair by the hearth.

She went and placed a hand on the woman's shoulder. "Nae. I think I shall work in the herb garden."

"Rain is coming," warned the woman as she kept tending to her current task of stitching.

"Or I might go in search of some berries?"

The woman's face lit up, and she dropped her mending. "I can fetch what meager items we have and make a few tarts."

"Did you not say someone found a jug of honey in the cellar as well?" asked Elspeth, hoping the account was accurate.

"Aye!"

Elspeth removed her hand. "Good. Then after I tend to the garden, I shall go on a quest to bring back berries."

With a renewed sense of purpose, Elspeth made her way out of the kitchens and quickly strolled across the bailey. Glancing upward, she indeed noted the looming threat of clouds. Indecision plagued her. Rain would surely arrive, but when?

"The herb garden can wait. We need berries," she mumbled.

The pithy bleating of a goat sounded behind her. Darting a glance over her shoulder, Elspeth spied the irksome animal with her nephew not far behind trying to capture the escaping goat.

Dropping her basket, Elspeth spread her arms and legs wide in an attempt to block the animal's path. She should have known better. It leaped and dashed around her.

Erik came to an abrupt halt in front of her. "By the hounds! Una escaped again, Aunt Elspeth!"

Chuckling softly, she ruffled the hair on her nephew's head. "It appears her fleeing her pen often might have saved her from the vile men who stole everything from us. She could have been a meal for them."

The lad scowled. "But Gunnar and I fixed the pen yesterday."

"And yet she escaped once again."

His eyes widened. "She used magic."

Elspeth folded her arms over her chest. "Una is a *goat* and not capable. After I have collected some berries, I will consider another area where we can keep

Una. Perchance she does not like being too near the stables."

"Berries, you say?" Erik smacked his lips in obvious joy. His appetite taking priority over the goat's lodging's.

She bent and retrieved her basket. "Aye, for tarts with honey."

"I ken where there are many," he admitted, running toward the gates.

"Wonderful. But we cannot go any farther than right outside the portcullis!" shouted Elspeth, making long strides after her nephew.

She waved at the guard in passing as she dashed across the bridge. Elspeth knew of the vines snaking a portion of the stone walls and headed in a northern direction. After several moments, she glanced all around. Most of the berries were absent from the bramble of vines, along with her nephew. Perchance some of the others had eaten the berries.

"Where are you, Erik? Did I not state to stay nearby?"

She followed the sound of his laughter, drifting between the ancient oak trees. Onward she walked until she came to the clearing overlooking the stream. Thunder clapped furiously overhead, and she knew her time was running short.

Glancing to her left, she noted the huge bush of blackberries. And still no sign of the lad.

"This is not a game, Erik! You had better not be stuffing your mouth with berries or you will not get any tarts." Her tone had taken on an edge of worry.

A breeze lifted the hair on the back of her neck as she allowed her gaze to travel down to the stream. She squinted in the gray light and let out a gasp. "*Magnar*," she whispered.

Overjoyed at seeing her husband, Elspeth dropped the basket and took off running. Her cloak slapped furiously at her legs, but she gave no care. Worry infused her at seeing her husband back so soon. Perchance someone was injured on their journey, or the threat of Halvard was gone. Nevertheless, she wanted to wrap her arms around him and bury her face against his chest.

"Magnar!" she shouted, slowing her stride down the hill after she almost slipped on a soft patch of leaves and mud.

Yet as she drew nearer, fear clutched at her heart like a falcon's talons. Coming to a halt by a pine tree, she studied the man. Something was horribly amiss.

Her husband had one lone habit. Magnar clenched his right fist when troubled. This man clenched his left fist.

Elspeth knees went weak as the blood drained from her face with the reality of what she now knew. She pressed a hand to her stomach. "*Thorfinn*."

The man turned around. His growl cloaked her like the stench of foul meat. "How fortunate. The prey has come to the hunter."

Elspeth shuddered and stumbled backward. His features mirrored those of his brother, except for one— a deep crescent scar from his right eyebrow down to his cheek.

Shaking his head slowly, he ordered, "Do not flee. I am swifter. And do *not* attempt to scream."

Shoving aside the bile that threatened to heave from her stomach, she straightened and looked beyond the man. "Where is Erik?"

Thorfinn arched a brow. "If you come willingly, he lives."

Determined not to easily yield to the terror of this man's plan, Elspeth's mind sought to think of something to say. "Can you not speak with your brother? You must mend this rift," she pleaded.

"*Magnar* is not my brother!"

Lightning flashed in the sky behind him, causing Elspeth to flinch.

He stalked closer and inhaled sharply. "You reek of him."

Fury squashed her panic, and she dug her hands into the folds of her cloak. "Magnar MacAlpin is my *husband*. And if you take me, he will kill you, Thorfinn. This will gain you nothing."

His mouth twisted into a sneering smile. "Not if my blade enters his heart first."

"Why?" she asked in desperation to fathom his intent.

"Because you are the source of power," declared another man approaching from her side, carrying the body of her limp nephew over his shoulder.

Unable to stop herself, Elspeth lunged at the man. "What have you done to him?"

The blow to her face came hard and swift. Staggering back into Thorfinn, Elspeth tried in a feeble attempt to wrestle free from his iron grip. "Release me," she mumbled as pain clouded her vision.

He complied but kept his stance far too near.

"Bind her mouth and hands," ordered the other man. "I have nae desire to hear what spews from her." He dumped Erik's limp and possible lifeless body onto the ground, adding, "When you are finished, bind the lad as well. I will fetch the horses."

The man drew closer. Elspeth refused to cower in front of him. The smile he gave her never reached his eyes. "I can sense the power on you." He ripped apart her cloak and regarded her with contempt.

Elspeth gasped and clutched at her pendant.

"It is what I felt and was shown in a vision. You wear Odin's blue stone." The man glanced sideways at Thorfinn. "Be on guard when we reach Halvard. Do not speak about this until I have confirmation."

Thorfinn gave the man a curt nod, watching as he departed through the trees.

When the dizziness and pain subsided, Elspeth looked down on her nephew. A large purple knot began to form on the side of his head. Lifting her head, she stared into the stony expression of her enemy. "Allow me to tend to his wound first and make sure his breathing is sound."

Ignoring her request, Thorfinn yanked her by her arm away from her nephew. She staggered as he drew her near his satchel and withdrew a fair amount of rope.

"*Please*," she begged, fighting the burning tears that threatened to spill.

Elspeth noted the hesitation and offered up a silent prayer he'd soften to her plea.

With a curse, Thorfinn relented and shoved her toward Erik. "You have only a few moments. If Ketil returns and sees you have not been bound, his wrath is far viler than mine."

"Thank you," she said softly and went to her nephew.

Slumping down to the ground, Elspeth placed her

hand over her nephew's nose. When his faint breath brushed over her palm, she let out a sigh of relief. With careful fingers, she examined the swelling on his head and the surrounding area. Bending near his ear, she whispered, "Erik, you must wake." Gently cradling his head onto her lap, she tried to stir him awake.

"Leave him. He lives," ordered Thorfinn.

She gave the lad one more shake on his shoulders. "Erik, *wake*."

On a mumbled groan, the lad turned from her and emptied his stomach onto the ground.

Elspeth tenderly swiped her cool fingers across his brow. "Take deep breaths in and out."

"He...he is *not* Magnar," mumbled Erik.

Before she could wipe the spittle from his mouth with a portion of her cloak, she was pulled away from Erik and forced to stand.

Thorfinn pointed to her hands. "Hold them outward."

It took all of her control not to strike out at Thorfinn. Elspeth battled the words she wanted to hurl at the man. Gritting her teeth, she grudgingly yielded. She watched in anger as he secured them tightly. When he was done, she asked, "And my mouth?"

"Unless you are prone to fits of screaming, you can go without the binding." He gripped her chin so tightly, pain shot to the back of her jaw. "Do not *misuse* my trust."

After releasing her, Thorfinn went to her nephew and quickly secured another portion of the rope around his hands.

Returning to her side, he placed his hands on her shoulders. "Do you carry any weapons on you?"

I will tell you nothing! And you cannot claim what is not yours!

His fingers dug into her shoulders. "Tell me, *Elspeth.*"

Hearing her name on his tongue made her ill. Attempting to be indifferent to the pain he was inflicting, she turned her head away and fought the wave of dizziness.

Thorfinn bent near her ear. "So be it. I asked and you denied me. Now I shall take."

With deft skill, his hands skimmed over her body, remaining too long over and under her breasts. When his hand delved lower, she fought the scream within her throat. He swiftly turned her around and bunched up her cloak and gown, revealing the small blade tucked in her boots. Thorfinn removed the weapon and tossed it aside onto the ground. She did not ken how much more she could endure of this torment while he touched her body in search of any more blades. Beads of sweat broke out along her brow.

"There are nae more," she confessed, fear edging her voice.

Immediately he ceased his actions and moved away to help Ketil who with the horses now approached.

Elspeth tried to calm her racing heart as she glared at her husband's twin.

If Magnar does not take a blade to your heart, I will.

Chapter Twenty-One

"Can you say for certain they have fled to the *Orkneyjar Isles*?" demanded Magnar, gripping his mug in silent frustration. The din of noise within the inn had increased with the mass of people entering to avoid the raging storm. He'd thought many more would follow, and some would be the enemy they sought, but it did not happen.

Rorik leaned his forearms onto the wooden table. "My man's account is accurate. He is a trader from the isles and overheard one of Halvard's men boast of returning with wealth and goods. They have forsaken their plans to stay in Scotland."

"As I have stated before, I judge Halvard is not a man to retreat so easily," disputed Magnar.

"Perchance he wants to enlist others from *Orkneyjar*?"

Shrugging, Magnar drained his mug and shoved it across the table.

"Do you seek a battle?" asked Rorik, his expression grim. "I ken we all wanted to rid Scotland of this vermin, but they have retreated."

Confused with this latest information, Magnar scratched at the three days' growth of beard on his face. "My instinct tells me differently. Even Steinar sensed they were returning to Steinn. Until I receive confirmation from Bjorn that their ship did depart, we shall remain here."

Rorik's expression grew taut. "Have you considered they took another path to Steinn?"

Magnar grunted. "Over a steep rocky incline and across a treacherous path?"

Leaning back, Rorik argued, "But a possibility."

"Nae. One of the men at Steinn spoke about the damage from heavy snowfall during the last winter. 'Tis not fit for any to journey through."

Rorik tapped his fingers on the rough wooden table. "Then clearly they have fled, or we would have encountered them along the road or forest to the coast."

"Aye," Magnar concurred.

The door to the inn crashed open and slammed against the inner wall of the building. A gust of rain and wind engulfed the men entering.

Magnar and Rorik both glanced sharply at the entrance, anticipating Bjorn's return.

"Loki's balls!" Rorik picked up his mug and guzzled deeply. "We have been trapped here most of the day."

"Relax. You will only inflame your beast," urged Magnar, doing his best to quash the turmoil within his own wolf. Between the threat of battle, being surrounded by others not their kind, and a raging storm, their wolves were restless—a circumstance that did not bode well in this strange mix of company.

"At least you allowed your wolf to roam most of the way to the coast," his friend responded dryly.

"Someone needed to tend to the horses."

The man grumbled another curse and stood. "More ale?"

"Aye *and* food. I have nae plans on going out into

this tempest."

Folding his arms across his chest, Magnar studied the group gathered inside the inn. Sturdy men hardened by life near the sea. None looked to be common travelers. In truth, he judged Halvard was unable to procure any men here in Scotland for his plan, despite his offer of coin. Many were loyal to King William. Magnar had heard the tales of men who had nae treasonous thought against the king. Their regard for their king was immense.

Your plans went awry and failed, Halvard. Perchance Rorik was correct. You left for the isles.

A deafening roar of thunder shook the roof of the inn. The serving lass stumbled on a gasp, spilling the contents of her tray onto the floor. Several of the men, including Rorik came to her aid.

Magnar lifted his head upward and sneered. "If you have journeyed across the sea, Halvard, I pray the Gods sink your ship before you reach the isles."

No sooner had one man shut the door to the inn than another came bounding through, bringing the fierce storm back inside. Fear slammed into Magnar's body. Abruptly standing, he tried to control his breathing. Unable to wait for the man to approach, he shouted, "Why are you here, Gunnar?"

Breathing hard, the man's grim expression hardened as he approached. "Erik and Elspeth are gone—*taken*."

Not caring who witnessed his display of fury, he snarled. "*Who?*"

Gunnar's lip twisted. "The stench of Thorfinn and another were found by the trees near the stream, along with this." He withdrew Elspeth's *sgian dubh*.

The howl of displeasure from his wolf filled Magnar. Unable to hold back his rage, he let out a roar and smashed his fists onto the table. The wood splintered and cracked in half. He barely heeded the plea from Gunnar and Rorik to temper the anger—his fury and pain too great. Darkness clouded his vision, and his wolf clawed to be released and seek vengeance. Kill the bastards who may have brought harm to his beloved—feel their bones crush within his powerful jaw. Rip the hearts from their chest and feast on their blood for stealing Elspeth from him.

"*Stop*," demanded Rorik. "You are shifting between man *and* wolf."

Within the murky depths of his wrath, Magnar battled the indecision to let loose the beast. His body shook with trying to control his raging emotions. The anguished howls of his wolf filled his head. He cupped his hands over his ears and closed his eyes. Piercing agony writhed within his mind and body. But the brutal force of a sharp blade slashed his heart into strips.

Rorik dared to move closer. "Unless you are prepared to battle us, we need you to cease so we can *save* them."

Magnar shuddered. *Control. Bind. Focus.*

Displeased, his wolf howled and then relented.

With his breathing labored, Magnar lowered his hands and slowly opened his eyes. "Sa...save *Elspeth*," he avowed in a raspy voice.

"And Erik," Rorik added quietly.

He gave a terse nod.

Gunnar solemnly handed the *sgian dubh* to Magnar. "Before you take my life, allow me to assist in rescuing Elspeth. If you find me unworthy for this task, then use her blade to slit my throat. 'Tis the only honor I ask of you."

Magnar's hand shook as he accepted the small blade. Rubbing his thumb over the worn leather of the sheath, he swallowed. He placed the precious item within the pouch on his side. Returning his attention to Gunnar, he noted the wariness and also the weariness within the warrior. Though his wolf cried out to take the man's life, Magnar must first hear his account—one he reckoned would not be cause for his death.

"When was the last time you ate or slept, Gunnar?" inquired Magnar.

Frowning, the man wiped a hand over his brow. "Since we found they had been taken."

"Rorik, see to some ale and food—*again*," ordered Magnar, glancing around the inn. "Should be an easy request, since most everyone has fled the building." *Most certainly from witnessing my outburst.*

"I cannot take any food or drink until we have rescued the lad and Lady Elspeth," argued Gunnar, shifting his stance.

Magnar let out a growl of displeasure. "If you want to remain with us on this journey, you will take sustenance. You are nae good to us in a weakened condition. While you fill your stomach, you can give your account."

The man nodded slowly. "Thank you."

Magnar crossed the inn and went to the hearth. With his pain and fury barely contained, he required distance to think. He looked beyond the flames.

Where did they take you, my kærr?

Rubbing his hand over his chest, he tried to ease the ache within. Elspeth had woven herself inside him.

More than lust. More than breeding an heir. He dared not say the word within his mind, yet there it was lodged within his heart. Had he always known? Possibly, but he refused to declare the word out loud.

Love.

His heart, body, and mind loved Elspeth. The fear of losing her forever twisted his gut, and he banished it with a single thought. He curled his hand into a fist.

"I shall search the ends of the earth to find you, Elspeth," he stated with conviction. "Be strong, my wife. You are a true shield-maiden." He clutched his torc. "Hear my prayer, Freyja. Never have I asked for anything from you, until now—until I can rescue them, keep Elspeth and Erik safe. Let nae harm befall them. Use your shield to protect them."

When the door to the inn blew open once again, Magnar looked over his shoulder. "Thank the Gods," he muttered and went to greet Bjorn.

"What news?"

Bjorn wiped the water from his face. "One longship departed three days ago for the isles. Yet another one left this morn. The man described Thorfinn and one man, along with a woman and child."

Scrubbing his hands vigorously over his face, Magnar shifted his stance. His beast demanded to be set free. "Gather the other men."

Bjorn cast a sideways glance. "Loki's balls! Why is Gunnar here?" His eyes grew wide as he turned back toward Magnar. "The woman and child are—"

"Elspeth and Erik," confirmed Magnar. "Have Ivar find any ship to take us to the isles and onto the shore. Anything will do, since we will leave all but one of the horses behind. I assign you to follow with the weapons.

Once on the isles, we can shift into our wolves and catch the lad and Elspeth's scent. You can follow on horseback with the weapons. Task Gilmore with informing the king and Sutherland of the enemies' actions. The rest of the king's men can ride back to Steinn with our horses."

Bjorn rubbed his nose. "With the storm, none will be willing to take us across."

"If they refuse, offer to buy the ship."

The warrior snarled. "Death to Thorfinn."

Placing a firm hand on the warrior's shoulder, Magnar ordered, "His death is mine—nae other shall claim his life! Now go."

"Can I claim second death?"

Narrowing his eyes, Magnar shook his head. "I reckon Gunnar will want that privilege, though I have yet to hear his account on how they were seized."

The man hesitated briefly and then stormed out of the inn.

"You have woven your charm within my warriors, beloved. Be strong. We are coming for you both." Magnar blew out a frustrated breath and raked a hand through his hair.

And in a moment of clarity, his hatred for Thorfinn grew.

He reached for a chair and scraped it across the floor to the table. Reaching for the jug of fresh ale, he poured a hefty amount inside his mug, sloshing liquid over the sides.

"Venison stew and bread," announced Rorik, shoving a trencher toward him and Gunnar.

Magnar gestured to Gunnar. "Quickly give me your account."

As he devoured the meal, he listened with rapt attention as the man gave a detailed report of the day Elspeth and Erik had been snatched from Steinn. He then explained further how he tracked them through the forest and to the coast, where he had come upon some of the king's men. After he alerted them to the disappearance of Elspeth and Erik, they directed him to the inn.

Wiping his mouth with the back of his hand, Magnar pushed aside the empty trencher. He grabbed his mug and drained the entire contents. Placing the mug back down, he regarded the warrior. "You are not to blame, Gunnar. 'Tis not the first time my wife has disobeyed an order."

"If I might add, the guard did state he overheard Elspeth shouting at Erik to not go any farther from the main entrance."

Magnar rolled his shoulders. The effort mildly eased the tension that coiled within his body. "Nevertheless, as soon as we can procure a ship, we depart. Thorfinn has taken them across the sea."

"For what purpose?" demanded Rorik, pounding the table with his fist.

His lip curled in disgust, recalling how he thought to bring his brother into the brotherhood. "For the blue stone of Odin. I believe Thorfinn sensed the power and wanted to possess it for himself. He would have heard the tales growing up with the Northmen."

Rorik dropped his hands to his sides and stared at him in disbelief. "Then you ken the reason why he is taking her across sea."

"To take her to the blue caves and the temple of Odin on *Orkneyjar* where he can force her to give him the stone over the ancient flame," confirmed Magnar.

Rorik shook his head and let out a low growl. "He is a fool to think Loki will challenge Odin. Does he seriously believe the God will give him the power to take what is not his to claim? And they cannot wander inside without consent from the men who guard the caves sacred to Odin."

Rising slowly from his chair, Magnar regarded both men. He understood the grave situation they faced. "Even so, they have already departed. We can only pray that the God of the Sea slows their progress but grants us a swift passage across. Furthermore, I alone will battle Thorfinn to the death. There shall be nae argument. Finish your meal and then join me down by the pier."

Rorik lifted his mug. "Let victory be ours!"

"Aye!" echoed Gunnar.

Magnar steeled his emotions as he reached for his axe and cloak. Fury and fear would only serve to cloud his mind and body. When he reached the entrance to the inn, he threw back the door, letting the brutal sting of the wind and rain slash across his face.

****

With one hand on the rope attached to a barrel and the other wrapped firmly around the limp body of her nephew, Elspeth's body ached and her muscles burned as she desperately tried to remain seated inside the longship and not be tossed outward into the punishing seas. The wind howled in her ears, and the tempest of the storm battered her face. Several times, Erik heaved what little he had in his stomach onto the deck of the ship. He muttered an apology and then yielded to silence.

Raw determination to keep them both alive had filled her when they first climbed on board. Did not Gunnar tell her she was a shield-maiden? How strange to think they were now heading to a land that was home to her ancestors, including her grandmother. She had never considered the isles her home—nae. The Northmen dwelled there. They came and slaughtered many in her country.

Yet Norse blood flowed through her veins as surely as her Scottish heritage.

Elspeth shifted to ease the onslaught of pain and water but to no avail. The storm was merciless.

Another wave crashed over the side of the ship, filling her mouth and nostrils with the salty bitterness of the sea. Great spasms racked her body while her stomach heaved its watery contents onto the deck. The skin of her fingers burned in agony against the coarse rope, and her wrists were raw from the bindings she was made to endure as they traveled to the coast.

The sea pitched the ship upward once again— before slamming down with such a violent force, her arm twisted. Pain gripped her in its talons as she tried to straighten her limbs. How long had they traveled? Time ceased to exist. One hour—one day bleeding into the next?

With her resolve slowly fading, Elspeth bent her head on a silent prayer the storm would relent.

Do you even ken where we are, husband? I fear we are not going to make land, and I will never have a chance to tell you what is inside my heart.

Squeezing her eyes shut, she battled the terror threatening to plunge her into its embrace. A sudden urge to rip the pendant from her neck and fling it out into the sea filled Elspeth. Her left hand uncurled from the rope. She clutched the stone through the material of her cloak, and her fingers tightened.

Then nae one will have the power, if you are truly lost forever.

Opening her eyes, Elspeth drew in a shaky breath, prepared to set free the blue stone.

When a sliver of sunlight pierced the storm-cloud sky, she sighed. The light touched the side of the ship and spread toward her. Hope surged forth within Elspeth. She dropped her hand. Reaching her fingers toward the light, she waited for the warmth to touch her skin. A lone tear trickled down her cheek.

I must have faith that you are coming, husband. For if I surrender the stone into the arms of the sea, I doom Erik and myself.

Shouting from one of the men snapped her out of her thoughts. She blinked in an effort to bring her vision into focus. Seawater continued to sluice down her face. Turning her head so she could hear better, Elspeth strained to make out what they were arguing over. She shuddered upon hearing Thorfinn's voice, so like her husband's. Apparently, the storm had sent them far west, instead of east to the inner main isle. Now they had to adjust their course and travel farther.

Elspeth snorted at the twist of fate. She stared at the backs of both men, praying the ship might toss them into the water and spare the lives of her, Erik, and the few crew members attempting to cross an angry sea.

Are you watching us, Grandmother? Do you help to guide the ship to a safe haven for us? Is not your homeland out there? If we cannot return to Scotland, then bring us safely home to Orkneyjar where Magnar can find us.

With a renewed sense of strength, Elspeth took hold of the rope again.

Chapter Twenty-Two

"Steer the ship to center and then bend to the left!" bellowed Magnar, wiping another blast of seawater from his eyes. Thank the Gods the storm had abated, but the sea was ruthless.

He pointed to the southern inward dip of the land near the coast. "Look! There is another ship. They have landed at *Hamnavoe*."

"How can you be certain 'tis them?" asked Rorik, coming to his side.

He pounded his fist against his chest. "She is here. Nearby." Magnar held back the knowledge that since he declared his love for Elspeth within his heart, a burst of unexplained power and connection to his wife grew inside of him. At one point on their journey across the sea, he thought he heard her speaking to him. And in response, he called out to her within his mind. Was this part of the powerful claiming his father had spoken of? He had no answers, save one. His love for Elspeth grew with each passing hour.

Glancing sharply at his friend, Magnar hoped he'd fathom and trust his direction.

Rorik braced his hands on the side of the bow. "The storm is lessening. Their travel across the sea must have taken them beyond the caves."

Magnar agreed. "Aye. This will mean it will take them more time to travel across the land."

"What if some did not survive the storm?" asked Rorik quietly.

Returning his attention to the land, Magnar reflected on Rorik's words and considered his friend's unspoken meaning. *What if of Erik had not survived?* He gritted his teeth. *Nae! You are strong, young chieftain.*

Directing his thoughts to their plan, Magnar studied the surrounding landscape—treacherous, wet, and mud-filled. The trees were few, but the hill they needed to ascend was a steep, rocky incline. Once over the crest, they could descend without delay to the caves below.

However, Magnar's concern happened to be with a certain tribe of men loyal to Odin. Any seeking entry into the temple of Odin without consent might face the blade of a warrior. Or worse, have the skin flayed from their body. He found nae fault with harm coming to Thorfinn and the others, but the tribe might not be so forgiving to a woman and child attempting to enter. No female was ever allowed, and surely not a young lad.

He blew out a soft curse. Magnar prayed to the Gods they would not encounter the tribe on their quest and would permit him and his men to seek justice.

As they drew near land, Magnar tempered the increasing strain to shift into his wolf. Since Bjorn was tasked with taking care of their weapons, he knew the man had already drawn his blade. Glancing over his shoulder, he smiled inwardly. Bjorn sat in quiet contemplation with his sword—whispering words while he sharpened the steel.

Magnar returned his focus to the edge of the shore where they would land. Digging his fingers into the rough wood, he tried to settle his wolf. He would not shift until they all departed. And then he would plunder the land in search of his beloved and Erik.

The ship slowed on her approach, rising and dipping within the sea.

Magnar lifted his head. *Hear my prayer, All Father. Though Thorfinn is my blood kin, I cannot abide by his reckless actions. We shared the same womb, but he is my enemy and yours. Grant me the power to bring justice for you and for my wife.*

The clouds separated, and a shaft of sunlight broke free. Magnar searched the hills to see where the light landed. Deeming this a message from Odin, he pointed outward to the area. "We travel there!"

The other men came forward, each nodding their accord.

Magnar regarded each of his warriors. "I do not ken what we face or the dangers. If Loki interferes, death may claim us all. Offer your own prayers for a swift victory." He hesitated, unsure how to proceed with the next. Shifting his stance, he lowered his voice. "Once we come upon Elspeth, I am unsure how my wolf will respond to seeing her in danger. You must each give me your word not to hinder me in any way. I fear if you do, I cannot hold back my wolf. At the moment, he is barely contained."

Bjorn stepped forward. "May Odin guide our path, and Thor's hammer smash our enemies."

"Aye!" bellowed the other men, raising their fists outward.

Magnar acknowledged each of his men with a nod, and then returned his focus on the approaching shore. His wolf paced furiously, knowing the time to shift was drawing near. He quickly removed his tunic and tossed it to Bjorn. The rest of his clothing would be cast aside once they were on land.

When the ship touched the shore, Magnar jumped over the side and landed with a heavy force onto the ground. He knelt on one knee, thanking the Gods for safe passage. Rising slowly, he scanned the area. His body shook with a fierce need to let loose the beast.

Be patient, my friend. We shall find her.

Soon he was surrounded by his men. They strode silently with purpose across the small shore and upward onto a small rise toward a cluster of trees. Immediately, Magnar rid himself of the rest of his clothing, leather greaves, and boots, as did his men.

Giving one last look at his men, he uttered softly, "For Elspeth and Erik."

Magnar dropped to the ground and inhaled. He dug his fists onto the soft earth. On the exhale, he shifted into his wolf.

The wolf's cry of displeasure echoed all around him, yearning to rip the heart from those who had taken Elspeth. He lifted his head, sniffing the air and his surroundings. Turning north, he lowered his head, and his lips drew back on a snarl. Without waiting for the others, he sprinted forward through the trees and out into the open landscape.

The scenery blurred as Elspeth's scent spurred him faster. The others swiftly joined him, and they moved as one, beginning their treacherous ascent up the hill. Mud, leaves, and rocks flew out from under them, each wolf doing their utmost not to crash to the bottom. His wolf narrowly missed a boulder that had dislodged from the speed of their climb. Raw determination kept him fighting and clawing to reach the top. With victory almost in sight, his front paws landed on a patch of small rocks and mud. He fought for several moments to find a solid patch of stone to avoid falling into death's embrace below. Lunging forward, he ran the remainder of the way to the top.

When the rest of his men successfully reached the crest, he paced to the edge. One by one, all the wolves padded to his side. He shook his body, ready for the battle that was coming. Indifferent to any who heard him, he lifted his head and howled savagely.

****

Thorfinn regarded both men with intent. This was not the battle he foresaw between Halvard and the Seer. Granted, Ketil had not been content with a few of Halvard's decisions. Yet this latest was now a concern for Thorfinn. Halvard judged he had been betrayed. And he was correct. The Seer had another purpose—one Thorfinn found he could not follow or agree upon.

Secrets, lies, power, and plans that have gone awry. We should never have returned here.

"Tell me again about the blue stone of Odin?" Halvard's laugh was bitter. "Now that we have killed one of the men who have guarded the caves, you owe me your account."

Halvard's men surrounded them—each holding a hand on their weapons at their sides.

Ketil narrowed his eyes. "Why must I repeat myself to you? Did you not understand?"

Halvard took a step near the man. "If I had not witnessed your arrival, you would have gone on ahead to the caves *without* me. You crave the power for yourself, Ketil. I only wanted to hear you spout your lies before I rip your tongue from your mouth."

"'Tis not for me," argued Ketil quietly, flicking the edge of his dirk with his thumb. "And I would be careful of the words you speak this day."

Thorfinn realized the danger he now faced, and he clenched his hand.

Halvard slowly turned toward him. "You!" He spat on the ground in front of Thorfinn. "I should have known you would have betrayed me, *wolf*!"

"How have I betrayed you?" challenged Thorfinn, doing his best not to kill the man where he stood.

"Will you take the stone from her?" demanded Halvard, pointing to the woman tied to the trunk of a tree.

He looked beyond the man and at Elspeth. She regarded him with hatred, even in her untidy and soiled appearance. Furthermore, the lad kept his fixed gaze on him as well, while he sat beside her. *Not only have I betrayed these men but incurred the anger of your husband. Death will take one of us.*

Halvard and Ketil were arguing for two separate plans. Their joined cause to wrest free part of Scotland was simply a deception for another gain of power. And each was determined to seek it for themselves.

Uncertainty no longer plagued Thorfinn. There was only one decision he could confess to. "I do not desire to claim the stone. To suffer the wrath of Odin is not what I seek."

Ketil sneered at him and shoved him aside. "You are nothing but a *traitor*." He made his way toward Elspeth.

Halvard gave him a look of contempt. "It appears you have made many enemies today, wolf." He dared to lean near Thorfinn. "You should have alerted me to the Seer's plan."

"And what if I had?" asked Thorfinn with malice. "Would you slay him? The Seer? You ken what our people would do to you. They will strip all the skin and flesh from your bones while your heart continues to beat. You have forgotten honor."

The man's face transformed to one of horror, and he took a step back. "Not if they knew their Seer was foolish enough to go against the Gods and become one himself. 'Tis part of what he craves."

Thorfinn frowned in confusion. "What are you not saying?"

Elspeth's scream tore them away from their conversation. Ketil was bent over the lad with a blade to his throat.

His decision now made, Thorfinn stormed over to Ketil. He dared to grasp the Seer's wrist and removed it away from the lad's throat. "Are you mad? Leave him!"

"You shall regret this moment, Thorfinn! Remember my words well." Ketil stood and sliced through Elspeth's bindings. He pulled her across the clearing, heading for the caves.

"What are you doing?" asked Halvard, stalking after the Seer.

In one swift move, the Seer shoved the woman to the ground and thrust his dirk into Halvard's heart. The man stumbled back in shock. Blood oozed forth from his lips and trickled down his chin as he tried in a feeble attempt to remove the blade from his chest. On a guttural curse, the man pitched forward onto the ground.

Halvard's men advanced on Ketil, but the man held

a hand up in warning to stay their movements. "Your leader had become weak. He had a sickness in the mind. Some of you have confessed witnessing this on our travels. Now is the time to choose wisely. Will you stand with me and the God Loki? Or shall I utter the words to curse you and your souls forever? Who will join me on this new path? If you are worthy, take up your weapons and guard the entrance to the caves."

The men all cast suspicious looks at each other.

The wolf within Thorfinn clawed to be released. He could smell the men's fear seeping forth from their skin.

Without waiting for their response, Ketil rolled the dead body of Halvard onto his back with his booted foot. Swiftly, he removed the dirk from the man's body and held the bloody blade outward. "Well? What is your answer?" His voice rang sharp, and his stare was penetrating.

They were all mad, and Thorfinn wanted no part of this deceiving gain for power. He watched as each made a solemn vow to follow the Seer on his venture.

When Ketil's gaze landed on him, he battled his next decision—one Thorfinn never thought to take. He inhaled sharply. The Seer would never trust him, even if he proclaimed his vow to follow. He had to thwart the man's quest and rid himself of this madness.

He tempered the beast within and stared at the Seer. "Take the blue stone of Odin."

A sinister smile curved the mouth of the man. "With a powerful wolf at my side, we can rule them all. Attend to me in the caves after you slit the boy's throat."

Thorfinn gave a curt nod and removed his sword

from the sheath on his back.

Ketil turned and yanked Elspeth's braid, tugging her to a standing position.

The woman's cry of anguish surrounded Thorfinn, but there was nothing he could do at the moment. He watched them depart.

When the last man faded from his sight, he turned and approached the lad. Crouching down in front of him, he spoke quietly. "You are a brave chieftain, Erik."

The lad jutted out his chin. "Give me a sword before death takes me. 'Tis my honor as a warrior. As it should have been for my father."

He scratched the side of his face. "Today is not your day to die, young chieftain."

Startled, Erik asked, "But you told that evil man you would—"

"If I set you free, are you strong enough to bring the others here?" interrupted Thorfinn, angry at the mention of Thomas Gunn. The man's death still haunted him.

The lad's eyes widened as he looked around. "Aye, but what others?"

Thorfinn slashed at the bindings holding Erik firmly against the trunk of the tree. He stood and pointed outward. "Steadily make your way in this direction. There you will come upon the Sutherland wolves."

Erik managed to stand and rubbed a hand over his nose. "You must save my aunt," he ordered.

Fisting his hand on his hip, Thorfinn shook his head. "One wolf cannot save her, but many can stop him." He nudged him forward. "Go quickly."

Erik started forward and then paused. "Why not join them—the wolves?"

Thorfinn laughed wearily. "Because my home is here, and Magnar belongs to Scotland. Furthermore, since I brought harm to his wife, he shall seek revenge. 'Tis his right."

"I will speak to Magnar about this honor you have done for me," affirmed Erik and darted into the trees.

He raked a hand through his hair. "Nae matter the amount of good deeds I do, they will never be enough to wipe away the stain of what I did by stealing Elspeth."

After sheathing his sword, Thorfinn silently retreated from the menacing and forthcoming battle.

Chapter Twenty-Three

Coming to a halt before a thick group of pines, the wolf glanced in all directions before slowly entering. His long strides took him into the center. His ears twitched, hearing the sound of footsteps crossing at a fast speed. Jumping onto a fallen log, he inhaled sharply. The other wolves lumbered around him—all aware of who the intruder was bounding toward them.

When the lad stumbled and fell, he let out a curse.

In a gray shimmer, the wolf shifted into Magnar. "Erik?" he asked on a low rumble.

The lad bolted forward through the limbs of a tree.

Magnar crouched and opened his arms. "You are safe, young chieftain." His voice tightened with strain as he held the quaking lad.

Each wolf shifted and stood in a circle around them.

"You must save Elspeth," demanded Erik in a voice choked with emotion.

Magnar drew back, trying to rein in his beast. "How many?"

Erik swallowed. "Ten, including the evil Seer."

"*Seer?*" echoed Magnar, dread filling him. "Do you ken his name?"

Erik's face twisted with hatred, and then he spat on the ground. "*Ketil.*"

Rising slowly, Magnar looked at Steinar. "Go fetch

my clothing, boots, and axe from Bjorn. I sense him nearby."

"'Tis worse than we thought. Your brother and Halvard traveling with a Seer," mentioned Rorik. "With magic, he can force Elspeth to give him the stone."

Magnar nodded solemnly.

Erik went and sat on the boulder. His shoulders sagged as he dropped his head forward. "Nae, nae 'tis not them. They are gone."

The burden of what he'd endured showed on his small frame, and Magnar turned toward Rorik. "Fetch a water skin for the chieftain."

Bjorn entered and tossed Magnar his clothing. After dropping his boots and axe on the ground, he said, "The caves are beyond the clearing of the trees."

Quickly putting on his tunic and trews, Magnar ordered, "Go observe but remain hidden. Given Erik's account, there are ten men, and one is a Seer called Ketil."

Bjorn's hand tightened around his sword. "Observe as wolf or man?"

"Man." Magnar turned around to face the others and added, "Whatever happens, you must *not* shift into your wolves. If Ketil is successful in taking the stone from Elspeth, our beasts will control us. Do you ken my meaning?"

Each acknowledged Magnar with a grunt or nod, while he watched Bjorn silently slip away. Reaching for his boots and axe, Magnar went to sit beside the lad.

Rorik returned and handed Erik the water skin. The lad guzzled deeply. When Magnar deemed he had enough, he asked, "Who is gone?"

Erik coughed and sputtered on the water. He wiped

a shaky hand across his mouth. "Ketil killed Halvard. He then ordered Thorfinn to slit my throat. But he did not kill me. Instead, he cut the rope and freed me."

Stunned into silence, Magnar stared at the lad. *You freed the lad but not my wife?*

Erik handed the water skin back to Rorik. "He knew you were coming and showed me the way to you, so you can save Elspeth. Then he left."

"Holy Odin," proclaimed Rorik, raking a hand through his hair.

"Even with this revelation, Thorfinn's blood is still mine," protested Magnar, putting on his boots.

"Nae!" shouted Erik, slamming his fist into his palm. "In the end, he acted with honor."

Standing slowly, Magnar regarded the young warrior and pondered his words. Aye, his brother did act honorably when faced with a grisly deed. Yet the time of reckoning with Thorfinn was coming—be it with words or weapons.

Magnar placed a gentle hand on the lad's small shoulder. "I shall think upon what you have revealed." This was all he could mention to one so young and weary. His wolf however demanded blood vengeance.

Erik sighed. "Thank you."

Releasing his hold, he asked, "Will you promise to remain hidden, Erik, while we rescue Elspeth?"

Rising slowly, Erik placed a fist over his heart. "I give you my vow to stay in the trees."

Gunnar stepped forward. "Allow me to guard him. Call out to me if you require my sword arm."

Magnar smiled inwardly. He had hoped one of his warriors would come forth. He knew they all wanted to take part in this battle and refrained from asking them to stand guard with the lad. "You may stay with the chieftain. I reckon five of us can vanquish ten."

"Aye!" affirmed his men.

Magnar raised his axe overhead. "To victory! If death takes you, may you enter Valhalla with honor!"

Lowering his arm, Magnar stormed out of the trees with his men swiftly following behind him.

When he reached the clearing, he made careful strides across the land. Beyond the last hill, the temple of Odin beckoned to him. His beloved was there, and his breathing became labored. With one final prayer for his wife, Magnar sealed off all emotions and took off running.

His steps quickly led him up and over the crest of the hill, and he scanned the area below in search of the enemy. Bjorn was stooped down behind a large boulder not far from the entrance with his gaze fixed on him. *Where are they?*

Bjorn shrugged, as if he heard Magnar's unspoken question.

Yet what drew Magnar's attention away from the caves were the five men striding forth toward him.

His men stood ready—each weapon poised for battle.

Magnar gripped his axe tightly, the leather biting into his skin. "These men do not travel with the Seer," he uttered quietly, noting their shaved heads and the blue markings covering their scalps and upper body. They were dressed only in trews and without shoes. He judged them to be those that guarded the temple. Loyal only to Odin and no other.

The tribe of men halted their progress.

Forgive me, All Father, for if they have killed my

beloved, their blood will stain my weapon.

Magnar took a step forward. "I am Magnar MacAlpin, son of Andrew—"

"Grandson to the great Berglund from *Kirkjuvágr*," interrupted one of the men, coming forward. He tilted his head to one side and leveled his spear near the ground.

"If you ken *who* I am, then you must ken why I am here." Magnar's voice was cold and exact.

"Aye. We have waited for your return. I am called Dagr."

Tension knotted Magnar's shoulders. "Does my *wife* live?"

"Not for long. Loki now uses the man called Ketil to try and force her to give him the stone of Odin." With his staff, he drew a line across the muddy ground. "'Tis a battle between two men and the Gods."

His patience snapped. He did not care about a battle between Gods. "Then we waste time discussing what has happened." Magnar motioned for his men to move forward.

The man held up his spear in warning. "*Nae*! There is nae need for your men. We have purged the threat of the others."

Magnar dared to take a step toward the man. "Purged?"

"Dead," he replied flatly. "The battle is now between you and Ketil. As I stated, between *two* Gods and *two* men. We can do nae more for you." He leveled his spear against Magnar's chest. "You are the only man allowed to enter. *You* must claim what is yours— what was given by Odin. If you fail, *many* will die."

****

252

Elspeth spat out the blood within her mouth. The man's fury at her repeated attempts to deny him the pendant had been rewarded with a hard smack to the mouth and a fist to her stomach. She gathered she'd met the face of evil with Halvard. She was wrong.

Ketil was a hideous monster.

The pain within her body from being beaten by the Seer was merciless, but she would not relent. Her resolve grew with each hour. For reasons she couldn't fathom, Elspeth sensed the presence of Magnar. Once, she thought she heard him howl and call her name. To ken he was coming gave her the courage and strength to withstand the harsh assault from this monster.

Besides, to surrender the pendant might mean death for Magnar and all the wolves.

I would willingly give my life to safeguard the life of my husband—the man I love.

The vile man paced in a rage around the blue and golden flame in the center of the cave. Its light towered within their darkened space. He pointed, cursed, and shouted at the flame as if expecting some great reward. She strained to understand his language, noting the repeated word of the God Loki.

A chill of foreboding cloaked her. Even her grandmother had refused to utter that God's name out loud. To her grandmother, the God was cast out for a reason, and all those that followed his path were doomed to endure a violent death.

She swept her gaze across the cave and at the entrance. If Ketil continued with his madness, perchance she could flee. And hope soared when she couldn't see the other men positioned near the entrance. One moment they were standing there and the next, they simply vanished.

Anything is better than remaining here with this monster. Dear God, let him keep speaking his drivel.

Elspeth took a hesitant step forward. Her stomach clenched, and she swallowed. She then dared to take two steps, and then three. The light from the entrance beckoned her to keep moving and not look back. As her steps drew her near freedom, Elspeth realized silence now reigned within the cave. Fear kept her from turning around or glimpsing over her shoulder.

Run!

Yet before she could take one more step to flee, Ketil wrenched her back by her braid. Sharp pain extended from her head down her neck. He leaned near her face as she trembled—his breath hot and foul against her cheek.

"Do you think to flee, woman? My men would surely halt your escape." He touched the tip of his blade against her neck.

Without giving her time to respond, he dragged her across the rugged floor of the cave and back toward the shimmering flame. She stumbled in an effort to maintain her balance. This time he brought her nearer the flame. Grabbing her bound hands, he inched them closer to the light. Strangely, Elspeth felt no heat. However, her body began to weaken.

"What is hap...*happening?*" she stammered, trying to pull back. "Stop!"

"Silence!" Ketil ordered, his fingers digging into her outstretched arm. "Soon you will do my bidding."

Beads of sweat broke along her brow, and Elspeth fought a wave of dizziness. She squeezed her eyes shut. Her breathing became labored as if someone was squeezing her body in two. Was death coming for her? A part of her yearned to surrender to the glowing light—to allow the burden of what was happening to cease. But her mind fixed on one.

"Magnar!" She screamed, his name echoing all around her.

I am here, Elspeth. Do not give in.

She shook her head in refusal, and slowly opened her eyes. On a choked sob, her gaze met his from across the cave. "*Magnar!*"

Even with the threat of her husband standing inside the cave, Ketil refused to move her away from the flame.

"Come to watch your wife surrender and give me the stone?" Ketil's voice grated harshly against her ears.

"Are you not curious as to where your men are?" asked Magnar, taking another step inside.

Elspeth clenched her jaw so tightly, she feared it would snap. Fighting another wave of dizziness, she kept her focus on the man she loved. His eyes were cold black shards, but she knew the love within. She did not fear the wolf. Man and beast had come for her.

"Nae doubt by you and your men. And if you take another step, I will end her life with my blade before you can save her."

"Wrong! You have offended the tribe who watches over the flame of Odin."

Ketil shrugged. "Then they feared doing harm to me."

Magnar leveled his axe at Ketil. "You are a fool! Either you remove your hands from my wife, or I shall cut them off. 'Tis your choice, *Seer!*"

"You are nothing, wolf," the man taunted. "When I have claimed the stone, your head is the first to be severed. I will shove it on a pike and roam Scotland to show what a weak leader they had. Forcing your men to become my thralls is next. Their first duty is to bring me the head of your king. The reign of the lion is done, along with Odin's."

Her husband snarled. "You dare to oppose both—king and God? With what? A blue stone? You do not understand the power and wrath of All Father."

While keeping her arm secured near the flame, Ketil shouted, "Enough! You chose the wrong God, *wolf.*"

Tears burned Elspeth's eyes, and drawing any air into her lungs became difficult. Her resolve to not give in was ebbing quickly. Her mind tried to fathom a solution in the dark recess of the blackness beckoning to her.

And there it shone—pulsing with hope. It had been there all along—waiting for her to understand.

"I am ready, Ketil." Elspeth ignored her husband's cry of protest. "Allow me to remove the pendant."

He pressed the blade firmly against her throat. "If you lie, I'll slit your throat," he avowed, his spittle marring her cheek.

Upon my death, I ken my husband will take yours. Yet he shall have the power of the stone.

"Aye," she whispered.

Magnar's roar of displeasure surrounded her. "Nae, beloved!"

Ketil loosened his grip but remained by her side.

Her hands shook as her fingers grasped the pendant. Time slowed and the air grew thick. She loved them both—Magnar and the wolf. While she slowly removed the pendant, her thoughts were for only one. The stone grew heavy in her palms. The words caught in her throat, and she felt the sting of more hot tears brimming within her eyes.

Death or life—this was her decision.

Holding the stone in front of her, she found the strength to utter the words swift and true. "From my body to yours. From my blood to yours. I surrender the stone of Odin to the man who holds my heart and love."

With everything she had left in her body, Elspeth flung the pendant outward toward Magnar.

She watched in a haze as his powerful strides bridged the distance between them. Ketil's scream resounded heavily in her ears, and he thrust her violently to the side. In a blur of shouting and chaos, the battle between men and Gods began in earnest. Elspeth barely heard her name being called as her head slammed into a hard surface.

A blinding tempest of dazzling colors surrounded her body, and Elspeth surrendered to the dark abyss of what was surely death's welcome.

Chapter Twenty-Four

Magnar allowed the power to consume him. It grew—flooding his body and mind. The stone pulsed within his palm. Magic unlike he had ever encountered seeped into his skin and that of his wolf. The air was sweeter, the light brighter. He dared to look beyond the veil of mists, summoning more power beyond the stars. Everything faded—the cave, his men, the enemy, even Elspeth.

Displeased, his wolf howled in protest.

Magnar rubbed a shaky hand over his eyes and blinked several times to focus his vision. *Control the power as you would the beast!*

Even though he had severed the hand of the man who held a blade to his beloved, Ketil continued to remain standing. Blood gushed forth from the stump, drenching the man's clothing and the ground.

"Do you think this is finished?" screamed Ketil. He lifted his mangled arm. "You have judged falsely the command I control. Your woman is dead, and I seek the protection of Loki!"

Magnar shook with fury. The tempest of strength swirled around him. Lifting his hand, golden flames sparked on the end of his fingertips. "Death will be your reward!" he bellowed. The ground around and beneath them shook with the power he held.

Before he had a chance to end the life of the

monster, a blinding windstorm filled the cave. Magnar stumbled back and shielded his eyes. A great howling filled his ears. His wolf clawed and lunged against him in an effort to be freed. He gasped, trying to take in air.

And suddenly everything ceased.

Magnar blinked, noting nothing had changed within the flame.

He cast his gaze in all directions, searching for Ketil. The man had simply vanished.

"Nae!" he roared, furious at the man's escape.

When he spied Elspeth slumped against a boulder and blood pooling around her head, he ran to her side. Dropping his axe and the pendant on the ground, Magnar knelt and cradled his beloved. Holding her pale, bruised, and lifeless body in his arms he surrendered to the pain ripping his heart into pieces. All the emotions he had steeled away for the battle burst forth. In one swift slice, his heart shattered, and he roared out his agony, allowing the grief to pour forth.

"Wake, *my kærr!*" He kissed her cold lips, trying to breathe life back into her. "You cannot leave me," he pleaded, tears streaking down his face.

He rubbed the heel of his palm over her heart. "Feel my warmth. My heart beats for you and nae other. Hear the words within your heart and mind, Elspeth."

"Move aside, MacAlpin," ordered the man who approached to stand at his side.

Magnar battled the rage to cut out the man's heart. How dare anyone who thought to touch his beloved. "Do not," he warned in a voice raw with pain.

"I can save her."

The man's words slammed into Magnar, and he glanced sideways at one of the men from the tribe. He hesitated briefly and with a terse nod, he lowered Elspeth gently to the ground. Standing, he moved to one side, refusing to distance himself from her.

Magnar watched as the man drew forth an oval gem from his pouch. Wanting to hurry this keeper of the cave, and knowing he couldn't, he fisted his hand and waited.

Closing his eyes, the man chanted the ancient words of healing. Within the darkened corner, golden light reflected inside the gem. While he continued to speak, the man lowered the gem across Elspeth's forehead, eyes, nose, lips, and then he placed it over her heart.

When Elspeth gasped, the torment within Magnar released on an exhale, and he slumped onto the ground. "Praise Odin," he muttered.

The man returned the gem to his pouch. "Fetch me some water," he ordered softly.

Magnar stood and rushed out of the cave, only to be surrounded by his men and those from the tribe. "I need water," he demanded in a voice raw with emotion.

"Elspeth?" asked Rorik coming to his aid and handing him a water skin.

His smile tight with strain, he replied, "She lives—now."

A combined sigh of relief came forth from his men.

"And Ketil? Dead?" asked Bjorn.

Magnar shrugged, unsure on how to respond. His concern was now for his wife, and he hurried back inside the cave.

After handing the man the water skin, Magnar knelt near Elspeth. A tint of color had returned to her lips and cheeks. And when the first drop of water entered her mouth, his beloved opened her eyes.

His joy so great, Magnar bent and brushed a feather-like kiss on her lips and took her hand into his. "*My kærr.*"

"*Husband,*" she whispered, giving him a slight smile.

"The wound to her head must be cleansed. There are healing herbs and bandages where we dwell. You can bring her there," offered the man.

Magnar looked at the man. "Thank you. Will you give me your name?"

Smiling, the man stood. "Odin favors you. You have honored him this day. My name is Olaf."

"Do you ken what happened to the Seer?"

The man looked past him at the glowing flame. "Either Odin destroyed him, or Loki took pity and removed him from here."

"If I ever encounter him again, death will be his justice by my hand," vowed Magnar.

"I shall await you outside." Giving him a slight bow, the man departed.

Magnar picked up the pendant and regarded his wife closely. "So…you love me, Elspeth MacAlpin?"

Her smile filled him like the warmth of the sun when she replied, "With all my heart, husband."

His heart swelled at her declaration, and Magnar rewarded her with a larger smile of his own. "I love you as well, wife."

****

"You can cease carrying me like a newborn bairn, husband," protested Elspeth, squirming within his arms. "I can walk outside on my own."

Magnar's steps stilled, and he lowered her to the

ground. Wrapping his arms around her waist, he asked, "Bairn? Are you trying to tell me something?"

"Surely you can see I am able to wander without help. Two days of tending to me was plenty, but not *one* week. Even Erik has been seeing to my every need."

He placed a hand over her womb. "You mentioned a bairn!"

Her eyes widened, and a blush began to spread along her neck. She lowered her head against his chest and whispered, "Nae. I am not carrying our child."

"Yet," he added and cupped her chin. When her gaze met his, he kissed her tenderly.

Elspeth broke free from his embrace. "When can we leave?"

Confused by her tone, Magnar brushed a hand down the back of his neck. "I had hoped to show you where I spent time on *Kirkjuvágr*. Where I was born. Erik desires to visit the area as well."

She twirled a lock of hair around her finger. "I would favor seeing the place you were born and spent time in. Is the home large enough for all or only for us?"

Now his thoughts grew troubled. "You wish to dwell with my men?"

Laughter bubbled forth from her, and she grasped his hand. "Nae!" Again, the stain of roses crept upward to her face. Standing on her toes, she bit his lower lip. "I miss you in my bed, Magnar."

He let out the breath he had been holding. Grasping her firmly against him, his mouth covered hers hungrily. His kiss was urgent and demanding, while his hands skimmed down to her lush bottom. Elspeth's moan filled him, and he rubbed his swollen cock against her, aching with a fierce need to take her.

When he heard two of his men approaching, Magnar broke free and drew back.

Elspeth licked her lips. "Now that is a *kiss*."

"Have I not been giving you many kisses, wife?" he protested.

"Not the ones I crave." Placing her hands on his chest, she added, "You have been treating me too tenderly. Do you fear I shall shatter into tiny shards? I am strong, Magnar."

How could he confess the numbing helplessness he had felt when he thought she had died? He would have begged Odin himself to bring her back to life. Magnar rubbed the stone that was around his neck. He had the power to do almost anything, except summon the words to bring her back to life. If not for Olaf, and the truth his wife was a true shield-maiden, he feared all would be lost to him.

"Be ready to travel before the light of dawn graces the sky tomorrow. The men and Erik can accompany us. They can stay with Berulf while we'll lodge at the former home of my parents. I ken your nephew will enjoy my friend's company."

Her entire face transformed to one of joy. She slipped her hand over his cock and squeezed. "I require your healing touch," she whispered. Quickly releasing him, she sauntered away while humming a tune.

"Where are you going?" he asked, though he probably knew the answer.

She waved a hand over her head. "To gather flowers and speak with Erik. I heard he was going to catch some fish."

Magnar let out a growl and turned from her appealing form. With his men not far, he had to quash his burning desire.

He did not have long to wait as Rorik and Gunnar came striding forth from the trees. "Should I ask what you have been doing?" He fisted his hands on his hips.

Grinning, Rorik looked at Gunnar. "And here I thought he would be fond of the good news."

"The only good news you can offer is the head of Ketil," grumbled Magnar, still frustrated by the man's disappearance.

Rorik's good humor vanished. "Sadly, nae. Be assured we will find him."

"We have a ship to take us back to Scotland when you are ready," announced Gunnar.

Magnar shifted his stance. "I decided to stay for a while. I wish to show Elspeth *Kirkjuvágr* and the surrounding area."

"A wonderful idea!" declared Gunnar and smacked Rorik on the back.

The man grimaced. "I think I shall remain nearby."

Magnar's brow creased. "Fear you will encounter Ragna?"

Though the truth showed in Rorik's eyes, he replied, "Nae, nae!"

"Good. You can stay with Berulf. There will be nae need for you to wander away," ordered Magnar.

His friend gave him a scathing look and stormed off.

Gunnar scratched the side of his face. "Why does he hate her thus?"

Magnar chuckled softly. "He does not. Do not be fooled by the loathsome words he spews out about the woman."

Gunnar tapped a finger against his chin in thought. "I think I shall go join Erik and Bjorn by the river."

Smiling, Magnar stepped around his friend and walked away. There was something he needed to do before they departed. It had haunted him since the dreadful day in the caves. He had thought to speak with Elspeth but banished involving her in the decision. When he woke this morn, he understood it was time.

Even his wolf agreed.

Steadily making his way through the trees, he considered his decision one last time. A chance to accept what had been given to him. Magnar reached the clearing and descended onward to the caves. The tribe's leader stood at the entrance. From what the others within the tribe had shared with him during the past few days, each man would guard the entrance for one full day.

Magnar halted before him. "I have made a decision."

Dagr pushed away from the rock wall. "What do you seek, MacAlpin?"

Letting out a sigh, Magnar removed the pendant from around his neck. He rubbed his thumb over the stone. "I have all the power I judge necessary to help my king. I have nae desire to become snared in a war between Gods. In truth, the power of the stone is far too tempting for men. It should remain with Odin."

"Are you certain?"

"Aye. In the wrong hands, the pendant can destroy worlds."

The man moved aside. "You are a warrior for Odin, son of Alpin. Toss the stone into the golden flame. There it shall be given back to Odin."

As he started forward, Dagr tapped him on the arm with his spear. "You are correct. The power of the stone does not give life, yet it can destroy. You have made a wise decision this day."

Giving the man a brief nod, Magnar stepped inside. For a moment, the horror of almost losing Elspeth slammed back into his thoughts. He let out a shaky breath and banished the images. Striding across the cold cavern, he halted before the towering flame.

Magnar knelt on one knee. "Once, you gave this gift to our people. But I judge this too much for men. I have tasted the power of the stone. In that moment, I felt I had become a God." He shook his head solemnly. "You have granted me the wisdom and power of the wolf. 'Tis enough."

He stood and regarded the stone one last time. "Into your hands, All Father, I give back what was bestowed to us."

When he tossed the stone into the flame, Magnar watched in stunned silence as a great hand reached forth from the golden light, catching the blue stone within its grasp.

Retreating swiftly, he paused outside the entrance. Magnar placed a fist over his heart and faced Dagr. "Long life to you and those that guard the caves and the temple of Odin."

Smiling, the man clamped a hand on his shoulder. "And may Odin bless you with many years as well. Come and visit us again."

Magnar retreated to the trees, eager to be with his wife and share his decision.

As soon as he entered the dense thicket, his wolf

growled in warning. He halted his stride and withdrew his dirk from the sheath belted at his side. Inhaling sharply, he exhaled on a curse.

"Show yourself, Thorfinn!"

Wariness reflected across his brother's face when he emerged from behind a huge pine tree. Magnar studied the mirror image of himself, except for the scar near his twin's eye.

Unable to control his anger, he shouted, "I should thrust my blade into your cold heart! Even my wolf demands justice for what you did! But a young chieftain cautioned me on my choice, if ever we would meet."

"As you can see, I have not drawn my weapon," declared Thorfinn, slightly shifting his stance.

Bitterness seeped into his words. "Yet you did to my *wife*. You allowed her and the chieftain to come to harm. For what? Power? Is this what you wanted?"

"Nae!" Thorfinn pounded his chest with his fist. "'Tis what *they* wanted—a battle for what you possessed. Halvard for land and power, including your wife. And Ketil's plans were unknown until he sensed Odin's blue stone."

"So you are telling me you objected to this madness?"

"*If* I was in agreement with them, I would not have freed Erik. By the time I realized Ketil's plan, he already had Elspeth in the caves with him. There was nothing one wolf could have done."

Magnar attempted to quell the fury but held firmly onto his dirk. "Why are you here?"

His brother stretched his arms out wide. "'Tis my home. Unlike you, and where you have chosen to serve a king not loyal to our people. Furthermore, I reckoned we needed to meet at least once before you departed."

Snorting in disgust, Magnar glanced upward. "We are blood to both countries, Thorfinn. And as part wolf, I am honor-bound by an ancient edict to serve the King of Scotland. Whereas, you have become the enemy." Magnar hated the next words he would spout and returned his attention to his brother. "You ought to be with the brotherhood at the Sutherland keep. 'Tis your duty."

Thorfinn's eyes darkened dangerously. "Then I should have been allowed to live with my parents and raised with my brother! You do not ken the life I was forced to live, while the deeds of the great Magnar MacAlpin were spread throughout our lands." He spat on the ground. "Did you even think to consider what happened to me?"

Cursing softly, Magnar sheathed his dirk and went to lean against a tree. "I only learned of you a year ago. In anger, I spoke harshly to our mother and left *Kirkjuvágr* for Scotland. Sadly, our parents' reasons died with them."

"Despite what you have shared, I cannot undo the past or who I am. I belong here."

Pushing away from the tree, Magnar went to his brother. "Will you think on my words? A solitary man who is part wolf can be a lonely journey. King William is a good man and leader."

His brother grinned. "Ahh...but I am never alone. The wolf dwells within me. Scotland is your home, Magnar, not mine."

He refused to argue further. The offer to become an elite guard was there for his brother. "I once confessed the same about the *Orkneyjar Isles* not being my home. Recently, I have come to find peace with this land. Perchance one day you shall feel the same about Scotland."

Thorfinn shook his head and turned to leave. Glancing over his shoulder, his expression softened. "Long life, Magnar. Fear not, I will not plague your Scotland."

While Magnar watched his brother slip through the trees, an ache settled within his heart. How he yearned to speak more with Thorfinn. Aye, the anger at what he had done to Elspeth and Erik lingered but somewhere in their conversation, his bitterness lessened.

"Long life, Thorfinn MacAlpin. I pray Odin leads your steps back to me, and to the letter that awaits you from our mother." Placing a fist over his heart, Magnar added, "And if death takes you, may you storm proudly across the void to Valhalla where I pray we will meet again."

Chapter Twenty-Five

Elspeth observed her husband from the stone path in front of what he proudly proclaimed was now their second home in *Kirkjuvágr*. When she first entered the wooden structure days ago, she opened all the shutters, filling the entire living area with light and warmth. It was a lovely home with two levels and a large central one for eating and preparing meals, which also served to greet guests. And then there was an upper level with several open rooms. Love had filled this home once as she touched objects not used in many moons.

I love you, husband.

And I you, my kærr.

She found she enjoyed this new connection of speaking to one another within their minds. Magnar confessed that it was part of the magic when a wolf truly fell in love and gave his heart to another. However, most days she jumped when he intruded on her thoughts.

"I must learn to shield my mind, or I will never get anything done," she uttered softly.

Never, kærr!

She grinned.

A cool breeze swept over her, and Elspeth drew her cloak more firmly around her. Though they would be leaving soon for Scotland, peace had settled within her on this isle.

"Are you sure you have chopped enough wood?" she asked, strolling down the path toward Magnar. She admired the view he presented—his brawn back flexed with each swing of his axe.

He turned and wiped a hand over his brow, slick with sweat. "I ken Ragna leaves the comforts of her small home to tend to the garden here. Many a time, she has spent the night."

"Aye, *aye*, the Seer." Elspeth bent and fingered a flower petal. "'Tis a flourishing herb and vegetable garden in the back."

Magnar thrust the axe into the wood block. "She was a good friend to my mother."

"And you?" she inquired, bridging the gap between them.

Magnar laughed. "Do I sense jealousy, wife?"

Elspeth arched a brow in challenge. "I am nae fool. You have had others."

Her husband let out a low growl and wrapped his arms around her waist. "True. But when I took you as my wife, I made a silent vow to never take another to my bed." He tipped her chin up with his finger. "Now I make this pledge out loud. Never did I fathom the love or pleasure you give me, Elspeth. Each day, my love grows for you."

She cupped his cheek. "When I was taken, I feared to never tell you what was in my heart. My love for you kept me alive, Magnar. Strange how we started our marriage, aye?"

He pulled at a loose tendril of her hair. "For a brief time, I despised the king for forcing us into this marriage."

"I barely recall the words I mumbled at the

ceremony," confessed Elspeth, shuddering at the memory.

"At least there were words spoken by a priest for you. Did you think your God would condemn you for marrying a heathen?"

Dropping her hand, she reflected on that time. "I cannot lie, husband. I worried for my soul. However, God has shown me the power of love with you. Perchance your Gods and mine destined for us to be together." She smiled wistfully. "My grandmother would have adored you."

His mood appeared pensive. "I am sorry your pendant is gone—returned to Odin. I ken it was a gift from your grandmother. The only true item she bestowed to you."

Elspeth's gaze roamed over her husband's face. "There is nae need. When you spoke of the immense power days ago, I became frightened. The stone was nae longer mine. I gave it to you and in truth, I am happy 'tis gone. My grandmother had the gift of sight and possibly she knew the day would come when a true warrior would claim the stone. She did stress that I wear it on my wedding day, though."

Magnar sighed and leaned his chin on the top of her head. "To answer your earlier question, Ragna and I quarreled most of the time. She judges the wolves are mere beasts, and we should make an effort to control them. In truth, she has feelings for another."

They stood silently in the warm sun for several moments until Magnar spoke quietly. "And here he comes now."

Elspeth drew back and glanced over her shoulder and then back at him. "*Rorik* is the one?"

Placing a finger over her lips, he whispered, "Our secret."

She smiled against his warm skin.

Magnar released her and went to greet his friend. He smacked him on the shoulder. "What brings you to our home?"

The man grimaced, though he gave her a broad smile. "Now that Elspeth has healed, the men and I have come to an agreement and wish to discuss it with you."

Magnar pointed to his shoulder. "Knife wound still bothering you? You should have Ragna tend to the injury."

"Knife wound?" echoed Elspeth, coming to his side. Concerned, she asked, "When did this happen? Magnar mentioned nothing about one of the men getting injured in the battle. Goodness, you should have said something earlier."

Rorik gave her husband a scornful look and took her hand. "Please do not worry. 'Tis an injury not fought in any battle." He glanced sideways at Magnar. "And I would *never* let that witch tend to anything on my body. She would inflame the wound or curse me."

Rubbing a hand over his chin, Magnar explained, "He wagered he could take down all the wolves with one hand tied behind his back."

Dropping the man's hand, she asked, "As wolves or men?"

Magnar leaned near her ear. "We do not fight each other as wolves."

"And how would I ken this?" she scoffed and returned her attention to Rorik. "You fought and lost?"

A faint glint of humor shone in his eyes. "I was

winning until Ivar challenged me with a knife. Unprepared, I slipped and the blade caught me in the shoulder."

"Too much mead made you stumble," interjected Magnar.

"Oh, for the love of Mother Mary! You are all savages!" She turned to leave, adding, "When we have a son, Magnar, he will not be allowed such folly." Trying to keep the smile from forming on her mouth, she failed miserably.

"Are you with child?" asked Rorik, his tone one of shock.

Elspeth observed the man. He appeared eager to hear some kind of news. She clasped her hands in front of her, finding it odd to discuss this openly with another man. "Nae."

"*Yet*," added Magnar, once again.

"As I was saying earlier," mentioned Rorik, "the men and I have agreed that before we depart *Kirkjuvágr*, we would consider it an honor to recite our vow of protection to your wife."

Elspeth smiled at his kind offer. "You do not need to profess your vow, Rorik. I ken you already have shown me your loyalty when you came to rescue Erik and me."

Magnar came and wrapped an arm around her shoulders. "I reckon it a wise choice, Elspeth. As with our custom, during a wedding feast the men state their vows of loyalty and protection when their leader takes a wife." He gazed with love at her. "I would like to restate my vows here on the isles to seal the bond between our two lands and to each other, as well."

Tears misted her eyes, and her voice trembled

when she spoke. "With true wedding vows spoken with love."

"Aye, *my kærr.*" His smile broadened with affection.

Elspeth kept her sight focused on her husband. "Rorik, go tell the men to plan for a wedding feast."

"When can I say it shall happen and where?" he asked.

She shrugged, waiting for a decision from Magnar.

He lowered his forehead against hers. "In two days. We can speak our vows by the cliffs and hold the feast in the hall of our home."

"But we do not have plenty of food and drink for everyone," protested Elspeth. "Nor do I have anything to wear."

"Do not fear, all can be supplied by the others!" shouted Rorik as he took off running.

Placing her hands on the back of Magnar's head, Elspeth brought his lips near hers and whispered, "Then I agree."

And when he took her mouth in possession, Elspeth surrendered to the passion of his kiss.

****

Elspeth fingered the soft ivory gown with golden threads sewn on the edges of the sleeves and hem—a simple garment but a treasured one. Ragna had told her it belonged to Magnar's mother. She lifted her gaze above the hilltop overlooking the ocean. Not a cloud blemished the sky on this warm day. Her husband leaned against a tree, laughing and talking with his men. It was a day of surprises, beginning with the arrival of Berulf and the barrels of mead. Though she had never met the man, Elspeth had this immediate connection with the elder. He recalled tales of her grandmother and filled her with added memories to cherish.

Then there were the others who came with food and more drink. Thinking this was going to be a small feast, she was mistaken. Many had come to witness the great leader of the wolves marrying a woman from across the seas. They came to offer their own blessings with many of the women touching her womb and asking the Goddess to provide many sons and daughters. She embraced the prayers and the women in return.

And if she thought to walk the journey to meet her husband alone, she was wrong. The women kept her company, singing songs and asking about her life in Scotland. Even some of the younger women asked about the young chieftain, Erik. Had he been promised to another? How large were his holdings? Did he own many ships?

Elspeth responded to each one.

Smiling, she sought out her nephew amongst the group of men. He had proven to be a warrior many times during his short time as the new chieftain of Gunn. "I ken you are proud of him, Thomas, as am I," she expressed softly.

As if he heard her, Erik darted out from the men and ran to greet her. "Aunt Elspeth!"

She bent and opened her arms to him. Wrapping him in a warm embrace, she closed her eyes.

"'Tis a fine day," he proclaimed, squirming to be free.

Elspeth straightened. "One I feared we would never witness."

Erik stared at her closely. "You love Magnar."

"With all my heart," she confessed. Yet she noted her nephew had already concluded this for himself.

"My father would have been happy with his friend marrying you, Aunt Elspeth."

Her mouth twitched in humor. "More shocked, I believe, to ken I found love with the leader of the Wolves of Clan Sutherland."

"'Tis a good match, he would state."

Elspeth nodded in agreement. "Aye, he would."

One of the young girls started to approach them.

Erik gave her hand a quick squeeze. "I must return to the men."

"Do you not wish to speak with the young lass?" she teased.

His face twisted as if he had drunk sour goat's milk, and Elspeth fought the laughter bubbling within her.

"Nae, nae!" Without giving her a chance to speak more with him, Erik took off running.

Halting her progress, the girl sighed heavily, and her grin faded.

Shrugging, Elspeth gave her a smile to ease her displeasure.

"Are you ready?" asked Ragna approaching from behind her, holding a bunch of wildflowers fastened together with a thin blue cord.

"Aye!" she beamed.

"These are for you." Ragna offered the flowers to her. "Magnar confessed how you have a fondness for the wildflowers. Since I ken the hills where they flourish, he asked if I would gather them for you."

Elspeth gathered them into her arms. "Thank you."

"You have tamed the barbarian wolf of the *Orkneyjar Isles*," the Seer declared, glancing toward the group of men.

"Nae." Elspeth disagreed. "All I did was open his heart to love."

The woman shielded her eyes from the sun. "Then a perfect match. One should not have to change for love, aye?"

"I agree," added Elspeth, though she pondered if the woman was speaking about another wolf.

Ragna dropped her hand and linked her arm with Elspeth's. "Allow me to walk with you to your husband?"

"I would be honored."

"Do you still suffer pain in the head?" asked the woman.

"Slightly. They tend to come later in the day." Though Magnar had a way of easing the tension and pain with his fingers before he made love to her.

"Before you leave, I shall give you some herbs to mix with wine. It will aid in the pain and healing."

As they wandered through the lush grass, Elspeth's heart started to beat wildly. Her husband's appearance made her knees go weak. He wore a simple ivory tunic and matching trews. Drawing closer, she observed the same stitching around the bottom of his tunic as hers.

She glanced at Ragna. "Did you stitch the pattern on Magnar's tunic?"

Her gentle laughter rippled through the air. "You would not want to see my stitching. I am not fond of the task. He must have come upon his father's clothing in his parents' trunk. Both—your gown and the tunic were made for them by one of the elder Seers long ago." She paused, releasing her hold on Elspeth. "May your marriage be blessed with the love of not only our Gods and Goddesses, but your God as well. Go to your husband."

Elspeth embraced the woman and crossed the distance to meet Magnar.

His arm encircled her waist, bringing her to stand near a towering ash tree. She inhaled the scent of her husband along with the salty sea breeze.

He lowered his head next to her ear. "You are a beauty, Elspeth MacAlpin, and you must wear your hair unbound in this fashion more often." With a low growl, he rubbed his cheek against hers.

She melted into his strong embrace. "*Always* eager to please you."

Chuckling softly, Magnar drew back. "Before we state our vows, I would like to present you with a gift." He brought forth a pouch tucked inside his leather belt. Removing two silver cuffs, he placed one on each of her wrists. "These were my mother's, given to her from my father. Now 'tis my gift to you."

Elspeth gasped with joy at the wonderful gesture. "Are the stones amber?" She brushed her fingers over the smooth stones gracing across each of the cuffs.

"Aye," he affirmed.

She raised her head and placed a hand over his heart. "I shall treasure these always, though I have nothing for you."

His blue eyes bore into hers as he placed his warm hand over hers. "Contrary to what you think, your *love* is the most cherished gift I could ever have hoped for, *my kærr*."

Elspeth placed a kiss on their joined hands.

Her husband turned her toward the crowd. "Allow the first warrior to pledge his vow."

Rorik stepped forward. He placed his sword on the ground in front of Elspeth and knelt on one knee. In a loud voice, he proclaimed, "From the power bestowed upon me from Odin, my sword and strength is yours to protect and defend, Elspeth MacAlpin."

Rising, he gave a curt nod to Magnar and stepped aside for Bjorn. Soon all the Wolves of Clan Sutherland had declared their pledge to her.

Overcome with emotion, Elspeth let the tears of gratitude fall freely.

Magnar took her hands and brought her close. "My *kærr*, never did I deem our marriage would be one of love. You have filled a void that I did not seek to ever fill." He brushed the back of his fingers over her cheeks, adding in a voice raw with emotion, "You are the star of each night, you are the sunlight of every morning, and you are my greatest quest. I shall be a shield to your back, and you, to mine. Until my last breath and beyond, I shall always love you, Elspeth."

She blinked as more tears slipped down her cheeks. Her voice trembled when she spoke. "*Once*, I called you a heathen, not seeing beyond to witness the true character of the man. Husband, warrior, *and* wolf—all who possess great honor and love for me. In return, my heart opened completely, and I fell in love with you, Magnar. Each time I say the words of love out loud, I find I am unable to breathe. My love is deeper than all the oceans and as great as all the stars in the night sky. Forever I am yours, *husband*."

Scooping her into his arms, his gaze roamed over her face. "I *love* you."

Before she had a chance to repeat her words of love, he ravished her mouth in a fiery kiss that made her dizzy with passion.

The crowd broke out into boisterous laughter and shouts of approval.

Breaking free from her lips, he asked, "Are you ready for the feasting?"

Elspeth wrapped her arms around his neck and giggled. "I don't believe the hall is big enough for all our guests."

He started forward, and the crowd parted for them. "There is room for all. Many will come and go throughout the day."

"Magnar?"

He gave a wink when he passed an elder woman. "Aye, wife?"

"Why are you carrying me? I have nae pain in my head."

Amusement flickered over his face, and his eyes crinkled with mirth. "My men have made a wager that I do not have the strength to carry you to our home."

She gaped at him. "You do realize how far it is, aye?"

His laughter was a full-hearted sound as he shifted her within his arms. "Aye, most definitely!"

"Then why are you agreeing to this folly?" she demanded, pulling on his earlobe with her fingers.

He looked affronted. "Because they reckon with all my attention in bedding you, my strength has weakened. I must prove them wrong."

"Men!" Yet Magnar's smile disarmed any ill word she wanted to spew out. She loved him far too much. She twirled his hair between her fingers. "What is the wager?"

He blew out a breath. "If I lose, I must endure another game of *skinnleikr*. Except this time, I have to have one arm tied around my back."

Elspeth pursed her lips. "And if you win?"

"They must do all the chores at Steinn for one month, including cleaning all horse and human muck."

She wrinkled her nose in disgust. "I suggest you win, husband."

"If I can manage the hill, we are bound for home, wife."

An hour later and with sweat dripping down her husband's face and neck, Magnar brought her to standing in front of their home.

"Someone fetch me a horn of mead for my victory!" he bellowed.

Taking her hand, he led her inside and to a wooden chair by the empty hearth. Sunlight and candlelight danced along the food-laden tables—from trenchers of cod, salmon, and dried herring to loaves of bread, pickled vegetables, and cabbages with onions. She almost swooned at the sight of so many delicious berries.

Elspeth licked her lips as a woman placed a horn of mead into her hands and gave another to her husband.

Magnar remained standing while draining the entire contents.

Smiling, she took a few sips, relishing the cool liquid within her parched mouth.

As the hall continued to fill with more people, she spied Rorik making his way to them.

Lifting his horn, he proclaimed, "Long life to you both!"

"You need to shift, Rorik, so you can completely heal," suggested Ragna. She approached from the side, lifting her horn of mead at Elspeth and Magnar.

Rorik glanced over the rim of his horn at her. "Nae. Nae need."

She shook her head and gave Magnar a pleading look.

"I will not order him, Ragna," he stated.

Shrugging, she turned to Rorik. "You are stubborn to not let your wolf aid in your healing. I noticed your shoulder plagues you."

Rorik glared at her. "Hold your tongue, *witch*," he hissed out.

She tossed the remainder of her mead into his face. "You forget who I am, *wolf*!"

Elspeth watched as Ragna's fury and hurt reflected over the woman's features before she stormed from the hall.

"You have forgotten your manners," scoffed Magnar. "Given Ragna is a healer, she was only offering her thoughts to you."

"Loki's balls," snapped Rorik, wiping the mead from his face with his hand. "She need not concern herself with me." He gave a slight bow. "Forgive me."

They watched as he swiftly departed the hall.

Magnar shook his head solemnly as he took a seat beside Elspeth. He held his horn outward when a woman came by with a jug of mead.

"Thank you," he offered quietly as she filled it.

Concerned, Elspeth placed a hand on her husband's arm. "Let us worry about your friend in the morn."

Magnar snorted. "'Tis not worry for the man, nae. Only how long it will take for him to see what he refuses to acknowledge."

"I love you, husband."

He kissed her soundly and then stood. Magnar lifted his gaze to those gathered near them, and he smiled. "You have honored Elspeth and me in sharing this day with us—one filled with love. May the Gods and Goddesses continue to favor you and your families."

A rousing cheer echoed all around Magnar and Elspeth.

Epilogue

Steinn Castle ~ Late September 1206

Magnar gazed upon his wife's lush form within the solar. "I have bolted the door, my *kærr*. Why are you backing away from me?"

"You ken we are expecting guests," she replied dryly, fingering a quill on his desk.

"Sutherland and the king will not be here for another week," he countered, stalking toward her. "And to answer your unspoken question, he is not sending me on any commissions. My time shall be spent traveling between Steinn and Vargr. With Steinn as another stronghold for the wolves, this will expand our strength. Erik has also given his consent for this to be a training keep. Despite what I stated in the beginning of our marriage, I have nae plans on leaving for other areas of Scotland. Rorik is my second in command and capable of taking over some of my duties for the king."

Her hand stilled. "What of Thorfinn? What will you tell the king?"

"Unsure." He paused in his pursuit. "My brother is now an enemy of the king, and I must tread carefully in my account to him."

Elspeth tapped a finger to the side of her head. "I sense they will be arriving sooner."

Concern filled him, and Magnar closed the distance

between them in two strides. "Are you now gifted with the sight? The healers say any shock to the head can cause visions."

Her brows furrowed, and she took a step back. "Nae, *nae.*"

Magnar took advantage of her waving hand and grasped it firmly. He silenced her protest with a smoldering kiss, thrusting his tongue into her warm mouth. She tasted of apples, and he ached for a bite. With his other hand, he started to unravel her loose braid, eliciting a moan from his wife.

Elspeth broke free, and then nipped along his chin with her teeth. "You will have to take me hard and swift."

"Touch me," he encouraged, yearning for more. Nuzzling her neck, he could smell her desire for him. His need so fierce, he craved to lick the scent from her skin.

Elspeth drew back with a beguiling smile. He watched in a lust-filled haze as she slowly undid his lacings and slipped her hand inside his trews.

"Aye," he muttered, trying not to spill himself into her hand. He enjoyed watching the play of emotions across her face, especially the way her tongue darted out along her lower lip. As if she wanted to devour him.

When her hand slipped lower to cup his balls, he groaned. "Enough," he rasped out.

She pouted in protest.

"Turn around and place your hands in the middle of the desk.

Her eyes darkened with desire, and she slowly complied.

Magnar freed his throbbing cock and with the other

hand, he bunched up her gown to reveal her heart-shaped bottom. His eyes feasted on the soft ivory flesh. Bending over her body, he whispered into her ear while his hand caressed the bare skin, "Now spread your legs."

Loud voices within the bailey halted the pleasuring of his wife's body and his.

Barking out a curse, he retied his laces and went to the arched window. He pounded a fist on the side of the stone wall. "By the hounds!"

Elspeth's soothing laughter floated by him.

He glared at her. "You are correct, wife. Sutherland and the king have arrived."

"And you will be with them for many days, aye? I heard there was a hunt planned." She straightened from the desk and smoothed the folds of her gown.

"Aye," he bit out tersely returning his gaze to the men gathered below.

He heard her sigh heavily. "'Tis a pity. I shall go attend to the kitchens and see to the preparations."

Magnar refused to be discouraged, even for his king.

His smile came slowly as he made his way back to Elspeth. Her fingers were deftly plaiting the hair he was overly fond of, and he reached out to stop her movements. "There is plenty of mead, bread, and cheese in the hall, aye?"

She tried to pull free. "You ken the hall is never empty with so many men—I mean *wolves* in attendance."

He shrugged. "They are always *hungry*. As I am for you, wife."

"The king is here. *Stop*," she protested, though

desire still flared within her emerald depths.

"Do you trust me?" He breathed the words against her full lips.

Her mouth parted. "Always, husband."

"Come with me to the stream. Everyone will be busy tending to our guests."

Elspeth wrapped her arms around his neck. "And what shall we be doing by the stream?"

His blood burned with need to bury himself deep into her. Magnar's love for her consumed him—filled the hollow emptiness, and he reveled in the powerful sensations.

Letting his fingers slip free from her tresses, he replied, "I will remove your gown, taking care not to *rip* it from your body."

"And then?" She trembled within his arms.

"I will take your body swiftly on the grasses by the cool water. And then slowly by the ancient oak."

She groaned and leaned her head back. "What else?"

He kissed the pulse at the base of her throat. "While I taste your sweet honey between your legs, I want to hear you scream my name as you take your pleasure."

"What are you waiting for?" Her voice husky with need as her heated gaze met his. "If we leave now, nae one will notice. We can slip out the back entrance near the cellar."

Magnar grasped her firmly around the waist and lowered his head. "I love you, *wife*."

Before Elspeth had a chance to respond, he took fiery possession of her lips in a kiss—one that pledged a lifetime of love.

Note from the Author

As a man, Magnar MacAlpin was not prone to patience. As a wolf, he was far worse in his demands to see this story written.

On my trip three years ago to the Orkney Islands, I discovered a vast landscape steeped in ancient legends, ruins, standing stones, and my fictional world of the Wolves of Clan Sutherland. They emerged quietly before I took my journey across the northern seas and entered with force once I arrived in Kirkwall. Magnar announced his presence (and literally shocked me) in the opening chapter of *Destiny of a Warrior*, and again when he slipped into the ending of *To Weave A Highland Tapestry*. A character who constantly demanded his story be told *now*. I finally surrendered (on my terms), giving him a woman who would constantly challenge him. In the end, Magnar *The Barbarian* was tamed. However, he may disagree with me.

In addition, I have woven King William *The Lion of Scotland* into this brand-new story and series. I've always been fascinated with this king. In my research, I became drawn to his particular attempts to gain back certain lands and castles in England after they were stripped away under the reign of Henry II. The negotiations for their return with Kings Richard I and John met with no success.

I hope you've enjoyed Magnar and Elspeth's love story—one that took you on an epic adventure from northern Scotland to the Orkney Islands. Who is next? I believe you might have guessed. His love conquests are many. But only one has captured the heart of this man—she is also the one woman who despises everything about Rorik MacNeil.

Until then, may your dreams be filled with Irish charm, Highland mists, and the Wolves of Clan Sutherland!

Other Books by Mary Morgan

Order of the Dragon Knights ~
Dragon Knight's Sword, Book 1
Dragon Knight's Medallion, Book 2
Dragon Knight's Axe, Book 3
Dragon Knight's Shield, Book 4
Dragon Knight's Ring, Book 5
~*~

Legends of the Fenian Warriors ~
Quest of a Warrior, Book 1
Oath of a Warrior, Book 2
Trial of a Warrior, Book 3
Destiny of a Warrior, Book 4
~*~

Holiday Romances ~
A Magical Highland Solstice
A Highland Moon Enchantment
To Weave A Highland Tapestry

A word about the author...

Award-winning Celtic paranormal and fantasy romance author Mary Morgan resides in Northern California, with her own knight in shining armor. However, during her travels to Scotland, England, and Ireland, she left a part of her soul in one of these countries and vows to return.

Mary's passion for books started at an early age along with an overactive imagination. Inspired by her love for history and ancient Celtic mythology, her tales are filled with powerful warriors, brave women, magic, and romance. It wasn't until the closure of Borders Books where Mary worked that she found her true calling by writing romance. Now, the worlds she created in her mind are coming to life within her stories.

If you enjoy history, tortured heroes, and a wee bit of magic, then time-travel within the pages of her books.

Visit Mary's website where you'll find links to all her books, blog, and pictures of her travels:

http://www.marymorganauthor.com